Little Black Dresses,
little White lies

· LAURA STAMPLER ·

SIMON PULSE

New York   London   Toronto   Sydney   New Delhi

SIMON PULSE

An imprint of Simon & Schuster Children's Publishing Division
1230 Avenue of the Americas, New York, New York 10020
First Simon Pulse hardcover edition July 2016
Text copyright © 2016 by Laura Stampler
Jacket illustration copyright © 2016 by Lucy Truman
All rights reserved, including the right of reproduction in whole or in part in any form.
SIMON PULSE and colophon are registered trademarks of Simon & Schuster, Inc.
For information about special discounts for bulk purchases, please contact
Simon & Schuster Special Sales at 1-866-506-1949 or business@simonandschuster.com.
The Simon & Schuster Speakers Bureau can bring authors to your live event.
For more information or to book an event contact the Simon & Schuster Speakers Bureau at
1-866-248-3049 or visit our website at www.simonspeakers.com.
Book designed by Karina Granda
The text of this book was set in Adobe Garamond.
Manufactured in the United States of America
2 4 6 8 10 9 7 5 3 1
Cataloging-in-Publication Data is available from the Library of Congress.
ISBN 978-1-4814-5989-1 (hc)
ISBN 978-1-4814-5991-4 (eBook)

For Mom and Dad

I'M SWAYING BY MYSELF AT BOBBY MCKITTRICK'S summer kickoff party—surrounded by couples whose Dance Floor Make-Outs are so intense, so ravenous, I'm kind of worried someone's going to drop down dead due to suffocation—when I get what might be the most important phone call of my life.

Of course, I don't realize the magnitude of this moment when I see the unfamiliar number flash on my phone. I don't even recognize the area code. To be honest, I'm just excited to answer a real call instead of a fake one, the kind I usually pretend to get during awkward party lulls. So I don't think twice when I answer it on the dance floor, loudly shouting "Hello?" over an even louder "Keg stand! Keg stand!" chant crescendoing from the corner of Bobby's backyard. (As a graduation treat, Bobby's older brother is giving the departing seniors a tutorial in college-party etiquette, which apparently involves kegs and then dangling people by their feet above said kegs as they chug beer upside down.)

My hello is answered by an indecipherable garble.

"Sorry, I can't hear you!" I shout again.

("Keg stand! KEG STAND!")

Still gibberish.

"Wait, wait, stop! Just hold on one sec!"

I try not to spill my one-third beer, two-thirds foam–filled red party cup as I maneuver around the blindly gyrating Dance Floor Make-Outers to a less populated part of the yard and sit on the outdoor swingy-bench next to a passed-out dude whose face is decorated with a drawn-on, very accurate portrayal of male anatomy. Real classy, guys.

Rule number one for aspiring writers is to steer clear of clichés, which makes living in Castalia, California—where every social gathering feels like it was ripped from a bad teen movie—less than ideal.

"Okay," I say into the phone. The bench swings as I sit. "Try again."

I hear a loud sigh on the other end of the line, followed by an exasperated and syncopated, "I *said* is this Har-per An-der-son?"

"Yeah." I take a sip of my drink. "Who's this?"

"Well, *finally,*" the female voice on the other end says.

"And you are . . ." I start to wipe the foam mustache residue off my upper lip. This is one persistent telemarketer.

"This is McKayla Rae from *Shift* magazine."

I stop wiping. And maybe breathing.

"Harper, did you hear me? I said that this is *McKayla Rae,* the assistant managing editor of *Shift* magazine."

Yup, definitely stopped breathing. Clearly I misidentified who was at risk of asphyxiation tonight.

"Harper?"

Finally my brain tells my lungs to breathe and my mouth to speak.

"Sorry. Yes! This is Harper! Oh shit, I said that already, didn't I? I mean, *not* shit. Forget I said 'shit.' I mean, yes! Yes, I heard you, McKay—er—Ms. Rae."

Okay, so my brain didn't specify that my mouth should speak eloquently.

"McKayla."

"Right, McKayla. Sorry."

"Stop saying 'sorry.' Women overapologize for things they have no reason to apologize for. *Shift* Girls are strong. *Shift* Girls don't say 'sorry.' Ever."

"Sor-sounds good." I just barely catch myself. "I am no longer sorry about anything under any circumstances. Got it."

God, I hope that didn't sound sarcastic. I take another gulp of foam.

"This is important because, Harper, I've called to let you know that you are now a *Shift* Girl. Or, you will be if you accept our summer internship."

I drop my cup on my sandals, spilling lukewarm beer on my toes, and don't even care because Oh My God.

Which comes out as "OMIGOD!"

"I take that as a yes?"

To say that my night has taken an unexpected turn would

be an understatement. Up until about two minutes ago, I had resigned myself to an anticlimactic three months before my senior year of high school spending my days working behind the counter at Skinny B's Smoothies with my best friend, Kristina, and my nights going to kickbacks so similar to one another, they start to feel like reruns, all destined to be shut down by the Castalia Police before midnight.

Granted, I had aspired to a summer that was slightly more glamorous than memorizing antioxidants and blending acai berries into drinks for aggressive water polo moms. (Think soccer moms, only taller.)

Shift was the dream.

Because even though I'm having trouble stringing words together while McKayla waits for me to say not just "yes" but "hell, yes," I want to be a writer. Badly.

And not only is *Shift* the biggest teen magazine in, well, any-where, but it's also the only magazine (well, anywhere) that hires interns who are still in high school. Usually I find rah-rah, children-are-our-future, teary-eyed teen-empowerment mission statements kind of cheesy. But when I saw *Shift*'s Facebook post calling out to sixteen-to-nineteen-year-old aspiring journalists, I applied. I didn't tell anyone I applied, but I did. Writing and rewriting an "edgy per-sonal essay" to serve as a sample blog post for weeks. Pining after the job more than I pined after Adam Lockler, my preppy school's one brooding hipster. And then quietly mourning its loss to an "edgier" contender, just like I mourned the loss of Adam when he started seriously dating our school's resident beat poet, Sylvia ("like Plath"), whom he also conveniently anointed his successor as editor in chief of the *Castalia Chronicle*. ("EICs have to be fearless, Harper. You'll be much happier doing copyediting. You're *really* good with punctuation. And don't get me started on your fact checking!")

If I get one more rejection, I'm going to . . . Wait.

"Wait," I say, regaining the ability to speak. "Didn't I *not* get this internship already?"

I *definitely* didn't get this internship already. In fact, I think McKayla was the one who sent me the "I hate to inform you," "very strong applicant pool," "but I loved the sample blog post you included in the application," "Keep writing!" form rejection e-mail months ago.

"Yeah," says McKayla. "About that . . . Well, as you know, we had a very strong applicant pool—"

"I think I remember that from the e-mail."

"But we liked your application essay—"

"I remember that, too."

"Okay, I'm going to level with you here. No, you weren't my first choice for dating blogger."

Wait, *dating blogger*? That wasn't listed on the application. I checked the box to intern for the Arts & Culture section. I had wanted to write about books and movies, spend my summer seeing Broadway musicals. I'm suddenly aware of how sticky my toes feel.

McKayla barrels on. "But our first choice had a little bit too much fun—how shall I put this—getting firsthand dating material this year and just informed me that she can't do the internship because it now conflicts with her *due date*, which would have been nice to know one trimester ago." McKayla pauses. "*You* aren't planning on going into labor before August, are you?"

"Definitely not!"

I mean, not unless Immaculate Conception is making a comeback.

"Fantastic. Just get yourself to Manhattan by this Monday morning and it's yours."

"Wait, this Monday as in three days from now?"

"Is there another 'this Monday' that I'm not aware of?"

I can hear her drumming her fingernails. Before I can respond, she says, "Look, Harper, I get that things are moving fast, but that's journalism. It's after one in the morning here and I'm still putting out fires at the office because this is *Shift*. This place makes careers. An internship here, and colleges will be lining up to accept you."

Her sales pitch has the advantage of being totally true. I've read about what past interns have done after a summer at *Shift*. And I could use colleges lining up. When I didn't get editor in chief, the Castalia High college counselor told me that getting into Columbia with an application all about how I want to be a journalist was going to be challenging. ("Got any other talents?" Mr. Buchanan asked. "Can you code? Universities love girl computer coders!")

McKayla sighs. "I'd love to have you on board, but if you're even thinking of saying no, tell me now. I have a list of other rejects who would be on a red-eye to the city ten minutes ago."

I don't have to think about it.

"Yes."

"Yes, meaning . . ."

"Yes, I'm in. I'm a hundred percent in! I was just surprised because—"

McKayla cuts me off. "Great. Check your e-mail for details. Welcome to *Shift*."

She hangs up before I can say thank you.

What. Just. Happened?

I have to tell someone.

I have to tell Kristina, who's currently making out with a University of Michigan–bound water polo player in the middle of the pulsating Dance Floor Make-Out throng. She locked in on his chlorine-blue eyes within ten minutes of getting here.

But Kristina won't mind being pulled away. My blond-haired bestie, whose personal mantra has been "carpe that effing diem"— which roughly translates to "seize that freaking day"—ever since she saw it cross-stitched on a pillow on Etsy last year, is never lacking in the make-out-partner department. A varsity swimmer who's so good, she's already getting recruited by Stanford, she's fluent in hot jock. Boys practically throw themselves at her. I'm the one who—

Just as Sharpie Face guy's head comes crashing down on my shoulder, my reality comes crashing in as well.

Shit.

I'm now the *Shift* summer dating blogger.

Which would be awesome save for the teeny, tiny, infinitesimal detail that I know absolutely nothing about dating. I'm not a leper, just easily flustered. I'm the girl who has crushes on hipster editors in chief from afar. The girl who observes rather than jumps to action. And the one time I took Kristina's advice to go out of my comfort zone and actually get set up on a date, well, that ended in disaster.

Not that McKayla would know that I'm completely unqualified, given the "edgy" sample blog post I submitted. *Shift* asked intern applicants to write an "eye-catching personal essay" with a headline that "people in the Twitterverse can't help clicking on." Something "scintillating." But when I paged through my black Moleskine notebook for ideas, it became clear that my life had nothing scintillating about it. But my notebook isn't just for writing about myself. I love jotting down weird observations, funny things people say, and other people's stories for future writing inspiration. And I was inspired. Kristina *does* always tell me that I'm way better at recounting her hookup horror stories than she is.

I know I should never have pretended Kristina's scintillating life was my own—I should never have written about *that* story of hers for my application blog post—but in an act of writer's-block-fueled desperation, I did.

How's that for being a killer fact-checker, Adam Lockler?

And now, because I was an idiot, because I wrote about something I know nothing about (and debatably betrayed my best friend, who can *never* find out), I'm going to have to turn into some sort of dating guru. In three days.

I'm *so* metaphorically screwed.

Before I have the chance to descend into a full-blown freakout, Bobby McKittrick walks over to see what's going on with

Sharpie Face, who's slumped on the bench next to me. This interrupts my spiral into total anxiety.

"Lookin' good, Harper," he slurs, giving me a once-over after he checks his comatose friend for a pulse.

Wait.

While Bobby isn't exactly a Nordic god masquerading as a graduating senior like Kristina's Dance Floor Make-Out partner, he's kind of cute. He's also famous for getting super drunk and making out with a different girl (or two or three) at every party he throws. Kristina and I always laugh about it during our end-of-night debrief. But tonight, maybe it wouldn't be so bad to be one of those girls. Maybe it will be easy. To throw myself into the lion's den and get a preview of what may be in store.

I'm going to have to learn on the job.

• 2 •

THE CASTALIA PD PULLS UP AT 11:01, AND EVEN though absolutely no one should be surprised that the party is getting broken up this early, absolutely everyone starts scrambling to stomp out joints and empty the contents of their red party cups into the surrounding vegetation.

I, however, welcome the interruption. Because what started out as an exercise in flirting has ended up with Bobby making out with my chin. And while I'm no expert, I'm fairly certain that that doesn't count as foreplay, just bad mouth-eye coordination.

"Um, do you need to go deal with this or something?" I ask, trying to find a way to subtly wipe off the lower quadrant of my chin. (Note: there is no subtle way to do this.)

"Dammit, just when we were getting to the good stuff." Bobby groans. "I'm gonna have to go sweet-talk the five-oh for a bit so they don't call my parents and shiz."

Good stuff? Five-oh? *Shiz???* Oh, Bobby, no.

"Ya know," he continues, "you could hide out in my room

while they clear everyone else out. Keep the party going?"

"Tempting"—not tempting—"but I'm going to call it a night."

"I have pot!"

I give Bobby a conciliatory pat on the hand.

"Good night, Bobby. And," I add, before walking away, "thanks?"

The funny thing is, I'm not even being sarcastic. Because even if this was the sloppiest of sloppy experiences, even if I had no idea what to do with my hands or if I should close my eyes or if Bobby could tell that Kristina and I stopped for fries before coming to the party, mission freaking accomplished! Turns out, I'm fully capable of (sort of) making out with guys whenever I so please. Granted, this particular guy was horny and drunk and uses "dawg" in his everyday vernacular . . . but still.

Could I be a dating goddess who has simply never unleashed her powers? A guru who has never honed her skills?

Maybe this won't be so bad after all.

"So." Kristina's voice breaks me out of my self-congratulatory inner monologue. "What did I miss?"

For the past hour she's been occupying herself with a Greek god up against Bobby's mom's bougainvillea vines rather than the comings and goings of the party.

"Um . . . nothing?"

"Come on, Harper, give me the report. Who cried, puked, and did something that will bar their future selves from running for public office?"

"Um." How do I put this?

"Come on," she says. "You know I live for your narrative skills.

What were you doing if not taking meticulous mental notes?"

I pick a red petal out of her bangs.

Fine.

"Bobby."

Kristina grabs my arm. "No. Effing. Way."

"Well, not *doing* doing, obviously. I just wanted to kiss someone. . . . So I did." I put my free hand on my hip because that's a casual pose, right? "You can close your mouth now. It's not *that* big of a deal."

"Okayyyy, but you never make out with randos at parties, so this is at least a little bit of a big deal," she says, kindly leaving out the fact that I pretty much never make out *period*.

But then Kristina's confusion is replaced with a glint of excitement.

"Wait! Does this mean you'll be a make-out bandit with me this summer?" she asks. "We'll have the best time winging for each other! We can, like, drive to San Francisco on weekends and flirt with genius Silicon Valley boys who dropped out of college to sell their apps!"

"Ah yes, I can't wait to spend my time away from the Skinny B's counter driving two hours to flirt with eighteen-year-olds who probably have the social skills of eighth graders." I lead us through Bobby's back gate. The party's clearing out.

"Yeah, but eighth graders whose companies have millions of dollars in investor funding and can take us out on their yachts on weekends! We're going to have the best summer ever!"

Except *we* won't.

I mean, hopefully we'll have the best summers ever, but, if you note the plural, they'll be two completely different summers. Rather than a shared one.

Because in three days, I have to be sitting at a desk approximately three thousand miles away for an internship I never told anyone about. Not just Kristina, my parents.

"Oh God, I have to go home. Now."

I start booking it toward my street, hoping that my mom and dad haven't gone to bed yet. If I power walk, I think I can make it before they finish up their wild Friday night tradition of binge watching BBC crime dramas on Netflix. They're currently working their way through a series about two elderly British women who solve grisly murders when they aren't busy pursuing their true passion: gardening.

"What's going on with you, Harper?" The clopping sound of Kristina's Rainbow sandals get louder as she catches up. "I think this is the fastest I've seen you move, like, ever."

Kristina's and my friendship predates her emergence as a sports star—although she *was* in the shark lane in our pre-K swimming lessons when I never made it past guppy. And even though I don't exactly click with the other jocks at school, she's like my sister. Like my parents' second child. After her dad took off, Kristina started spending even more time at our house. I mean, she's even in charge of making pancakes when she sleeps over every weekend, since the entire Anderson family seems to have some strange genetic disorder that renders us incapable of flipping things in frying pans.

The longest we've been apart is when she had to go to Connecticut for all of spring break sophomore year for her dad's wedding, which came complete with a shiny new stepfamily, and *that* was a total disaster. So how do I tell that person, *my* person, that I'm essentially abandoning her to fend against blenders and protein powder on her own, with zero warning?

"Harper?" Kristina grabs my arm. "Okay, now you're starting to freak me out. Did something happen with Bobby? I'm going to *murder* him—"

"No, it's not that." I stop abruptly, causing Kristina to stumble over her flip-flops. "It's just . . . I'm so sorry, but we can't drive to San Francisco this summer."

"Oh." Kristina looks at me quizzically. "That's okay. I mean, we can—"

"No, that's not it either. We can't *anything*."

And then I take a deep breath and tell her (almost) everything. With a dozen different variations on "I'm sorry." How I got a writing internship in New York at the very last minute. How I have to take it.

I do, however, leave out the small, minor details explaining how exactly I got the job—or even that I'll be writing about dating. The whole truth wouldn't benefit either of us right now. She never needs to know that I kind of, sort of, 100 percent misappropriated her own salacious story as my own.

After a too-long silence, Kristina asks, "How did I not even know you went out for this?"

"Because there was no way I'd get it!" I say. "And having to tell people I got rejected *again*, which I *was* . . . God, I probably wasn't even at the top of the waiting list. I probably only got it because I was the first girl to answer the phone when the editor called. I—"

"Listen to me! I'm surprised because I had no idea you were going for it, which is something best friends usually tell each other, by the way. I'm not surprised you got it. You're a really good writer." Kristina's the only person who's seen not only the articles I've written for the *Castalia Chronicle*, but excerpts from my private notebook. "You deserve this. I was just really excited for our summer together."

"Same."

"And now you're going to have this awesome adventure without me, and you'll be totally over me after you make a million super fashion-y, intellectual New York friends."

"No!"

Kristina's by far the coolest, best person I know. I can barely deal when she's home sick, because there are a hundred things I want to tell her all day. Also, while people are okay with me as her sidekick, I constantly feel like I'm crashing conversations and tables in the cafeteria when it's just me.

Kristina, without me, is still golden. But the thought of me, on my own, making a better set of friends with ease seems so ridiculous that it takes me a minute to realize that Kristina's eyes are wide and kind of glassy and totally serious.

"You are legitimately a crazy person! I won't make any friends on your level. I'm just going to make a big bowl of cantaloupe friends. Probably not even ripe cantaloupe."

Kristina sighs. "Why are you changing the subject to melon? You didn't smoke any of Bobby's pot, did you?"

"No," I say, "*cantaloupe friends*. Nobody craves cantaloupe in their fruit salad, it's just there. The ultimate meh filler fruit." There's a slight chance that the almost imperceptible movement at the corner of Kristina's lips is the beginning of a smile. "Cantaloupe friends are just who you make do with in extenuating circumstances so that you don't, you know, starve to death socially."

"So what kind of fruit am I?"

Strawberry? Blueberry? If I screw this up, I might be her rotten apple.

"Pineapple. Definitely pineapple. Exotic but something you want to eat every day."

Silence.

"I'd rather be a mango," Kristina says finally.

"Perfect! You're my mango."

Kristina stops fiddling with her hair and links arms with mine. "Well, as long as you're just hanging out with filler fruits . . ."

One mango down. Two parents to go.

Parents who shout, "Girls, keep it down! Lady Pendleton just found a dead body in her sage bush!" as I crack open our creaky front door.

But tonight, instead of making fun of my parents' strange BBC addiction like I normally would, I put a finger to my lips. I lead Kristina past the smiling Vishnu (my dad's an East Asian history professor) and the massive bookshelves (my mom's an English professor) to the couch where my parents have a burnt-orange throw blanket pulled up to their eyes.

We sit down on the couch next to them. Kristina gives me a

reassuring smile—even though I know she must be kind of mad still—and I look at the TV screen as they fast forward past a particularly gory scene involving garden shears. I have twelve minutes and forty-seven seconds of the episode left to get my thoughts in order.

It's gonna be a long night.

• 3 •

IT'S 6:29 MONDAY MORNING, AND MY TIRED EYES jolt open to the monstrous roar of a blender.

But I'm not at Skinny B's, and there are no intimidating forty-somethings with pitchforks shouting things like "Blend faster!" and "Where's my wheatgrass?" Once the clock on the unfamiliar bedside table next to me strikes 6:30 and my iPhone starts blasting Taylor Swift, I know where I am.

"Welcome to New York," Taylor sings, kicking off my very carefully curated, in-theme playlist.

And I'm back to reality. Hard as it is to believe, I, Harper Anderson, am waking up in Manhattan to start my first day at *Shift* magazine.

Un-freaking-believable.

At first, I didn't think it was going to happen. When the Netflix went off and the truth came out, Mom and Dad made it very clear that they were both less than pleased about a lot of things. Namely:

- The fact that I applied to an internship without telling them. ("I didn't think I'd get it. . . . I mean, I *didn't* get it.")

- The fact that I needed them to fund a last-minute flight for said internship—or at least let me reallocate some college money for the ticket. ("I won't need college money if I don't get into college. Think of how good this will look on my applications!")

- The fact that said last-minute flight would take me across the country for an entire summer. ("Mom! Stop crying! Of course I'm not going three thousand miles away because you're overbearing!")

I kind of left out the whole dating blogger part of the equation when I talked to them, too. For now, let them think I'm making coffee and fact-checking inspiring stories about fifteen-year-olds overcoming extreme adversity to start world-changing nonprofit organizations. We can leave the conversation about their daughter's new role as resident Rosetta Stone of Hooking Up for the five minutes before my first post comes out.

After substantial cajoling on my—and even Kristina's—end, my parents relented. They even seemed a little bit, dare I say it, *excited* about the whole thing. ("Obviously!" Kristina, who was no longer showing any signs of sadness about my imminent departure, told me when we were tucked under my polka-dot comforter that night. "It's exciting.")

"Welcome to New York," Taylor belts, repeating the refrain. It's 6:31. "Welcome to New York—it's been waiting for you."

The upbeat pop anthem is met with a loud grunt reverberating from the corner of the guest bedroom I've been placed in.

One condition of going to New York was that I live at my Aunt Vee's Upper East Side apartment. And let me say that after arriving here late Sunday night, *that will not be a problem at all* because what I expected to be a shoe box is actually a sweeping penthouse the size of my family's entire home . . . but with a view of Central Park.

The only catch is that I have to share my bedroom with a very unhappy roommate, currently making disgruntled sounds from a little plush bed surrounded by doggy toys. Princess—who is quite possibly the fattest pug in the universe, or at least the northern hemisphere—does not approve. Of me or my music choices.

"More of a Beyoncé kind of girl?" I ask the pug, who somewhat resembles a sausage with tiny legs.

Princess gives me a withering stare before flopping her head back down to resume her favorite position: Princess in repose.

I, however, cannot repose. Because of all the things I can and probably will colossally mess up at my first day on the job, being late will *not* be one of them. (Note: Control the controllables.)

My "Welcome to *Shift* magazine!" e-mail—which I can recite from memory because I've read it so many times—says new interns have to get to the office by nine a.m. sharp to get security badges and computer passwords, and do whatever other mysterious things prestigious magazines make interns do on orientation day. I wouldn't know. I've never worked at a prestigious magazine before. I've never worked anywhere that didn't make you wear a hairnet.

I pry myself out from between sheets that might be made out of actual silk and drag myself toward the guest closet, which is filled with my newly procured, work-appropriate wardrobe. I tip-toe past Princess—her tongue is out and she's back to snoring—out of our room toward the sound of the roaring blender.

"Good morning, sunshine!" A very chipper Aunt Vee is in the kitchen making smoothies. "I hope you like spirulina! Your mother and I were all about it when we were roomies—and spirulina wasn't even cool back then."

She throws a handful of green sprouts into her murky concoction.

It's probably worth noting that Aunt Vee isn't my actual aunt. Rather, when my mom moved to New York to start Fordham's PhD program in English forever ago, she rented a room in Aunt Vee's then–Upper West Side apartment. Aunt Vee's the last person Mom lived with before she found Dad.

"Live with Vee? Are you sure about that, honey?" Dad asked Mom while driving us to the mall to pick out a bevy of discounted, knee-length skirts, which my mom insisted were what the dress-for-success businesswoman wears to work. "Isn't she a little bit . . . nuts?"

From what I've gathered from piecing together snippets of stories, when Mom was spending her nights raging in the library, her older roommate was at after-after parties, trying to re-create the "good old days" of Studio 54, where she regularly did cocaine off male models' abs with Andy Warhol.

"It will be fine," Mom said. "The woman's in her sixties. I'm sure things have slowed down."

Luckily for Aunt Vee, her surgically enhanced face, which is now turned to me with an expression of abject horror, looks closer to forty.

"What are you *wearing*?" asks the woman who's decked out in skintight, neon-colored, head-to-toe workout spandex.

"Um, a skirt suit?"

"It's so *beige*. And synthetic." Aunt Vee is trying very, very hard to be nice and not frown. (The Botox helps.)

"I think it's actually a cotton blend," I say, looking down at my new, sensible work flats.

Oh no. Is this all wrong?

This is all wrong.

"You can't go into a fashion magazine looking like you just walked out of some discount superstore," Aunt Vee says.

(Let the record show that I love Target.)

Also: "We actually got it from the Gap outlet."

(I also love outlet shopping.)

Aunt Vee shudders. "My closet. Pronto. This is an emergency."

Aunt Vee is officially over the spirulina. She pivots and stalks toward the master bedroom with a sense of purpose. Her jet-black bob bobs up and down at her chin with every step.

I follow behind, scurrying past the gigantic wall of windows in her living room, which overlooks the park. I just barely take in the view of the treetops emerging from the shadows as the sun continues its ascent. That's okay, though. I quickly learn that the view *inside* Aunt Vee's closet is far greater than anything nature could provide.

We walk through the double doors off her dramatically all-white bedroom and are immediately enveloped in exploding colors.

"This"—Aunt Vee spreads her arms wide, her fingers sweeping the climate-controlled air of her closet—"is where the magic happens."

There are animal prints, sparkling fabrics, and shoes. So, so many shoes.

"'Summer' is on the left."

I turn my back on the furs—"All faux and PETA approved, Harper, so don't look at them like that!"—of winter and fall and walk toward Aunt Vee's summer selection.

"This is crazy-town," I say. And it is. Aunt Vee's closet is fancier than any store we have in Castalia.

"*Au contraire*, Harper. Couture is the facilitator of sanity."

Aunt Vee starts pulling out floral dresses with plunging necklines and sheer tops. She is literally waving leather short-shorts in my direction.

I don't know what to say.

"Um, I'm not really sure it's a good idea to wear *shorts* on my first day of work."

"These aren't shorts. They're *leather* shorts. It's a completely different genre."

"And . . . that makes it more work-appropriate? Because when Mom and I talked about—"

"Who do you think your mother comes to when she's in need of fashion advice? Or, at least, she used to before your parents up and moved you all to the middle of nowhere." Aunt Vee has the pained look of a woman on the second day of a juice cleanse.

Some people think that being from California automatically means that you live somewhere cool, like San Francisco or LA. Aunt Vee knows better.

"It's not that bad," I say, feeling a surprising tinge of Castalia loyalty. "And we're not *that* far from San Francisco. Kind of."

Aunt Vee sighs.

"You're using *San Francisco* as your fashion talisman? Harper, hoodies pass as formal attire out there."

The woman has a point.

"All right. I'm open to your stylistic expertise." (Aunt Vee responds with a squeal.) "But no shorts. Please."

I'm bent over picking up a dress that fell from Aunt Vee's arms when she stops squealing and shouts, "Stop! That one's perfect!"

She drops the rest of the clothing she was considering on the floor and pushes me toward the full-length mirror.

"See?" she raises the short (very short) white linen dress—decorated with intricate stitchwork around its low neckline—in front of my thin, five-foot-two-inch frame. "See how the cerulean embroidery makes your eyes pop? They look so blue."

"It won't show too much cleavage?"

Aunt Vee and I both give my minimalistic boobular region a long look over.

"I honestly don't think that that's going to be an issue, Harper."

"Point taken."

"Now"—Aunt Vee scans the closet—"we need some accent pieces." She snatches a pair of blue strappy heels from her wall of shoes and throws them in my direction.

"These shoes," she says. "And . . . *this* purse."

She hands me a canary-yellow bag that even smells brand new.

"I don't know," I say, holding it carefully. "I'd be worried I'd scratch it."

"Well, try not to. It's a Birkin."

I show no sign of recognition.

"Oh dear, I have so much to teach you," she says comfortingly. "Let's just say a Birkin costs more than a Mercedes. Only a small one, though."

Oh, hell no. Heels I can manage. (I think.) Heels the first day on a job make sense. But I definitely don't want to carry a small Mercedes on my arm. There's absolutely no way I could handle the constant fear of scuffing it. Not to mention the constant fear of being judged as the seventeen-year-old who brought a Birkin to the first day of an internship. "Thank you, Aunt Vee, *thank you*. But I can't. It's too much."

"Too much?"

"Too much!"

"Well, you're no fun at all, but I *suppose* a Birkin could be overkill." She puts her hand on my shoulder and I breathe a sigh of relief. "Maybe it's more second-week appropriate."

Our bonding moment is interrupted by a buzzing sound

coming from the pocket on Aunt Vee's butt. She unzips the back of her yoga pants to retrieve her iPhone. The back of the case has a picture of Princess wearing a tiara.

"So sorry, Harper, but I'm going to have to run to a PiYoCo class."

Blank stare from me.

"Pilates-yoga fusion with an emphasis on working your core. Everyone's doing it! But before I go, I demand a quick little fashion show to make sure it all works."

Like that, she's off to her spirulina, and I'm in the closet alone for the first time. I take a long, slow breath of the lavender-scented air.

"Wow," I say to the abandoned yellow Birkin. I put it back incredibly carefully between its green and purple brethren. "What just happened?"

I take off my beige blazer, beige skirt, and white button-up to replace them with everything I've collected from what has proven to be both my most and least expensive "shopping spree" ever.

"Harper!"

"Coming!" I give myself another look in the mirror, and I've got to say, the tiny stitches of blue do make my eyes pop against my pale complexion and dark hair.

I look good.

Princess grunts at the second disruption to her beauty sleep when I go back into *our* room to grab the big, black H&M bag I got with Kristina on a trip to SF so that I can show Aunt Vee the finished product. (I guess I'm the finished product.)

"Oh, Harper!" Aunt Vee clasps her hands together. "Now *this*

is a first day of work outfit. You're a knockout! There's just one last thing. . . ."

Uh-oh.

Aunt Vee unties a scarf from the handle of her workout bag. "I suppose I understand skipping the Birkin, but can we at least tie this onto your purse? It will really pull the piece"—Am I the piece?—"together."

A scarf. I can handle a scarf.

"Thanks so much, Aunt Vee." I take it and knot it where the base of the strap meets the body of my bag. The royal-blue, gold, and cream design looks very midcentury. Kind of like something Audrey Hepburn would have worn to cover her hair on a windy day. "It looks great."

"Well then, my work here is done. Have Lothar downstairs call you a car and charge it to my account. The subway gets so hot and crowded during the morning rush that the humidity and body heat will completely ruin your fresh aesthetic."

Even though I studied the intimidating subway maps and have memorized my route, I don't argue. I have a lot to process, and my day hasn't really even started yet.

I had hoped to get to work a good half hour early so that I could grab a real New York bagel and drink an iced coffee on the edge of the office building's iconic fountain while mentally preparing for my first day, but after my fashion show for Aunt Vee, that clearly isn't going to happen. I'll be lucky if I get there with thirty seconds to spare.

I fly out of the Fifth Avenue apartment's foyer as soon as the car arrives.

I fly out the door.

I fly down the stairs.

And then I'm literally flying through the air. That is, until I'm not. There's a loud *thunk* on the ground (me) and a high-pitched yelp (not me).

"What the *hell*?" When I try to get up, I realize that my legs are tangled up in . . . leashes? A Pomeranian scampers over my fallen body and a yelping Goldendoodle inspects my (now-bare) foot with his wet nose. Towering above us all is a tall figure with a messy flop of brown hair—his face obscured by the sun. His hand descends and I stretch mine out, getting ready to be helped up. But his diverts to scoop his dog-walking wards away from me as quickly as possible. As if I'm toxic.

"What the *hell*? You bulldozed directly into Atticus. You almost impaled him with your shoe!"

The very pissed-off dog walker points accusatorially at the Golden, who, yelp aside, shows no sign of damage from the alleged bulldozing. Thank God.

Unscathed, the puppy is enthusiastically chewing on my right shoe, which must have flown off upon impact. But Dog Walker doesn't care. He turns his finger from Atticus to me (note: I'm still lying on the ground, injured for all he knows), ranting, "This is what happens when idiots text and walk."

Excuse me?

"I think you're kind of mischaracterizing what happened." I unwrap a leash from around my calf. "Besides, I was *not* texting and walking. I was . . . okay, I was Google Mapping and walking."

Totally different.

"Well, there's an alternative to, 'I'm so sorry for my recklessness and animal endangerment,'" he says.

"As opposed to your gentlemanly, 'Are you hurt? Here, let me help you up and extricate your sandal from my dog's slobbery mouth.'"

I stand, lopsided. Even in my single heel, I come up only to his chest, putting me at direct eye level with the words "Varsity Lacrosse" written across his T-shirt. Well, that makes sense. Some might call him cute, what with the height and the freckles, but I know better. That endearingly crooked nose is probably a result of one too many lacrosse sticks to the head. Total Neanderthal Jock. The kind who would never talk to me in the halls at school unless I came as a package deal with Kristina.

I hobble over and try to pull my shoe away from the Goldendoodle.

"You do not get to call him slobbery right now." Neanderthal Dog Walker takes the now-dripping-wet footwear away from Atticus.

Under completely different circumstances, I would take this one-on-one, male-female interaction as an opportunity to practice bantering—a true dating master needs to master the art of banter . . . I read it online—about how my name and the dog's name were both inspired by *To Kill a Mockingbird*, but instead I wave my shoe in his direction and shout, "If the salivary gland fits!"

I shoo the Pomeranian away from the spilled-out contents of my bag—"Now you're attacking Poncho!" Neanderthal Dog Walker shouts—and pick up my compact mirror to try to assess the damage to my, as Aunt Vee put it, "fresh aesthetic." Ugh, make that my slightly wilted aesthetic.

"You are not checking out your hair right now!"

I unleash my best withering side eye. "You know, just before right now I thought that the rumors about New Yorkers being giant assholes was a lie. Thanks for proving me wrong."

Jerk.

I dramatically fling my bag over my shoulder, teeter to the car Lothar the doorman called, and slam the door. I put my shoe back on.

"You all right, miss?" the driver asks as I scoot in.

My shoe is somewhat damp.

"Yeah, I'm good. I'll be good."

Maybe if I say it loudly enough, that will make it true.

• 4 •

KRISTINA AND I SHARE THE SECRET SHAME THAT
it took both of us three—that's right, *three*—tries each before we
passed our driver's license tests. The failure bonds us, like a friendship bracelet.

But after my car ride from the Upper East Side to *Shift* in
Lower Manhattan, I realize that we just took our road tests in the
wrong city. Because based on how nutso the drivers here are, I
think that we would have been the freaking star students at the
New York City DMV.

"Oh my God, watch out!" I shout from the backseat of the
black car as it careens down Broadway, weaving between taxis. And
to think that I was worried he would be going too slowly.

The driver responds to my concerned cry by cutting off a bicy-
clist who really shouldn't have opted out of wearing his helmet
today. Just as I cover my eyes, the car makes an abrupt stop.

"We're here."

I look between my fingers and see a very pissed-off (*but* very alive) Citi Biker flip us off as he races past the exterior of a building I've studied relentlessly in Google Image Search.

The Bosh Media Building.

In Castalia, a four-story office is considered a high-rise. But in Manhattan the high-rises are high. So high, in fact, that from my vantage point in the back of the car, I can't see even halfway up the architectural marvel that is Bosh Media.

It literally glimmers.

These walls, which are made out of reflective glass, house all the Bosh Media publications, which range from *Gilded Putter* (for golfers) to *Disrupting* (for techies) to *Shift* (for teen fashion slaves) to *Iconic* (for adult fashion slaves). Pretty soon, five days a week, between the hours of nine and six, it will house me, too. That is, if I can make it up to HR in the next, oh God, I only have three minutes!

I thank the driver and get out of the car as quickly and carefully as humanly possible. I definitely don't want to flash all my potential new coworkers before I even get into the building. (Like the Birkin, that kind of behavior might be more "second-week appropriate.") I maneuver myself out of the vehicle with my dignity intact, walk past clusters of "I ♥ New York" tourists saying "cheese" to their selfie sticks in front of the Bosh Media fountain, and check my white dress for paw prints in the building's mirrorlike windows. Phew.

I give my reflection a quasi-confident smile as I walk toward and then through the rotating doors, into the—oh my God. There's an actual waterfall right smack in the middle of the lobby. A waterfall of skyscraper proportions. There are gigantic koi swimming in a large pond under the streaming water.

Where the hell am I?

I ask a hulking security guard as much, although in politer terms. He points me toward a front desk, where I show a receptionist my driver's license in exchange for a day pass. I hand my purse over to get x-rayed as I walk through a metal detector, and am then directed to take the first elevator on my right to HR, which is located on the thirteenth floor. My slightly unstable heels click to the first elevator bay.

Shit.

Everyone is wearing a suit.

I squeeze into an elevator and notice an older woman in beige and very sensible work flats giving me a not-so-subtle head-to-toe. Her eyes linger and widen when they get to my bag.

Might I repeat? Shit.

When the elevator dings, I can't get out fast enough, almost tripping over my heels as I exit. A stabilizing hand grabs on to my elbow.

"New intern?" a smiling lady (*in a skirt suit!*) asks.

I nod, pulling down on my dress to create the illusion of modesty.

Skirt Suit gives me a far kinder head-to-toe. "Let me guess. Based on the outfit you're either working for *Shift* or *Icon*?"

"*Shift.*"

"All right, hon, the other girls are waiting in Huddle Room B to start orientation."

She steers me down the hall toward whatever the heck the huddle room is and pauses in front of the door. I'm semi-scared to open it and see what's going on on the other side.

"Thanks."

"You're welcome, dear." And then, before she leaves me to fend for myself, "Nice scarf."

I take a breath before I push the door open to—OH, THANK GOD. I have never been happier to see leather short-shorts in my entire life. A group of five extremely well-dressed Amazons with perfect hair and gravity-defying heels towers over a snack table with coffee, an untouched basket of pastries, and . . . a bowl of cantaloupe. No way. I have to Snapchat a picture of the orange melon to Kristina. I start giggling, which very quickly turns into awkward laughter as soon as I notice that all five pairs of eyes—framed by impeccably applied colorful liner—are staring at me like I'm a crazy person.

"Sorry," I say. "It was just the cantaloupe. . . ." Um, how do I even begin to finish this sentence?

"Do you want some?" A girl who put her printed-out "Gigi, Arts & Culture Intern" name tag on the bottom of her white leather short-shorts motions to the bowl of fruit. With hair swept into voluminous black curls and a light brown complexion that contrasts starkly with her all-white ensemble, Gigi looks like she shouldn't only be writing for *Shift*—the girl should be on the damn cover.

"I take that as a no?" she asks in an unidentifiable but very sophisticated-sounding accent.

Oh no, I'm being awkwardly silent.

"Yes! I mean, no. No, thanks!" Nervous laughter. "I actually kind of hate cantaloupe. Such a filler fruit, am I right?"

It turns out the only thing worse than awkward silence is awkward rambling. Jesus, Harper, get it together.

Gigi pops a piece of the melon into her mouth and raises her eyebrow toward Sun-Hi, Fashion Intern; Abigail, Health Intern; and Brie, Beauty Intern.

Brie, like the cheese.

Which makes me realize that I haven't had any breakfast yet and could so go for some cheese right now. Or maybe one of those untouched doughnuts. But I don't know how my anxiously unsettled stomach will react to food, so I reach for a Diet Coke instead. Maybe the carbonation will be settling. So what if it's only nine in the morning?

"Starting early, huh?" Jamie, Viral Content Intern, asks as she grabs a water bottle. "Don't worry, you definitely won't be the only Diet Coke–head at *Shift*. I interned here last year and people drank it like it was coffee."

That was nice. Quick, say something funny back. Anything.

"I'm an addict too," I reply. "Hopefully HR won't make us start going to Aspartame Anonymous meetings."

Yes, she's laughing. I'm getting back in my groove. I pop open the tab on my Diet Coke and hear an ominous fizz.

"Watch out! It's exploding!" I hold the erupting can of Diet Coke as far from my body as possible and swivel so that it misses Jamie, Viral Content.

"Are . . . you . . . joking?" The accent makes the accusation sound even scarier.

I take it back. The only thing worse than awkward silence and awkward blabbering is awkwardly spilling your drink all over your new coworker's cute, probably really expensive, all-white outfit. Swiveling away from new friend Jamie meant swiveling toward newly anointed-with-Diet-Coke enemy Gigi, whose once-pristine clothes are now absolutely covered in sticky, brown, sugar-free soda.

"No, I'm serious." Her voice is almost at a whisper. "Is this a joke? Because I'm not laughing."

"I'm so, so sor—"

"Get me a napkin, maybe? Help me, maybe?"

Oh God, where are they? I put my bag down on the wet table and start scrambling to find napkins.

The other interns gasp audibly.

"Careful!" Brie, Beauty, sputters out in a Southern drawl. "The soda's going to get on your scarf."

"Oh, don't worry about it," I reply, still searching for that damn napkin. "Seriously, not a big deal."

"Isn't that *vintage Hermès*?" Sun-Hi, Fashion, asks.

Oh?

"You can't ruin the Hermès," Brie says. "That would be, like, *murder*."

"I can't watch this." Sun-Hi snatches the bag away and starts dousing my scarf in fizzy seltzer water. Brie then unties the scarf and dabs the silk material with paper towels—where did she *find* those?—to prevent any possible stain. She clutches it to her chest . . . which, unlike mine, is the *opposite* of minimalistic. Sun-Hi, whose face has looked sullen since I entered the room, is now wearing a scowl.

At least if I had said yes to the Birkin, I would have known that I was carrying precious cargo. I really have to start studying designers when I get back to the apartment.

"Seriously?" Gigi looks from the interns cooing around my scarf to the dark splotches seeping into her once-white high-waisted shorts and lacy white crop top. "You think that menace"—I'm the menace—"deserves help more than me? The innocent victim?"

I stop myself from correcting her "me" to "I" on the assumption that my copyediting would result in my murder.

Well, this day is off to a fan-freaking-tastic start.

I'm a naturally clumsy person, but this is just ridiculous. I blame Neanderthal Dog Walker. He totally got me frazzled this morning and threw me off my game.

Before I have the chance to apologize profusely, we're interrupted by the nice Skirt Suit I met in the hall.

"Change of plans, ladies. We're going to have to do orientation later. Request from the forty-second floor is that we get you all upstairs ASAP. McKayla is ready for you now."

"Wait, we're meeting McKayla *now*? I can't go in looking like this." Gigi motions to her outfit, which now resembles a Rorschach splatter test. "Can I quickly buy a jacket from one of the shops downstairs?"

"That is an . . . unfortunate situation," Skirt Suit says after looking at Gigi's outfit, "but no can do. Request from the forty-second floor is that we get you all upstairs ASAP."

"I'm a *really* fast shopper."

"I'm sure you are."

"Can I run to the loo to try to wash off?"

"Sorry, hon, but I'm not in the mood to get fired today. In McKayla-speak, ASAP means five minutes ago. Or else. So let's move it, ladies." She snaps her fingers and we shuffle to the door.

If I thought my side eye to Neanderthal Dog Walker was threatening, Gigi's is deadly. It could be the subject of an entire chapter in *The Art of War.*

· 5 ·

THE ELEVATOR DOORS OPEN TO A WALL THAT HAS THE *Shift* logo written on it over and over again in big bubble letters.

"Welcome to *Shift*," Skirt Suit says, just in case we missed the literal writing on the wall. She swipes her Bosh Media ID card in front of a sensor, which unlocks a large glass door. "Come this way."

The office's main entryway is decorated with blown-up magazine covers signed by that month's celebrity and leads into an open office space filled with electric-blue tables, beanbag chairs, and a variety of desk setups.

"So cool," says Abigail, Health, hypnotized by a woman in wedge sneakers who's typing furiously while power walking on a treadmill desk. "Sitting kills, you know."

Luckily I see staffers who are more my speed. Which is stationary.

Some are hunched in an ergonomically unfriendly manner over their giant computer screens, others at their standing desks, and there's a group of them gossiping by a watercooler that reads "Evian." No one so much as turns her Technicolor ombré-highlighted head when we file past in a neat row.

McKayla Rae is facing us when we enter her corner office, staring down each intern as we walk through the plate-glass door, one by one. Her arms are crossed as she leans against a large window that overlooks the Hudson River.

The décor is chic and austere. The walls are gray; the furniture is gray; the accent pieces around the room, metallic silver. McKayla, on the other hand, stands out against her surroundings. Her emerald-green wrap dress. Her dramatic red hair.

The message is clear: In here, you pay attention to McKayla and McKayla only.

While Gigi shrinks to the back of the intern cluster, trying to strategically place her big bag in front of her even bigger Diet Coke stains, Jamie beelines directly toward McKayla to shake her hand.

"It's *such* an honor to meet you," she says, arm outstretched. "I'm Jamie Sullivan. I interned here last summer and am so excited to be part of the website's viral team."

McKayla doesn't extend her hand.

"Can we . . . not?" she says. Jamie opens and then closes her mouth. She puts her rejected hand into the pocket of her dress and slouches back to the group. "If you can all manage to control yourselves, let's keep the ass-kissing to a minimum, 'kay? My sit-down with Taylor and Karlie got moved up, so I really don't have time for hugs and braiding each other's hair."

I don't know what's more terrifying, the ease with which she totally shut down Jamie, just for being polite, or the fact that she's on a first-name basis with Taylor Swift and Karlie Kloss.

She gestures toward the charcoal couches and stares until we take our spots. She remains standing. Only when we're quietly seated under framed photos of McKayla posing with celebrities ranging from Miley Cyrus to Hillary Clinton does she continue, slowly drumming her fingernails, decorated with Mondrian-inspired nail art, on her crossed arms. McKayla demands complete focus, deference, and a touch—no, a slap—of fear.

"Trenton Bosh hired me six months ago to take *Shift* from its current status as the biggest teen magazine in the country to the most clicked-on website," McKayla says.

Jamie raises her hand.

McKayla shakes her head, features sharp as a knife. "I'm going to be honest. I have no interest in any of you. I'm interested in your work. You're here to complete research for whoever tells you they need it, whenever they say they need it, and to write whatever I tell you to write. I don't want Shakespeare, I want edgy. I want stories that go viral, that people click on. I want thousands and thousands of clicks. If you aren't prepared for that, leave. But if you are, and if you do it *well*, you'll be rewarded. Or at least one of you will be. In a way that *Shift* has never rewarded an intern before."

Jamie raises her hand again.

"Seriously?"

Jamie drops her hand.

"As I was saying. The reward." We all sit forward, and McKayla suddenly beams, relishing her captive audience. "I'll be watching your stories all summer, and the intern who writes the pieces that get the most clicks will get rewarded not just online but in *print*. I've decided to reserve a two-page spread in the magazine to profile our most successful *Shift* Girl. Not only will you star in a photo shoot, complete with hair and makeup, but you'll be featured as our 'Teen Journalist to Watch.'"

The interns let out a collective, quick gasp. Afraid to make too much noise.

"And this won't go in just any magazine issue. It's going in our *September* issue. Back-to-School High Fashion is even bigger than May Prom. Millions of people are going to read it. The winner will be revealed in August, at the end of the internship. But you want this. The prestige of becoming the face of the future of journalism will open up more doors than you can imagine. It will impress everyone: your parents, your teachers, your future employers, who, if you play your cards right, could be us."

That.

I want *that*.

And I'm not going to let a few negligible deficits like no knowledge, experience, or edgy personal stories in my supposed area of expertise keep me from getting it.

"Internships here aren't for the faint of heart. We strive for excellence even from the lowest rung on the ladder, which you all *are*, so get ready to be on your A game at all times." McKayla stops her lecture abruptly. What was finally a cool smile has transformed back to a grimace on a dime. "Why are none of you writing this down?"

Our silence is broken as the interns crinkle through their bags to get out their notebooks. Jamie click-click-clicks and shakes a ballpoint pen, coaxing ink out of the tip. I can't help but smile. If this is our first test, I'm going to pass. I always have my black Moleskine on me. Every good journalist carries something to write on. But when I reach into my bag, I don't feel its smooth-to-the-touch cover. It's not like my keys, which always swim away from my fingertips like a goldfish. The Moleskine isn't small. It has nowhere to hide.

"How am I supposed to take you seriously if you don't come prepared?" McKayla says to me and me alone. Everyone else is scribbling away. "First impressions are *everything*. And you—which one are you?" She looks at my name tag. "And you, Harper, are . . . nothing."

"I'm sorry, I—"

"And *don't* say sorry. *Shift* Girls are not sorry. Haven't I told you this already?"

I feel my chest flush as my mind races. That notebook, which I *definitely* put in my bag this morning, contains almost all the physical evidence of my personal writing. This is not happening.

"Oh no, you're not about to *cry* are you?" McKayla says.

"No, I . . ."

"This is your one pass. Grab a notebook from the supply closet on your way out and be sure to have it with you at all times, because I won't be so nice next time."

"I have extras if Harper needs one," Gigi says, sporting a smug smile as she holds up a four-pack of long reporter's notebooks. "I always come prepared."

"Did you come prepared with a spare outfit in your Mary Poppins bag too?" McKayla's eyes go from Gigi's gigantic purse to her wrecked shirt, smacking the grin off Gigi's face. "Listen, ladies, as representatives of the company, *Shift* Girls always have to look their best, in and out of the office. Don't be the stain on the pristine *Shift* image." She levels her gaze at Gigi. "You're lucky your ID photo will be from the neck up."

"Actually, that wasn't her fault—" I begin, before McKayla hushes me and puts up her hand.

Gigi's eyes burn into my head. She has graduated from side eye to full-on glare.

McKayla looks down at her loose, gold watch, which hangs off her thin wrist like an oversize bracelet. Must be time for Taylor and Karlie. We're scooted out of her office with the promise that her assistant will set up one-on-one meetings for each of us with McKayla this week to go over specifics for what we'll bring to the site this summer. "If you last the summer."

The treadmill desk lady is now lightly jogging as she yells at someone on the phone, but after that meeting, I think we're sweating more than she is.

What have I gotten myself into?

• 6 •

"DID YOU OWN IT? BECAUSE YOU LOOK LIKE YOU owned it. Your outfit's on point."

I FaceTime Kristina the second I step out of the Bosh Building's rotating doors.

"My outfit might be on point, but I wasn't," I reply, sitting on the fountain's ledge, speaking quietly into my headphones' mic in case anyone from *Shift* passes by.

I tell her that the other interns hate me, the boss hates me, *and* I kept doing that thing where I get nervous and blabber a lot, followed by that thing where I get nervous and fall into complete silence.

"And to top it off, I was at peak klutzy mode."

"Like, lovable leading lady in the first quarter of a romantic comedy clumsy?"

"Like, worse than sixth grade volleyball clumsy."

"Ouch." Kristina pulls off her hairnet to let her scalp breathe, causing her blond hair to cascade across her purple Skinny B's work shirt. She took a break as soon as I called.

"Things will get better," she says. "Especially when you start writing. Any word on what you'll be doing there yet?"

I could divert the conversation. I could just talk about how I have the chance to have my face in *Shift* freaking magazine, which I need to tell her anyway. But I want to be honest.

And so I say, almost in a whisper, "Dating."

Kristina is silent.

"I'm going to write about dating," I say louder. "I'm *Shift*'s new dating expert."

And then Kristina bursts out laughing. The power of her giggle fit makes the camera phone shake back and forth. I even hear a snort.

"Kristina, stop it!" (She doesn't stop.) "I'm serious. They picked me to be their summer teen dating blogger. Like, the resident expert of summer flings."

"Wait, you weren't joking?" Her head pops back in the camera's frame. Kristina puts on her concentrating face. "Sorry, I thought . . . um . . . how did that happen exactly?"

"I don't know." Okay, so I want to be honest-ish, but it isn't quite working. "I think it was a random-selection thing? And no one else was interested?"

The improvised words come spinning out of my mouth with surprising ease.

"Sorry, I didn't mean to laugh." Kristina is still laughing, but at least she's trying to cover it up. "It's just, well, don't you need to *date* in order to be the dating blogger?"

"I've been on a date," I say defensively. But then I get a feeling in the pit of my stomach. The sides of my mouth fall as I remember.

Apocalypse Homecoming.

Homecoming's the biggest event on Castalia High's social calendar. Limos are rented, dresses are long, and hairdos are highly flammable.

Every year, Kristina insisted we go as friends; lots of girls did this.

She said it was because she didn't want to commit to just one guy in advance when who knows how she'd be feeling come dance night. But we both knew that she swatted down offers left and right while absolutely no guys were buzzing around me. We just didn't talk about it.

Which was fine until she announced that she got us both dates.

"Shane Barrett for me, Dave Ulman for you," she said. "Unless you wanna swap. I don't care, they'll both look good in pictures."

"You're tall," I said. "Basketball players will make me look like a munchkin. Besides, he's so not my type."

"Picky, picky! Kinda unfair to judge Dave before you give him a chance."

All right, so my personal taste skews toward an imaginary skinny jean wearer with a J. D. Salinger book in the back pocket (bonus points if it's an obscure Salinger), and Dave only wore athletic shorts and dropped English after his junior year despite our guidance counselor's dire predictions about what would happen to his college applications if basketball didn't pan out. But, the list of Castalia hipster, book-loving guys of my dreams began and ended with Adam Lockler, who was otherwise engaged.

But when Kristina went so far as to get my parents on board, telling me how great it would be to "give it a try, HunBun," I relented. And since my mind is known to wander and write its own creative nonfiction, I let myself imagine an alternate reality of Dave Ulman and our coupledom. Maybe I'd have fun and even *like* Dave. Maybe he'd like me back. Maybe I'd teach him to give Salinger a shot and he'd get me to start liking basketball. Maybe I'd start making *glitter signs* for away games.

So I let myself get excited for the limo and the long dress and the hair spray.

Dave brought me a corsage, we took selfies, the whole she-bang. Even though I was nervous, after Kristina dragged me to the bathroom ("I *said* I have to pee. Harper? HARPER, COME PEE WITH ME!") so that she could tell me to get out of my head and also reapply my lip gloss, I actually started making eye contact with Dave and completing full sentences and being smiley and flirty and agreeing to dance.

And then, by some miracle, before I knew it, we started to Dance Floor Make-Out. In public, on my tiptoes, under twinkle lights.

It wasn't my first kiss, but the one before almost felt like an accident. A random spin of the bottle. Kissing Dave Ulman was the first time it felt intentional. Real.

The running dialogue in my head (which is *always* running) told me that things were actually going well. Very well.

Stupid, stupid, stupid. I feel stupid just remembering it.

"You're thinking about him, aren't you?" Kristina says loudly into her phone speaker, yanking me back into reality. "We do *not* think about D-Bag Dull Man. We do *not* think of the guys who have embarrassed us."

"But don't you ever think of—"

"Nope," she snaps definitively. "I'm over it. Forgot all about it. And so should you! Forget I questioned the dating blogger thing at all. This is awesome and exactly what we talked about at Bobby McKittrick's party—he was the appetizer for your summer smorgasbord of *going for it*."

"I don't know. At home . . ."

"You *aren't* home. Do you know how many cute guys probably *live* in New York? And they're probably your malnourished, brainy type, too." Kristina's face gets really close to her phone screen and her eyes widen. "Like right there. You should just go up to that guy right there."

I turn and see him. Leaning against the reflective outside of the Bosh Building, reading a book. I squint and see it's called *Beyond Good and Evil* by Nietzsche, that German philosopher my AP Euro teacher wouldn't shut up about. He's skinny in the way I like guys to be, with dark brown, almost black, hair. Something about his stance (slanted slightly to the right), his expression (slightly smug), his whole demeanor, emanates intellect and cool. Interesting and exciting. Adam Lockler on hipster steroids.

He looks up from his book and I see how insanely green his eyes are, even from behind the lenses of his sexy, thick-framed glasses. We lock eyes for a second and I quickly avert my gaze, embarrassed to have been caught.

"You should go up to him," Kristina goads, smiling goofily through FaceTime. "Get this party started."

"Ha. Ha." I emphasize each word so she knows how little I'm actually laughing.

"Harper, it's time you started to carpe that effing diem. You can date whoever and be whoever. You look the part. Act it."

"Carpe that effing diem," I repeat. "Maybe. In fact, I might have to steal that phrase for one of my blogs."

"Replication is the highest form of flattery," she says. I hope she means it.

In the background, someone shouts at Kristina that she needs to get back to work. Water polo camp at the pool across the street just let out and the moms need their Kale Koladas.

"No, wait!" I say when Kristina starts putting her hairnet back on. "Just give me a five-second update on your life before I lose you. What's happening?"

"Nothing much. My summer is morning swim training, afternoon Skinny B's, and nighttime whatevers."

"What else?" I ask when she starts combing her hair behind her ears, her signature sign of distress.

"My dad's been calling," she says. "He wants to see me."

Kristina hasn't seen her dad since the wedding disaster—that he unfairly blames Kristina for. "How do you feel about that? Is he coming to California for work or something?"

"Not quite." Kristina shudders. "He wants me to go to him. To *them* in Connecticut."

"You must be joking." As much as I would love for Kristina

to take a trip east and save me, I know that's not going to happen. She won't even mention the stepmonster and stepbrother by name. "But at least your dad is reaching out. That's kind of good, right? He's gotta be missing you."

She doesn't answer. Someone calls Kristina's name again, and she flips her mouth back into a smile. "Okay, now I for real have to go. The blender awaits!"

The screen goes dark before I have the chance to ask more.

When I look back for the green-eyed Nietzsche reader Kristina spotted for me, he's no longer leaning against the building but is following an important-looking man and his minions out of the building.

I should have talked to him.

Carpe that effing diem. But in baby steps.

• 7 •

I'M EXHAUSTED, AND NOT JUST BECAUSE I BUNK with a plump pug who suffers from severe sleep apnea—although Aunt Vee says the vet has recommendations to get Princess's snoring under control.

My first week in New York is a whirl of memorizing subway maps (I've either gotten off at the wrong stop or taken a train in the wrong direction every day); memorizing designer names (after the Hermès incident, Aunt Vee has decided to make me fashion flash cards: "I used to help your mother study too!"); and memorizing *Shift* rules so I can be the best intern McKayla has ever had.

Most of our orientation with the office and staff is led by a member of the editorial team who has been at *Shift* the longest. But even though her hair is gray, the reporter's face is really young. And not in a Botox-y way.

"I *love* your granny hair," says Brie, Beauty, during a training session where we tell random factoids about ourselves to get to know one another better. "So on trend."

Comparing your superior's hair to your grandma's should *not* be a compliment. But in the world of *Shift*, this geriatric dye job is clearly intentional, and apparently popular.

"How long have you worked here?" Abigail asks.

"Five years longer than McKayla," Granny Hair says. "Since back in the day, when a person could write maybe one story a day. Under McKayla, make that more like six if you're on the viral news team. And that's not including when she'll call you at two in the morning when she needs you to write about a newly trending topic. But I've survived since her takeover, so that's something. It's . . . uh . . . challenging."

"Six stories aren't challenging for me!" Jamie says. "And viral's the section where I have the best shot of getting a job here by the end of the summer."

And there's the interesting factoid about overambitious Jamie. Even though she's only nineteen, Jamie has already graduated from college and is gunning for full-time employment at *Shift* after her internship ends. She thinks that if she wins the magazine intern profile, they'll *have* to hire her.

My eyes go from girl to girl as I match them up to their "fun facts."

Brie is the social chair of her University of Texas sorority and an aspiring YouTube beauty vlogger, who has the ability to make anyone look like a totally different human being with contouring. (She showed us the videos.)

Gigi is a rising high school senior like me but at a boarding school in Switzerland—"The French part. Obviously." She's half

Filipina and half Nigerian, and has lived on every continent except Antarctica. She once owned a pet peacock.

Abigail wants to be premed when she goes to college, but her parents made her take this internship after they bought it at her high school's silent auction. ("Trenton Bosh's kids went to Holland Prep too.")

Sun-Hi, who prefers going by Sunny (even though her face is in a perpetual frown), just finished her freshman year at the Fashion Institute of Technology.

I can't think of anything interesting to say, so I panic and tell everyone I'm the editor of my high school paper (lie) in California (true).

"Where in California?" Granny Hair asks.

"San Francisco." (Lie. Why am I lying?)

"Love SF," Granny Hair says, and then thankfully moves on to show us the most important features of the office.

My favorite spot by far is the *Shift* open kitchen.

Stocked with free-flowing, complimentary food and drinks, the kitchen has exposed me to a whole new world of luxury organic snack foods I never knew existed, and has been a major enabler of my Diet Coke dependency. It also has a state-of-the-art seltzer machine that pours out bubbly water with specialized flavor combinations—the kumquat-lime is not to be messed with—and a regularly replenished up-for-grabs table filled with leftover lunches from meetings and pastries sent from public relations firms trying to get reporters to write positive stories about their clients via carbohydrate bribery. ("The calories don't count if it was sent by a

PR person, right?" people ask, staring longingly at rows of uneaten, designer brownies.)

The most intimidating office feature hangs literally over our heads in the bullpen. Projected on an always-on television set is something called the Leader Board. With real-time data updating every seven seconds, the Leader Board shows the ten best-performing articles on the *Shift* website. This is our key to the magazine feature.

"You want to make this board," Granny Hair warns. "And this is how you get there."

She points to a piece of paper hanging under the television screen that reads, THE NINE COMMANDMENTS OF CLICKINESS. It's McKayla's own religious doctrine.

Shift biblical law includes: "Thou shalt write only odd-numbered listicles" (readers don't like clicking on even numbers), and "Thou shalt embrace puns" (the Internet *loves* puns). My personal favorite commandment, however, is the eighth:

Thou Shalt Not Pitch a Story If You Can't Think of a Good Headline First

A headline is hands-down the most important part of an article. Yes, even more than the writing. Because if your headline is bad, who will even read the story? Sell your story and yourself, even if you have to embellish. Any click's a good click.

I'm quick to memorize all the commandments—you never know when there's going to be a quiz—but am slow to break into the *Shift* Girls' social circle. They all laugh simultaneously several times a day at their computers, which makes me think they have an e-mail chain I'm not a part of.

So Friday, in hopes of speeding up the friendship process, I get to work extra early and leave a Sprinkles cupcake on each intern's desk in celebration of a successful end of our first week. Buttering them up by means of buttery treats.

Jamie is already at her desk, chugging coffee and watching a YouTube video of a toddler twerking when I arrive. To the untrained eye, it would look like she's goofing off. But watching crazy You-Tubes is actually a big part of her job. Every day, Jamie and the rest of the viral team comb through Reddit boards and trending hashtags to round up a batch of "quick hits" to write up for the *Shift* website by ten minutes ago. One hundred fifty words tops.

"My goal for June is to publish at least two viral stories before they go up on BuzzSnap," Jamie says. "I've gotta prove that I'm fast so McKayla will hire me."

She puts out her hand to accept the cookies-and-cream-flavored cupcake without even looking at it. Her eyes never leave her computer monitor when she pops it into her mouth and starts to chew.

When nine o'clock rolls around and the rest of the interns begin trickling in with giant cups of coffee, they appear underwhelmed by the treat. I start worrying that I maybe shouldn't have ignored Aunt Vee's warning that I should "try to kill them with kindness, not carbohydrates, dear. They're very different things."

"What's this?" Gigi asks in an accent as silky as her gorgeous dress.

"Cupcakes?"

"I see."

"I thought it would be fun to—"

"Fun? Do you know what's not fun, Harper? Debilitating stomach pains. Given how many people suffer from gluten intolerance, I find this action to be *very* insensitive."

Crap.

"One in every one hundred thirty-three people has celiac disease," Abigail, the trusty Health intern, pipes up. She's chomping on sunflower seeds rather than cupcake.

"That doesn't sound right," Brie says. "In my sorority, like, one in every three girls can't eat bread. My big, my big-big, and my big-big-big—"

"Well it is," Abigail says, seriously and severely. "I'm pitching a listicle about gluten intolerance for the health section, and I've done my research."

"Regardless," Gigi cuts her off. "This is very rude, Harper."

She drops the red velvet in the trash.

As promised, McKayla finally begins calling us individually into her office for our one-on-one meetings. Sunny is the first to go in. We look up from our various research and fact-checking assignments to watch her walk confidently into McKayla's office, her sleek, asymmetrical black hair and a sleek, asymmetrical black dress swishing behind her as if she were hooked up to a portable wind machine.

During her twenty-minute meeting, we all pretend we have reasons to walk past McKayla's glass door and get a surreptitious look at how it's going. But stoic Sunny's face reveals no leads, before, during, and after the meeting.

"It's really not that bad," Sunny says when she comes out. "But, Jesus, how many times can one person say the word 'edgy' in ten minutes?"

Sunny says she spent most of the time pitching McKayla an article idea she thinks is magazine worthy. "Don't Call Us Lipstick Lesbians: The World of Lesbian Chic."

Because she's in a relationship nearing its second anniversary, Sunny is probably more qualified to be the dating blogger than I am. She and her girlfriend, Cassie, even have their own hashtag on Instagram. #Sussie. And based on the pictures, chic is the only way to describe them. The two met on the first day of Sunny's freshman year at the Fashion Institute. Cassie was randomly assigned to be her "fit model." Fitting, right? (Note: I don't usually think in puns, but I'm practicing *Shift*'s biblical mandate to embrace them in our writing.) Anyway, it was love at first stitch. (Oh God, that one doesn't even work. Let's hope there's a big learning curve for becoming a pun master.)

I get called into McKayla's office last.

"Why do you look like your cat just died?" McKayla looks up from her phone to acknowledge my presence and then goes back to typing furiously. "You look more sullen than Sunny. Smile, Harper. You should be slightly pleased to have the opportunity to meet me one on one."

"So sorry!"

"*Shift* Girls don't say sorry. Maybe write that down this time."

"Of course!" I underline the words *NEVER SAY SORRY!!!* three times in my flimsy spiral notebook from the supply closet. In spite of my best searching efforts, my beloved Moleskine was nowhere to be found in Aunt Vee's apartment.

"Well, you know why you're here." McKayla puts down her phone dramatically. "Let's talk about your blog."

That's all it takes to make me break into a completely natural, completely excited grin. She said "your" blog. As in *my* blog. This is real. I'm not about to wake up from this dream with remnants of acai berries under my fingernails.

"There are two reasons that you were picked to be our dating blogger," she says. "And they are . . ."

Pause.

"Because your first choice got pregnant?" Oh God, did I just say that out loud?

"All right, there are *three* reasons why you were picked to be our dating blogger. The first is that the American public school system failed to teach Tammy proper sex ed. The second, however, is the fact that you have a voice. It's arch, it's funny, and it's a little bit snarky, which the Internet *loves*. You'll need to be our high school readership's friend. Their gossip buddy. I want to build a brand here with a following of avid retweeters and Facebook posters."

Am I hearing her correctly? Because it seems like this is going *really* well.

"Thank you!" My entire body untenses. This will all work out.

Shift didn't want me because of Kristina's crazy dating experiences and the fact that I replaced the word "Kristina" with "I" in my application essay. They want me because of *how* I wrote about them.

"The last reason is because of the sample blog post in your application." McKayla is now making direct eye contact with me instead of her phone. "I love a good sex scandal."

Sex scandal?

Uh-oh.

Medieval minstrels could sing songs celebrating my virginity; Kristina, on the other hand . . .

"Of course I can't post that on the site. Pity," McKayla continues. "Just yesterday I had to go to all-out war with the oldies who are still in power upstairs to clear putting the words 'dick pic' in a headline. I'm still trying to convince them to let me run the word 'sexcapades.'"

"That's probably for the best," I say carefully. "I mean—"

"Yeah, whatever." McKayla waves away my concern like she's swatting at a gnat. She doesn't like interruptions. "Still, your sample blog is the kind of stuff I want. Be real. Be gritty. Don't sugarcoat things. No sugarcoating *ever*."

Am I the only person in this whole office who likes both carbs and sugar?

"No problem." I refuse to show any signs of self-doubt. I readjust my Peter Pan–collared shirt and ask if we can start talking about other ideas for real, edgy, "clicky" dating blog posts. (I've been preparing for this conversation all week and have taken note of McKayla's favorite buzzwords to make sure this goes as well as possible.)

"Yes, let's huddle on that." McKayla begins rhythmically drumming her nails, now painted to look like Pop Art, on her desk, waiting for me to talk.

"People like horror stories, right? So I could write about my worst date ever and, like, have *Shift* readers tweet their bad dates too."

"Well, at least there's social media involvement." She leans forward, yawning slightly. I take this as a threat; put her to sleep only if you plan to turn in your *Shift* intern badge before she wakes up. "But what was the date?"

I might have used Kristina's story to get my foot in the door, but I'm going to try to make it at *Shift* being as honest as possible. Luckily my only "kind of" date was more than "kind of" terrible.

"Well, this fall I went to homecoming with this really cute guy," I say. McKayla looks intrigued, like she's about to hear a secret. Something tells me that McKayla loves knowing secrets.

"But it turns out that he only went with me because he wanted to hook up with my best friend, which totally isn't a surprise because *every* guy wants to date her. Anyway, when I left for five minutes to get us punch, he even tried to kiss her—"

"Oh God, stop. Harper, this story is so boring and mopey and pathetic."

It *was* pathetic.

I remember seeing Dave's puckered lips descend upon Kristina's angry mouth when her date and I came back from our expedition to get punch, and hearing his booming assertion that he was sure she liked him too carry across the dance floor.

"What are you talking about?" Kristina seethed, pushing him away. "You're here with my best friend."

"But not really," he insisted. "C'mon, you knew I wouldn't be into her. She's not one of us. You only asked me to come along because you weren't that into Shane, and I didn't have the balls to ask you out before he did."

Kristina responded by promptly kicking Dave in the groin before her date could get to him. As it turned out, Dave had those balls after all.

"I. Don't. Like. Cheaters," Kristina declared over his writhing body.

McKayla's voice rips through my memory. "Harper, that's *not* the kind of story that I'm looking for. Even if you're writing about a bad date—which you will, horror stories click *very* well—you still need to be the kind of girl *Shift* readers want to be. The pinnacle of desirability. Give me a better bad date you've been on."

I'm silent. There are no better bad dates. Or good dates. Or dates of any kind.

I feel another deep pang of loss for my missing Moleskine. The notebook is filled with funny quips and comments on Kristina's numerous disaster dates. One flip through, and I'd be set with a juicy tidbit. Not to publish, of course. I just need a quick fix for this meeting.

"It truly baffles me, Harper, how you can be so sharp in your writing and so bumbling in person. You should really work on that." Her phone starts buzzing.

She wraps up our meeting, telling me she'll want a draft of my blog on her desk every Monday (starting *this* Monday), so that she can go through it with a hacksaw. That way it will be ready for its weekly Wednesday publication.

"For this week's, you can just introduce yourself to readers, explain your dating mantra, and get everyone ready to read about your dating escapades. Easy."

Yeah, right. Easy.

• 8 •

I CAN'T BREATHE.

And it's not because the East Coast flora and fauna have unleashed allergies that my West Coast sinuses never knew existed. (Thank God for Mucinex.) And it's not because I'm in over my head at *Shift*. (Although, let's face it, I totally am.)

I can't breathe because out of all the places in Aunt Vee's gigantic penthouse that Princess could have chosen to lie—including her special-ordered, memory-foam dog bed—she has decided to sprawl out on my stomach, stubby limbs akimbo.

We're in the living room, spread out by the window, soaking up the last patch of light like lizards before the sun dips down behind the buildings to our west and into the Hudson River.

"Princess, I think we're bonding," I say, petting her on the back.

I might be projecting, but I think Princess grunts in agreement.

Unfortunately, my interspecies friendships are faring better than my intern-to-intern ones. The *Shift* Girls are all bonding with one another. And I wasn't invited. While McKayla was instructing me on how to conquer the dating blogosphere, I watched through her office's glass doors as the girls turned off their computers and got ready to leave.

"The Arts & Culture editor gave Gigi a bunch of passes to a movie screening," Brie explained. "Do you have another, Gigi?"

"Limited availability," Gigi said. "Maybe next time."

"Want me to take a red-eye and shank them for u?" Kristina offered when I texted her on my walk from the subway.

Harper: SHANK them?

Kristina: Been watching Orange Is the New Black. Alone. Bc u abandoned me. Is that a yes?

Harper: NOPE. (But reserving the right to change my mind...)

I'm lucky. Kristina has always been the kind of friend who would shank someone on your behalf.

Our friendship origin story goes back to my *second* first day of preschool, after my parents unceremoniously moved us from Sacramento to Castalia in the middle of the year, in spite of my very compelling requests to stay put. Making new friends sounded scary. Besides, my old pre-K had an endless supply of Popsicle sticks and googly eyes I'd grown very attached to.

So there I was, a shy girl hiding behind my parents' legs as a teacher showed us around Castalia Day, when a precocious four-and-three-quarters-year-old (apparently she was very specific when introducing herself to my parents) pushed her way through my dad's knees and asked for my name.

Like that, Kristina plopped a newly arts-and-crafted pipe-cleaner-and-pom-pom tiara on top of my head and claimed me as her own, dragging me around the room to inform everyone from the Play-Doh clique to the Tonka truck crew: "Harper's new. Be her friend."

I've never had to fend for myself socially without Kristina by my side. And from the look of things on the *Shift* Girls' Snapchat Stories from the movie screening, I don't know if I can.

"Maybe the two of us can go out on the town sometime," I tell Princess, flopping her ears up and down and up again, an activity so enthralling that I completely miss the approaching footsteps.

"Uh-oh, who let you near an animal?"

I jerk up and Princess tumbles off my stomach in one swift motion to a soft landing on the carpet. How do I know that voice? Who else is in the apartment?

"See, there you go again, knocking over dogs left and right. Should I be calling the Humane Society?"

The floppy-haired Neanderthal Dog Walker!

Is he *stalking* me? Is he back for retribution after our sidewalk scuffle? Am I about to be murdered before I even have a chance to go to the Guggenheim, get a frozen hot chocolate from Serendipity, and see a musical on Broadway?

"How'd you get in here?" I scramble in my bag for my iPhone. "Stay over there or I'm calling the cops?"

"Whoa, whoa, whoa. I think you have the wrong idea." Dog

Walker Stalker puts up his hands and backs toward the front door. "I'm here for Princess."

"How do you know her *name*?" I dial a nine, a one, and a one, and hover my finger dramatically over the call button.

"I'm her dog walker! I'm Princess's dog walker! Vet's orders."

Princess, too lazy to get out of the awkward position she fell into after her spill from my lap, gives an annoyed harrumph.

"This is only our second session. You can't tell me that that dog doesn't look like she's in serious need of some veterinarian-mandated exercise!"

His story is slightly credible. I've seen Princess plop her stomach into her monogrammed food bowl and drag it with her around the apartment so that she has easy access to food at all times. But of all the dog walkers in New York, couldn't Aunt Vee have hired someone else? Or maybe sprung for a puppy elliptical machine instead?

"Okay, if that doesn't help you chill, maybe this will," Stranger Danger says as he reaches into his backpack to pull out . . . a knife? Chloroform?

My missing notebook!

"You dropped it the other day during our, you know." He walks toward me like there are land mines embedded in Aunt Vee's hardwood floor and hands me the black Moleskine in not-quite-mint condition. "Sorry it's not in better shape. Atticus got to it before I did."

I run my finger over the soft cover, but its signature smooth texture has been replaced with what feels like inverse Braille, courtesy

of Atticus's incisors. When I flip through the pages, I see that por-
tions of dashed-off notes have been disrupted by chew marks. Sections of writing are lost to the smears of blue pen in areas that have
been particularly affected by slobber. I feel its loss all over again, as if
little pieces of me have been chewed up and obliterated, too.

Suddenly the land mine that Neanderthal Dog Walker was so
carefully trying to avoid goes off and, through absolutely no will of
my own, I just start crying.

And not cute crying. Ugly crying. The kind where your face
gets red and your breathing gets all gaspy and you realize you're
precariously close to becoming a snot monster.

Tell me this isn't happening!

I'm not just crying over spilled Diet Coke or a ruined notebook. Whenever I felt like I didn't fit into the social scene at school
perfectly, I'd imagine my alternate, fabulous life after graduation.
I'd live in New York. I'd be a writer. People would get me. But now,
here I am with this "opportunity of a lifetime," as McKayla puts it,
with the new clothes, job, apartment, and persona handed to me
on a platinum platter, and somehow I still can't make it work.

"Are you crying?"

But he isn't asking me about the state of my tear ducts in an
accusatory jerk way. The guy looks 100 percent freaked out.

And then he does something completely unexpected. Neanderthal
Dog Walker stops pacing, crouches down between me and a totally
over it Princess, and hugs me. Just wraps his arms around me and
holds.

And I do something even *more* surprising. I let him.

His arms anchor me while my mind swirls. They have a strange calming effect, and it doesn't take too long for my body to feel like it did after my mom's Xanax kicked in on my cross-country flight, when I finally stopped focusing on keeping the plane at a steady altitude through force of will (okay, so maybe I have some control issues) and just let go.

Reapproaching reality, I lightly wriggle my arms out of his hold so that I can sweep my hands under my eyes. Even waterproof mascara can only handle so much. The movement startles him.

"Oh man, was that not okay?" He withdraws his arms. "I'm not used to crying. At all. I go to an all-boys school and the only emotion my parents show is disapproval, so I went with my first instinct. That wasn't creepy, right?"

"Just one more thing to add to the police report," I say, turning to face him, his arms firmly folded across his chest and eyes turned back to saucers. "Oh God, sorry, too soon. I'm totally kidding. No police reports and no on the 'that not being okay' thing. The hug was actually surprisingly helpful. I just can't believe I lost it like that in front of someone I don't even know."

He smiles in a supremely goofy manner, as if nothing strange has transpired in the slightest, and extends a hand. "I'm Ben."

"Harper." His hands are rough. Maybe a casualty of the leash-holding.

"You okay, Harper?" He doesn't let go of my hand or my eye contact.

"Yeah, I think so." I never did well in staring contests. I look out the window and watch the sky transition into a deep orange as the sun begins to set over the park. New York sky *en fuego*. "Sorry again about being a total crazy person."

"You don't have to be sorry. I'm the one who came in here guns blazing," Ben says. "I swear I'm not always that big of an asshole. I've had a really crappy week. Not that it's an excuse."

"Tell me about it. Besides, I wasn't exactly a peach myself."

Princess snorts. No one has been paying attention to her for at least five minutes.

"I think that's my cue to do my job and walk the dog," Ben says. But he doesn't move. I don't move. "Hey, want to come with me and get some air?"

Is this a pity invite? My first impulse is to think of an excuse. It's not like I don't have any. I need to start writing my premier post to the *Shift* audience; I need to memorize my fashion flash cards.

Then I realize that I don't want an excuse to avoid Ben.

"Air sounds good."

Princess is less hot to trot.

It's hardly a surprise to learn that the pug, in all her roly-poly glory, is a part of Ben's "remedial group" of reluctant and unruly walkers. As soon as the leash is attached to her bedazzled collar, Princess lies down on her stomach, stretches all four legs, sticks out her tongue, and plays dead. It takes coaxing (note: coaxing involves a lot of fake bacon) to revive her.

"Your building is full of dogs who don't understand the concept of taking a walk," Ben explains as he drags Princess to an apartment down the hall to pick up his next confused client. "Wagner lives here. If you've never seen a dachshund chase his tail before, brace yourself, because your world is about to be rocked."

Apparently the longhaired, long-bodied Wagner hasn't always been an obsessive tail pursuer. Ben confides that Wagner is at the center of a mega custody battle between his uber-high-profile art dealer owners.

"His therapist blames the tail chasing on stress from the divorce," Ben says without a hint of irony. "They're considering putting him on a low dose of Lexapro."

"The dogs here are . . . *medicated*?" That's just the kind of anecdote I'd love to jot down in my notebook.

"Everyone here is medicated. You have no idea."

Ben tells me the personal histories of the dogs and their owners as I accompany him door to door to his other stops—Pepe the Frenchie at 4C, Poncho the Pomeranian at 3F, and finally Atticus, my nemesis, at 2A. While Ben clinks through his enormous key chain to find the right key, it sounds like the giant Goldendoodle puppy is going to scratch through the door. He bounds out as soon as the door opens and runs directly into Ben's leg.

"Atticus! Chill out!" Ben hands me the leashes as he tries to get ahold of Atticus, who is bouncing from the hallway's right wall to its left wall through Ben's legs and then directly into a not-having-it Princess.

"Are you sure that it was me who, how did you put it, 'bulldozed' maliciously into Atticus and not the other way around?" I can't help laughing as he wrestles with Atticus, who's now on a mission to lick the freckles off Ben's face.

"I might be overly protective of my dog family." Ben pushes Atticus off his face with one hand and deftly hooks him onto the leash with the other.

Ben practically drags the mismatched group of dogs out of the foyer and down the three stairs leading up to the building. We move from the air-conditioned lobby into the sticky heat of the New York City summer night. But I'm not complaining. There's a buzz in the air, and it isn't mosquitoes. The sun has set and sidewalks are teeming with people in suits heading home and joggers dashing toward the park and screaming "on your left" to meandering tourists staring at their guidebooks rather than the road ahead.

"I live a few avenues east," Ben says. "Cheaper real estate."

He's been walking some of these dogs since freshman year, when his dad told him it was time to get a job and learn some responsibility.

"But now he's pissed that I still do it. He says it's a total waste of my Saint Agnes scholarship to spend the summer walking dogs instead of doing one of those corporate finance internships my high school hooks juniors and seniors up with. My dad's all, 'How are you going to get into Wharton next year if you don't take your summers seriously?' Like I'd *ever* consider going to Wharton." He turns to me to explain, "Wharton is the business program at Penn—"

"I *know* what Wharton is," I tell him. "Believe it or not, word of the Ivy League has spread all the way across the Sierra Nevada."

"Anyway, I don't care about finance," Ben says. "I like the dogs, and the money people pay me to walk them is ridiculous."

While our group slowly traverses Fifth Avenue toward Central

Park (Pepe leads the pack; Atticus goes side to side sniffing people's shoes; and Princess defiantly, repeatedly, sits down in the middle of the road), Ben begins peppering me with questions. He nods when I say that I'm also a rising senior and does an overly dramatic eyebrow raise when I tell him I'm *Shift*'s summer teen dating blogger.

"So you're here for a writing internship? Oh man, I didn't let Atticus chew up the next great American novel, did I?"

"Hardly," I reply. "My notebook is mostly for, um, it's like I'm recording little snapshots of the weird things happening around me. Like something funny someone asks in class."

"I thought there were no dumb questions."

"Mary Taylor once asked if Shakespeare wrote *Titanic*. I think it's because she knew Leonardo DiCaprio was in that and a remake of *Romeo and Juliet*."

"I don't believe you."

"I'd show you proof, but Atticus ate it. Anyway, I record stuff like that. Weird observations. Snippets of conversations."

"You record your eavesdropping?"

"Instead of eavesdropping, can we call it active observation? *Very* active. But that's totally different from what I have to do at *Shift*. I'm actually going to have to write down the embarrassing things *I* do and say. Not just write down the highlights I hear from a first date crashing and burning at the table next to me at the coffee shop." I head toward the entrance of the park, but Ben is walking in a different direction. "Aren't we going into the park? Believe it or not, even though I'm living across the street, I haven't been inside yet."

"Nah, not yet. Let's walk uptown just a little bit longer." Ben directs the dogs north, and they follow behind like ducklings, realizing it's easier to trudge along by will than by force.

The crowds condense as we approach the Metropolitan Museum of Art. There are police on horseback and kids screaming to their mothers that they want a hot dog—no, *two* hot dogs. Caricaturists wearing headlamps are squinting in the dark at their canvases displaying sketches of women with pinched waists and accentuated breasts. But I just push past to take a look at the rows of stairs leading up to the Met, leaving Ben and the dogs behind.

I'm embarrassed to admit that the rush I feel is more credited to *Gossip Girl* than it is to the art. While the show was a big no-no at my house—"One of those kids will have an STD by the commercial!" my dad decreed. "Watch a musical with me and Mom instead!"—Kristina's mom didn't do television rules in elementary school. Those Monday nights are some of the few memories I actually have of sleeping over at Kristina's. We would eat tiny peanut butter Ritz Bits crackers on the living room couch, her pining after Nate the jock and me pining after Dan the brainiac, and watch Blair scheme her way to the upper echelons of the Manhattan elite while she sat on these very steps.

I take a Snapchat and write the words "Wish you were here!" in big orange letters with my pointer finger.

"I was wondering where you went!" Ben says, dogs in tow. Princess takes one look up at the stairs and lies down, in case anyone was under the false impression that she would be climbing them. "Catch!"

My hand-eye coordination sucks, but my reflexes don't. Before Atticus can get his teeth on it, I bend down and pick up . . . a new notebook.

"There's always a kiosk set up around here," Ben says. "I figured I owed you."

Rather than my understated black Moleskine—a favorite of Hemingway, Picasso, and other intimidating geniuses who sometimes make me question if I should write in permanent pen—this notebook is a bright yellow.

"I thought you could use something a little flashier," he says. Which I guess makes sense. This summer is all about doing rather than taking notes by the sidelines. Been there, done that.

"That's really nice." I notice that when Ben curls his lips into a half smile, a dimple appears in his left cheek. "And thanks. You really didn't have—"

"Look!" Ben's dimple quickly disappears, like a secret that's meant to be kept hidden. He whips out his phone and points it down. "Wagner is chasing his tail! I've been trying to get a video of this for weeks. Can you turn on the flashlight on your phone so I get good lightning?"

Wagner starts slowly, making eyes at his tail like it's a doe that's about to run away into the forest. Then he slowly bends his long body around to creep up on it from behind. Pretty soon Wagner is spinning, in hot pursuit. But the difference between a dachshund chasing his tail versus just about every other breed of dog is that the dachshund actually stands a chance of catching it. And in a triumphant moment, Wagner does. But that doesn't keep him from continuing to go round and round like a pinwheel, tail in mouth, in pure, unadulterated puppy bliss.

"I don't get Wagner." I watch him twirl under my temporary spotlight. A crowd has formed. "Isn't the fun supposed to be in the chase?"

"No way. The fun is what comes after."

I feel little baby butterflies leave their cocoon and start to flutter in my stomach.

"Got it. I'm definitely posting this on my dog Instagram." Ben stops recording. Wagner is panting on the ground.

"Your *what* Instagram?"

"I have a separate account for funny dog stuff," he says. "Anyway, as I was saying, games suck. My girlfriend wasn't into making me do the whole chase thing at all and I liked her even more for it. I like things as uncomplicated as possible."

Annnnnd the butterflies are dead. Smashed to smithereens. Stomped into oblivion.

Ben keeps talking, but all I hear is that one word.

Girlfriend.

Neanderthal Dog Walker, who might not be so much of a Neanderthal after all, has a girlfriend.

• 9 •

THE NEXT DAY I SPEND A LOT OF TIME SITTING
and staring at a blank Word document. I try to conjure the persona
of a super-cool, confident, irresistible dating expert—snarky mentor and best friend to millions of girls across the country.

Nothing comes to mind.

Instead I try to estimate how many *Shift* readers should actually be giving me the dating pointers.

Conclusion: a lot.

And so I sit and stare some more. Writing and rewriting possible openings in my head, but rejecting them before I even type
them out on the page. Is it possible to have commitment issues
with sentences?

Fully aware that my head isn't in the game, I allow myself to
take a break from not-writing, and procrastinate by rewatching the
first few episodes of *Gossip Girl* on Netflix and lightly stalking Ben's
relationship.

The girlfriend.

Her name is Delilah.

She goes to Ben's sister school, Saint Clementine.

And she plays varsity soccer. Because *of course* she does.

They met six months ago at a party, Ben told me last night as he led the way back to Aunt Vee's, cradling a wheezing and overexerted Princess in his arms. He explained that every month, a trust fund kid ("usually one who goes to Holland Prep") rents out a club to host a party. Said trust fund kid then earns back the cost of rental fees and proceeds to make a killing by selling party tickets at fifty dollars a pop to other trust fund kids on the New York private school circuit.

"That's so much more exciting than a keg in someone's backyard," I said to Ben.

"Are you kidding? Kegs in backyards sounds way better to me."

"Well, that's only because you don't have backyards here. It's a novelty."

"Nah, these club things aren't my scene. Too many pretentious douche bags." He readjusted a slipping Princess while making sure to maintain full control of the leashes. "But I'm glad I went to this one. Because otherwise I wouldn't have met Delilah."

Ben's left to his own devices this summer while Delilah—"the next Abby Wambach!"—is away at a prestigious soccer camp in New Hampshire. She left the morning we literally ran into each other, which explains his crappy mood.

I pause on an Instagram of Ben and Delilah playing flag football. Ben and Delilah celebrating a big lacrosse win. Ben and Delilah on a couples' jog, aka my personal nightmare, through the Central Park Loop. And then it hits me.

I shouldn't actually care that Ben has a girlfriend.

If I wanted to date someone like Ben, then I could have just stayed in Castalia. There are plenty of jocks there. Ben's not my type and I'm not his—just look at his Kristina-esque girlfriend. (Minus the broad swimmer shoulders, plus the soccer girl calves, and with darker blond hair.)

Any fluttering I might have felt in my stomach must have been the product of phantom butterflies, not real ones. My status as dating blogger has made me feel desperate to find a guy to write a dating blog about. Ben was just the first guy I met.

Besides, he'll be way better as a friend—something that I'm severely lacking at the moment. A low-pressure friend, whom I don't have to impress with encyclopedic knowledge of dating dos and don'ts, viral headlines, and designer names.

If I were an actual dating guru, I would tell myself that this summer isn't about rushing toward romance with the first guy I meet. Besides, he's going to be around walking Aunt Vee's obese pug every day—that would be so awkward when things (inevitably) fell apart.

In fact, I'm lucky that I don't have to worry about trying to find a lasting whatever with one guy. That's way too much pressure.

I've been known to fixate. But this summer isn't about *a* boy. It's about *boys*. Or "dating escapades" as McKayla put it.

Suddenly I find my voice and start typing.

MEET *SHIFT*'S SUMMER DATING BLOGGER!

Every week Harper's going to be taking you with her on her road to finding the ideal summer fling . . . or should we say *FLINGS*?

Hey, *Shift* Girls! My name's Harper and I've come from sunny California to the concrete jungle known as Manhattan to tell tales of my summer dating escapades. Like any girl who has rocked out to *Grease*'s "Summer Nights" during karaoke, you might be tempted to find a sizzling summer fling. And I'm here to tell you—DON'T DO IT!

Don't worry, I'm not saying that you shouldn't find a hot lifeguard on the beach to help you apply suntan lotion to that impossible-to-reach spot in the middle of your back. That would just be irresponsible! (Take it from a Californian, UV rays are no joke, ladies.) But why should you limit yourself to one lifeguard and one set of hands? Why have a summer fling when you can have summer flings?

The whole concept of a summer fling is that it's no drama, no strings, no heartbreak when you call it quits come Labor Day weekend. But let's be real, you're just a little bit hoping that you're going to find the Danny to your Sandy. But who wants to spend the summer agonizing about why the cute guy at your fro-yo shop hasn't texted you back after your melt-worthy make-out sesh (you know he saw your iMessage; you know he was typing; you saw the ". . ."!!) when you *should* be getting smaller samples of all the different flavors?

Everything and everyone is hotter in this season, so take advantage of it. The only thing that should be tied down this summer is your surfboard to the top of your car.

You can join me every Wednesday for more *Shift* Girl summer dates, dos, and don't-you-dares.

Carpe that Effing Diem!
Harper

· 10 ·

ONCE I STARTED WRITING, NOT STARING AT THE screen and thinking about writing but actually putting words on the page, I couldn't stop.

I wrote the blog post.

But *I* also didn't write the blog post.

It was as if I was creating a character—summoning and projecting a cooler and more confident version of myself—and her voice took over, if that makes any sense.

"This is exactly what I was talking about when I said you could be whoever you wanted," Kristina says when I try to explain. "It's not a character; it's you. The writing sounds like you. Okay, *maybe* it sounds like you had a million cans of Diet Coke, but it's totally your sense of humor."

"It doesn't seem off to you that I'm giving advice about having a summer fling versus flings when I've never had either? It doesn't seem like I'm lying?"

"It's *not* a lie. Just because you haven't done it yourself doesn't mean that it isn't good advice. Advice that you should be taking. It *is* way better to date lots of guys over the summer. Slash always." She pauses for a breath before continuing her monologue. "Look, if Mother Teresa wrote a listicle about ways to help poor people, but she personally hadn't tried each and every one of them, she wouldn't be *lying*, would she? The world would still be a better place if people listened to her. Harper, you're writing service journalism!"

"Service journalism? Okay, now who sounds like she's been smoking Bobby McKittrick's bad pot?"

But in spite of the Mother Teresa hyperbole, Kristina is making some sense.

My dating blog isn't a lie. And even if it is, it's a white lie. Told for the greater good. And who knows, maybe if I fake this character long enough, eventually I'll start turning into this new persona through osmosis or something. (I don't know, science isn't my thing.)

I send McKayla my column first thing Monday morning, as requested. She doesn't say anything. And as Wednesday approaches, I freak out that her silence might be a very bad sign. I spend the nights before I finally get McKayla's feedback tossing and turning, acutely aware of Princess's snoring patterns. (Three short grunts followed by a long snort, pause, repeat.) Instead of counting sheep, I count all the different reasons McKayla might hate it. All the different ways that things can backfire. What if she sees right through my blog and me? I can hear her saying how obvious it is that I have no idea what I'm talking about.

How it was a mistake hiring me after all. How I'm clueless and I can't even write. How Adam Lockler was correct and I should focus on fact checking. How I'm going to be fired in a blast of public humiliation and sent back to Castalia, where I'll be unemployed because Skinny B's already finished up its summer hiring.

But that's not what happens.

Because it turns out that McKayla actually *likes* it.

Okay, so she doesn't go so far as to utter the words "I like it," but she does say, "Cute," before setting it live on the website Wednesday morning. And since McKayla is short on praise, that four-letter word makes me smile just as hard as I would if she told me that she was submitting my dating blog to the Pulitzer committee.

I walk on a cloud, back to the bullpen.

"I gained, like, five pounds when I dated an ice-cream scooper last summer," Brie tells me later that morning. "How about you?"

"Huh?"

"Your blog post? Your fling with a guy at a fro-yo shop!" Brie's eyes glimmer. Or maybe it's just her glitter eyeliner, which she insists is going to be huge this fall.

"Oh, right!" I quickly recover. "Um . . . six? I gained six pounds?"

Sunny looks up from her computer screen and sighs. "It's so much better dating someone in the fashion industry than the food industry. I'll take free clothes over calories any day."

"I don't know, it would be a toss-up for me," I reply, hoping to find a way to make Sunny smile. "Fries over guys."

"Oh, you poor hetero-normative child." Sunny sighs again. "Besides, I'll take girls over fries any day."

"What's the best thing you ever got out of a date?" Brie asks Gigi. "I'll bet it's something fancy and European. Like Chanel Number 5."

Gigi smooths her hair.

"I think it's very *gauche* to kiss and tell," she says, looking straight in my direction, before explaining in a kindergarten teacher voice, "That means *tacky*, Harper."

"No way, kissing and telling is fun!" Brie breezes right over the insult as if it never happened.

"I'm sure Harper has an *army* of conquests she'd love to keep talking about," Gigi says. "Go ahead. Tell us all about having sex behind the bleachers, or whatever it is you do."

The interns look up expectantly. Even Jamie, who's never not busy cranking out a story.

"I already made the Leader Board today, so I earned a break," she says smugly. The TV screen hovering above our desks shows that her article about "7 Bizarre Pizza Hut Creations You Won't Believe Are Real" is sitting comfortably as the third most popular story on the website. "I could use a funny story."

I didn't know being a dating blogger would make people treat me like a show pony. Luckily I'm more prepared this time than when I was with McKayla, and I have one of Kristina's bizarre dates ready.

He had a nut allergy. She had no idea and ate a Snickers bar a few hours before they started to Dance Floor Make-Out at a party. Swelling ensued. Eli and the EpiPen.

I tell the story and everyone laughs except Gigi.

"So the cupcakes weren't an isolated incident? You like poisoning people for fun?" Before Gigi can go on, she's interrupted by swear words echoing through the office.

We all freeze.

"No, I will not go to the thirteenth floor!" the voice shouts again. I stand up to get a view of what's happening right in time to see Granny Hair, usually so nice and levelheaded, hang up her work phone and throw it against the wall.

"THIS IS NOT HAPPENING!" she shouts even louder. People sitting near the meltdown go over and start saying things to her in whispers that don't travel the span of the office.

"NO, I WILL NOT CALM DOWN! I GOT A CALL TELL-ING ME TO GO TO THE THIRTEENTH FLOOR. YOU KNOW WHAT THAT MEANS." Granny Hair pushes them away and marches to McKayla's office, her stilettos stabbing the floor. But we can see through the glass doors that her office is empty.

McKayla's assistant comes running, explaining that she's at an important meeting.

"Coward," Granny Hair says in a more muted tone. "I've worked here for *five years*. She's going to fire me and not even be here to do it. She's going to send me down to HR."

The assistant tries to calm Granny Hair down. "Please, Michelle, just go to the thirteenth floor. You don't want to make a scene. I don't want to have to call security."

"Well, someone needs to make a scene," Michelle says, before turning around to the rest of the office. "She's turning you all into hamsters on a wheel. I'm not sorry that I can't write six-plus stories a day, every day. I didn't become a journalist to do *this*."

She walks back to her desk, picks up her bag, and heads to the elevators. She passes the intern desks on her way out and scoffs.

"I'm sure one of you will replace me in no time."

No one says a word for a good ten seconds after she leaves, which sounds like a short time but feels like eternity.

Jamie is the first of the interns to break the moment of silence.

"Do you think that she meant it when she said that one of us would replace her?"

"Oh my God, did you really just say that?" I ask in disbelief. "I thought you guys were friends."

"Also," Abigail pipes in, "Michelle had been here for years. Her replacement is probably going to have more experience than an intern like us."

"Maybe an intern like *you*." Jamie motions to the Leader Board. "Michelle's stories never broke the Top Ten. She just wasn't ready to adjust her skill set and help turn *Shift* into a digital powerhouse. I'd be a great replacement—I'm cheaper and faster."

And modest, too.

"Maybe don't advertise how *cheap* you are," Gigi says. "Harper's right, maybe you should at least pretend you have a tiny bit of empathy for Michelle."

Gigi actually smiles at me. Which is kind of shocking, but mostly nice.

"I should be realistic," Jamie says, refusing to relent. "I just want to get in the game."

By the time McKayla comes back to the office, she doesn't acknowledge anything has happened. Granny Hair's long gone and Skirt Suit from HR packed her desk into a box hours ago.

No one brings it up. Out of sight, out of mind.

McKayla summons me into her office and my heart skips a beat, knowing my blog post didn't make it onto the Leader Board. It didn't even come close.

Before McKayla has time to deliver her reprimand, I apologize profusely.

"Don't be *sorry*," she says. "Be better. There isn't a lot of social media chatter about your blog. What girls have been tweeting about the most is that they want to know how they can actually get a fling."

"Wait, people have been tweeting in response to my blog?"

McKayla looks at me like I'm an idiot. "Twitter is one of the biggest promotional tools we have. You really need to start using social media in a professional capacity."

I nod.

"So for your next blog, let's give readers what they want," she says. "I want you to write a how-to guide. How to get a date."

• 11 •

"WHY DO YOU LOOK LIKE YOU'RE ABOUT TO throw up?" Ben says, unleashing Princess so that she can attend to her pre-bedtime nap. "I thought a summer fling would have put some hop in your step. No extra toppings on your fro-yo?"

I look up from my notebook page, which is titled "How to Get a Guy" with absolutely nothing under it.

"You read my blog?!" I ask.

"I needed new reading material. Princess isn't as good as Atticus at sneaking me your diary."

"Not a diary. A notebook. Totally different thing." I kick off my shoe in his direction.

"Yeah, yeah. What I'm saying is, of course I read your blog. It was good. Although I'm more of a one-girl kind of guy."

"Ah, yes, pining from afar."

"Not by choice!" Ben bends down to take a picture of Princess. She's positioned like she's posing for a boudoir photo, luxuriating on her back with her head hanging off the side of her royal-purple doggy bed. "I wanted to go upstate for the Fourth of July to visit Delilah, but she told me she was too busy. She said I'd get it if I took sports as seriously as she did."

"That's kind of harsh."

Ben shrugs. "It's true, I guess. What are you up to this weekend?"

"Researching my next blog, aka why I look like I have to throw up. Editor's orders: Actually finding summer flings." I pause and watch Ben position Princess's crown squeaky toy in the frame of his picture. With trepidation, I put on my casual voice and ask, "Any advice? On the best ways to approach guys?"

"Just wear a low-cut top and you're golden."

"Ew!" Princess jolts up at my cry.

"You're not the only sarcastic one here!" Ben says, scratching under Princess's (multiple) chins to calm her down. "Guys are easy. You could even ask us what time it is and we'd be interested. It's just about starting the conversation."

Well, that's good news. I'm capable of stringing sentences together. Most of the time.

"Do you need help finding guys? I have friends who'd love to go viral . . . not in an STD way."

"Gross. Wish it were that easy. Unfortunately, this blog is a how-to guide on picking up a guy. I'm going to have to find them for myself."

This weekend it's time to practice what I preach, out in the wild.

I had planned on going into the day with a theme song. Maybe play my "Pump Up" Spotify playlist to get me in the zone for flirting domination. But I left my earbuds at Aunt Vee's apartment, so I headed downtown to the soundtrack of the subway—which is basically people playing Candy Crush with the sound turned on and little kids screaming about how badly they have to go to the bathroom.

I get out at 14th Street, Union Square, and make my way to my preselected first stop: the Strand.

"You have to go; it has eighteen miles of books," my mom gushed, encouraging me to make the trip to the East Village independent bookstore. "I used to go all the time in grad school. There's a secret entrance to a rare books room that will make you feel so inspired."

And so after two weeks in New York, I've finally made my trip to:

1. See what on earth 18 Miles of Books—a slogan written on Strand coffee mugs and tote bags— actually looks like. (Answer: Everything from bestsellers to graphic novels to pulp paperbacks to hardcover French first editions crammed in every crammable nook and cranny.)

2. Put myself in the flirting vicinity of cute guys who read. (Ben says he isn't a big reader, more of a "visual kind of guy." I had to remind myself not to feel disappointed that he's guilty of my biggest deal breaker—yet another good reason that he has a girlfriend who isn't me. What Ben reads or doesn't read is Delilah's problem, and from what he's told me, she mostly sticks to reading playbooks.)

The store is packed with both books and literary-minded boys. But I don't know where to begin. Maybe if I just stand by one of the highly trafficked tables and say "hmm" a few times, someone will just strike up a conversation with me.

Not so much.

I move on to the next level as the aggressor: smiling. Maybe at an easy target.

I walk over to the graphic novels and turn all my focus toward a freckly redhead wearing a periodic table of elements T-shirt. I wait, smiling across the table from him intently, for what seems like forever until he finally looks up at me with a completely confused look on his face. Oh God, I'm not being flirty. I'm smiling like a maniacal clown, aren't I? I get a feeling in my stomach like I'm on a roller coaster and turn away quickly . . . directly into a cute clerk who was standing behind me. All the books he was holding go crashing to the floor.

"I, um, I—I," I stammer, and bend down to help him pick up what has fallen and accidentally bonk into his head, because obviously that's what I'd do right now. Periodic Table Dude laughs from the sidelines, proving that he never deserved my killer-clown smile in the first place.

Okay, time for round two. Refusing to give up, I head outside to catch my breath.

Harper: I am failing!

Kristina: I'm sure ur not.

Harper: Seriously. Incapable of having normal human interactions. How do I start flirting with someone in a bookstore?

Kristina: Maybe reach for the same book, let him take it, and then start a convo?

Kristina is a serious genius.

I walk along the discounted dollar-book carts that flank side of the store, shaded by its deep-red awnings, until I co across a boy who looks like he's about my age, wearing NYU shorts. Perfect.

I approach the cart he's at slowly, and as soon as he go inspect a book, my arm shoots out like a frog's tongue reachir a fly, and I literally grab it out of his hand.

"Hey, I was looking at that," he says, clearly annoyed.

(Note: A tad too aggressive, Harper.)

"Oh, sorry," I say.

In the hope that I can somehow fix this scenario, I myself from re-creating my clown expression and instead sm my eyes, known to the uninitiated as smizing. Unfortuna does not have the desired effect of getting NYU boy to smi

"So, can I have the book back?" he asks, eyebrows rai

"Sure," I say, still smizing. I don't even know what is. But as I start to hand it back, I realize that it's an ol *American Psycho*. I take a quick flip through its yello and see that it used to belong to the Rikers Island C Facility library.

Um, a book about a murderous investment banker that was possibly read by murderous investment bankers in prison? Yes, please.

"Actually," I say, with a change of heart, "you can't. I definitely want this."

"Wait, are you serious? You ripped it out of my hands!"

"Sor"—Don't say sorry. A *Shift* Girl is *never sorry*—"I mean, afraid so!"

His voice trails behind as I run inside with my dollar bill. All's fair in love and literature.

Even though I'm one point for literature and nada for love so far.

So the Strand didn't work. But I'm not resigned to failure. I walk up toward 14th Street and decide to restart my efforts at Union Square. One block wide and three blocks long, Union Square is as close as America gets to having a European piazza. (Not that I've technically *been* to Europe, but I've seen Pinterest boards.)

If I were wearing a strapless bikini under my dress—which Brie claims to do every weekend "because you never know when you'll end up at a rooftop pool!"—I would join the anonymous sunbathers on the central lawn. Ask someone to put suntan lotion on my back.

But I'm not. Instead I traverse the square's periphery, bordered by Forever 21 to the south and Barnes & Noble to the north, accepting samples of spicy pickles from the pop-up farmers' market but refusing samples of "Free Hugs" from someone in desperate need of a shower.

I try to figure out my next move. Ben said guys are easy. Just ask what time it is. Or for directions. I can *do* this.

But as soon as I go up to a group of guys asking them for the time, one of them brings up the very good point, "Aren't you holding your iPhone? Can't you look at that?"

Rude, but accurate. Definitely won't be asking *him* for directions.

But when I ask the next guy how to get to the nearest Starbucks, it turns out he only speaks something that might be Russian.

What was Ben thinking? What was I thinking? I can't do this and I don't know why I ever thought I could. No matter the city, I'm still the same girl.

"Sorry if I'm interrupting, but I couldn't help noticing that you look lost." The guy who makes this assertion is very skinny, with perfect teeth but an otherwise messy vibe.

"Um, kind of," I say, as I jam my phone back in my purse. He has long hair, a flowing linen shirt, and a hemp necklace with a small Vishnu pendant hanging from it. More of a hippy, granola vibe than I'm used to, but I can work with this.

"I was lost once."

Well, that's certainly a strange thing for him to say. But considering my day, I let it slide.

Hippie Hottie's eyes light up when I ask not for directions but about his Vishnu necklace. He's impressed that I know the four-armed Hindu god's name.

"That's just one of the many perks of being an East Asian history professor's daughter," I say.

Hippie Hottie asks if I want to hang out with him for a while. I shrug and follow behind.

Oh my God. This is happening.

We walk toward the south side of the park, past a group of people with shaved heads and orange robes, and sit. Their chanting and tambourines punctuate our conversation. Seeing my plastic bag from the Strand, he asks me what book I got and volunteers that he just finished the *Bhagavad Gita* (yes, he reads!), which helped him get in touch with the universe and his spirituality.

"Actually, do you want to borrow my copy?" he asks, pulling it out of his hemp backpack.

"Sure?" I lower my eyes and then bravely ask, "But how would I get it back to you?" I feel so obvious and cheesy, but he hasn't asked for my number yet.

"I'm here every Saturday and at Tompkins Square Park in Alphabet City on Sundays. This group I'm in gives out food to the homeless. If you're free, you should join in. We're very welcoming."

And like that, Hippie Hottie transforms into Hippie Hottie with a Heart of Gold. He asks, "Are you doing anything now? Want to maybe meet my friends?"

"Sure!" Is this going well? Could this guy turn into more than a bullet point in a listicle?

He picks up his hemp backpack, eyes sparkling, and leads me toward . . . no. Nonononono. Why is he walking toward the people with shaved heads and orange robes who keep singing "Hare Krishna" over and over as they bang on their tambourines?

The only guy who wants to talk to me is in a freaking cult.

Awesome.

Hare Krishna Hottie doesn't quite have the same ring to it.

————

"You flirted with a guy in a cult?" Kristina asks as soon as I book it out of Union Square and give her a call.

"Is that the kind of vibe I give off?" I ask. "Guys only want to talk to me to meet their cult-recruitment quota?"

"You did like Kool-Aid a lot in elementary school."

"You're evil!" I bury my head in my hands, which obscures my moaning, "What am I supposed to write my blog on now?"

"You have plenty of material," Kristina replies as if it's easy as pie. "Your problem wasn't in the methodology, just the execution. Just say it worked."

"But it didn't work!"

"*Say* it worked. No one will ever know."

I take out my yellow notebook and start brainstorming different approach tactics with Kristina, going over what I did and how I could have executed better, until we have a satisfactory, odd-numbered list. A list about how I calmly and expertly picked up guys.

A little white lie never hurt anyone.

7 STEPS TO PICKING UP A GUY

Good things come to those who don't wait.

After last week's ode to flings, some readers tweeted some very practical questions, namely: How exactly do you go about acquiring a summer fling or three? How do you get a guy to approach? My answer is, this isn't the 1950s—don't wait for some dude to tell you that you have "really beautiful eyes" (or some other pickup cliché)! Here are some tried-and-true tactics on how to effectively make the first move and get your summer love on:

Play pump-up music before you head out on the prowl. *There's nothing like blasting some T-Swift to get you in the zone.*

Let yourself get caught checking him out. *Don't turn away when he catches you making eyes (or burst into a hungry smile like you're about to eat him whole). Rather, you can confidently walk over to him and say, "I couldn't help notice that you were looking my way." Turning the tables will keep him on his toes.*

Bump into him. *Literally. Being clumsy can be cute, or so I keep telling myself. If you throw in a line like, "Cute guys always make me lose my balance," then he'll know you're interested. (Note: Try to be clumsy gracefully. The only thing you should break here is his heart.)*

Talk books. *Go to a bookstore and ask the guy browsing next to you if he has recommendations. You might nab a reader (hot) and a new addition for your summer reading list.*

Ask a cute stranger what time it is. *Or for directions. Or for whatever. Once he helps you out, ask if you can buy him an iced coffee as a thank-you. (Pro tip: Make sure you leave your fully functional iPhone inside your bag for this one.)*

Get involved. *Seek out someone doing an activity—volunteering, playing in a park soccer league, handing out flyers—and ask about it. (Just don't end up joining any cults.)*

If you feel awkward, fake it. *Fake it till you feel it. Confidence can be contagious, even if it's only pretend at first.*

Carpe that Effing Diem!
Harper

· 12 ·

AFTER MY BLOG POST GOES UP, I KEEP WAITING for someone to call me out. I had a nightmare that someone posted a Vine of me (literally) crashing and (metaphorically) burning at the Strand. Luckily no such video existed, but after the blog went up Wednesday, I still got called into McKayla's office.

"The blog was *cute*," she begins.

The way she emphasizes the word makes me realize that "cute" is not a good thing.

"But you still aren't making the Leader Board, which means your blogs need to take a new direction," she continues, drumming her now Rothko-inspired nails on her desk. "No more how-to guides. I want personal stories. Steamy hookups."

Steamy hookups? All zero of them?

McKayla catches the look on my face. "Like in your application essay," she says. "You *do* want a shot at that magazine feature, don't you?"

I do. More than anything.

And that becomes even clearer when she gives me a non-blog-related assignment. My very first for the magazine. Although absolutely no writing is involved.

> **Harper:** Wanna know how many A-listers Harry Styles has hooked up with in the past three years?

Kristina responds to my text almost immediately. Must be a slow morning at Skinny B's.

> **Kristina:** Ew. Creeper much? Why do you know that?

> **Harper:** My job is so weird.

McKayla has demanded I research not just Harry Styles and the rest of One Direction's hookup history, but all of young Hollywood's dirty laundry. For the past two days, I've been working on quite possibly the perviest project of all time with Gigi, who has made it abundantly clear that forced interaction doesn't mean we're bonding.

Gigi and I are making a flowchart of heartthrobs' overlapping hookups for the magazine. And we've researched it so extensively and fact-checked it so thoroughly that if there were an AP Celebrity Hookup exam, I'd get the top score. No question.

We won't get official bylines, but the words "Research by Harper Anderson and Gigi Bello" will be written in tiny, microscopic letters at the bottom right-hand corner of the spread for the whole world to see! (As long as they have really good eyesight and, on top of that, a magnifying glass.) To me, this is a big deal. My mom already said she's going to hang it on the fridge. If this is what microscopic letters feel like, how amazing would it be to be the star of a whole article in the glossy pages of *Shift*?

Gigi is less impressed.

"I can't believe that I have to work on this dumb flowchart when I should be one of the interns assisting on the Jenni Grace cover shoot right now."

"Jenni Grace is here? Now?" I ask. Kristina and I devoured a whole season of her CW show along with mass quantities of Indian food takeout last Presidents' Day Weekend. "I *love* Jenni Grace. How did I miss her coming in?"

"Of course you didn't see her come in," Gigi sneers. "*Shift* doesn't parade A-listers in front of the plebeians. What if some fangirl asked to take a selfie with her?"

Clearly she sees my fingers itching toward my iPhone. A selfie's the new autograph, right?

"This is so unfair." Gigi sighs. "I'm the one writing the '9 Things You Never Knew About Jenni Grace' listicle. I should *so* be in the photo studio right now. I've done so much research—I know for a fact she hates the techno music blasting through the walls right now."

"What else do you know about her?" I ask, excited to finally have a common interest with Gigi.

"She's allergic to shellfish; she's a virgin—"

"Really?" I interrupt. Jenni Grace and I have something in common, too?

"Is there something *wrong* with that?" Gigi says. "Besides, that's her least-surprising fact. *Everyone* knows she's saving herself."

"Oh, that's really cool." I almost blurt out that being a virgin myself, I'm obviously not judging. But I certainly don't want Gigi to know that particular factoid. Instead I go back to drawing lines between celebrity hookups. McKayla wants us to finish before she leaves early for the Hamptons at three. We have to work through lunch.

I reach into my bag to get my sandwich, offering Gigi half.

"Christ, Harper, how many times must I tell you that I'm gluten intolerant? I had celiac disease before it was even trendy."

"Sorry, I forgot."

"And if the bread didn't make me feel sick, that tuna certainly would. Who has that for lunch by choice?" Gigi pinches her nose and scoots to the other end of the couch. "Please excuse me while I move over here and try to avoid the stench."

Aaand bitchy Gigi is back in full force.

"I'll cover for you if you want to run downstairs and get food," I offer, making another attempt to bond.

"Unnecessary. I got lucky in the open kitchen."

Gigi opens up her bag of food and starts eating her . . . wait, is that . . . ?

"Gigi! You're eating mac and cheese!"

"Congratulations, you have the gift of sight!" She rolls her eyes. "Since *I* have the gift of *smell*, maybe you should see if there's any more on the up-for-grabs table and ditch the tuna."

"But you were just talking about how you have celiac."

"So?"

"So it's macaroni!"

Never breaking eye contact, Gigi defiantly shovels another spoonful into her mouth, slowly chews, and finally swallows, defiantly asserting, "It's from Ban Bread."

"I don't know what that means."

"In Nolita?"

"I don't know what *that* means."

"It's from this new gluten-free restaurant *everyone* is talking about North of Little Italy. God, Harper, it's like you don't know this city at all."

"I don't!"

Apart from the Union Square outing and my neighborhood dog walks, my New York exploration has been pretty limited thus far, mostly consisting of trips from Aunt Vee's apartment down to the office and back again. When I daydreamed in homeroom about escaping to New York, I assumed I'd immediately be catapulted into this fabulous life sans awkward transitions. I assumed that I would make fast friends, the kind of friends my mom made when she was here and young, and we'd go gallery hopping and to book readings and try to sneak into bars together.

"Besides," I say cautiously, "it's not like I've been invited out to any cool events."

Gigi looks down at her gluten-free mac and cheese (complete with gluten-free bread crumbs) and pretends that she hasn't been taking everyone but me to the cornucopia of cultural events she gets invited to as Arts & Culture intern.

"But," she says, "it's not like this is your first time in Manhattan, is it?"

"First time outside of the West Coast."

"Well, at least San Francisco is pretty decent. For an American city."

I stop myself before correcting her. I almost forgot that I told everyone during orientation that I was from San Francisco and not Castalia.

Our conversation is interrupted by a shriek: "Well, where in the name of all things holy did it go?"

A man is screaming and the waves of testosterone are crashing throughout the office.

"I swear it was right here," a voice squeaks back.

"Well, find it, Briana," he shouts. "Find it!"

"It's Brie."

"You're smelly Camembert to me until you get me Jenni Grace's mac and cheese. The talent is HUNGRY!"

As the Beauty intern, Brie sometimes gets to help out during photo shoots. Brie's tasks range from blotting the "talent's" T-zones with oil-reducing tissue in between shots to making sure that they never run out of Perrier. (Or, for the uptight celebrities, Perrier with a dash of vodka.) Other intern duties: resident whipping girl for whatever goes wrong.

"Has anyone seen a bag from Ban Bread?" Brie pleads, darting out of the kitchen and down the halls of the office, her once Pinterest-perfect hair falling out of its braids. My eyes dart to Gigi's half-eaten lunch.

This is bad. This is very, very bad.

"Tell me this isn't happening!" Gigi whispers, her fuchsia lips starting to quiver. This is the first time I've seen her uncomposed. She starts talking to herself in a panic. "I have to get rid of the evidence. What am I going to do?"

I go into friend-freak-out mode, one of my personal settings that Kristina has seen many, many times.

"You have to breathe," I say. "Maybe they won't figure out who took it. Just don't say anything."

Gigi stuffs the gluten-free mac and cheese back in its bag and stuffs the bag into the nearest trash can, not seeing the tall man in a fedora stomping our way.

"What the fucking fuck is that?" the angry-man voice says. Angrily.

"It's, it's, it was on the up-for-grabs table so I . . ."

This is painful.

Why am I standing up? Why am I walking over? Why am I cutting Gigi off to tell this seething, I'm guessing powerful, bizarrely dressed man, "You have it all wrong!"

He turns in his cowboy boots (another interesting choice) and his spurs make a sharp jangle.

"I have it wrong and she wasn't throwing our cover girl's specially ordered, gluten-free, truffle-oil macaroni and cheese in the garbage? That's *not* what I'm seeing right now?"

Now I'm telling myself to breathe.

"Of course she was throwing it away. But only because she saw it was gluten-free, truffle-oil . . . *lobster* macaroni and cheese."

Gigi is playing possum standing up. I continue my ramble.

"We all know that Jenni's allergic to shellfish! Thank God Gigi thought ahead and checked on the food. Otherwise we might have had to call an ambulance. The correct order is already on the way."

"When will it be here?" The photographer stares down Gigi.

"Soon," she says. "Very soon."

"Give it to Gouda and have her bring it down to the photo studio ASAP. Our talent is getting hungry."

And like that, he turns again and stalks off.

Gigi is staring at me as if I'd just grown a second head. (But maybe a second head with really good hair, since Gigi doesn't look entirely disgusted.)

"Why did you do that?" she asks. "Why did you step in? I'm sure you would have loved to see me get fired."

But then her eyes narrow.

"Unless you're in it for the long game." She points her finger in my direction like a talon. "And you're going to hold this over my head."

Does Gigi think that we're actually in an episode of *Gossip Girl*? I'm not conniving; why would she think I am? What's wrong with this girl?

Suddenly I'm no longer thinking this—I'm saying it.

"Seriously, Gigi, what's your problem? Guess what? I'm not gunning for you. I'm not plotting your downfall. I have more important things to worry about. The Diet Coke thing was an accident, and right now, the mac and cheese? Any person would do that. Any decent person, anyway." Clearly I've moved into the three-headed category. With really split ends. "Come on! In all your travels around the world, have you just never met decent people before?"

The words barrel out of me. I'm incapable of stopping until I'm done. But when I'm done, I'm terrified. How much worse could Gigi make my life if given the opportunity?

But Gigi doesn't look like she's about to attack. She looks stunned.

"Then, I guess, thanks." She says it so quietly, I can barely hear, and then lowers her head.

"Don't worry about it. Just worry about getting that mac and cheese ASAP. You might want to consider bribing someone to deliver it quickly."

Gigi nods. "I'll offer a big tip and tell the manager we'll tweet about Ban Bread from *Shift*'s main account. They'll love the free publicity. *Shift* has millions of followers."

After the food arrives in an unheard-of delivery time of fifteen minutes, Gigi turns to me and says, "There's a party tonight. I'll text you details."

· 13 ·

THE ONLY PERSON MORE EXCITED THAN I AM THAT
Gigi invited me out is Aunt Vee.

As a recovering seventies (not to mention eighties and nineties) party girl, she can't quite comprehend how it is that Princess
has a more active social life than I do. And no, being a third wheel
on the dog's walks, which I've been doing regularly, doesn't count
as a social life.

A typical conversation goes:

Aunt Vee: "It's only eight. Why are you home so early?"

Me: "Because it's a Monday?"

Aunt Vee: "It's New York! Mondays are the most delicious
nights to go out in New York. If I had a seventeen-year-old's ass
like yours, I'd be shaking it in the Boom Boom Room right now."

Me: "Do they even allow seventeen-year-old asses inside the
Boom Boom Room?"

Aunt Vee gives me a pitying look (note: Get a fake ID to avoid
social shaming at hands of "middle-aged" aunt) and proceeds to

stay out until three in the morning at a charity gala for the Society to Save the Spotted Pygmy Owls. "Those ornithologists sure know how to party!"

But that's all changing because Gigi actually makes good on her promise and invites me out with the *Shift* Girls to one of the awesome events she's always Instagramming.

The *Shift* Friend Ship is definitely on the horizon, I text Kristina.

> **Kristina:** Love u but even I can't condone that lame pun. Ur rly bad at this.

> **Harper:** I have to practice punning for work. Don't hurricane on my social voyage.

> **Kristina:** Pls stop.

Aunt Vee's reaction when I show her Gigi's text invitation verges on ecstatic.

> **Gigi:** Art show opening in Brooklyn tonight. Philistine Gallery @10. Everyone's going.

I'm part of the everyone. Going to an actual party with actual peers—unlike Aunt Vee's friend's Fourth of July gathering I went to, where I was the youngest person by at least three decades.

"And Brooklyn is so trendy now," Aunt Vee gushes. "The *New York Times* style section was just raving about the homemade lingonberry jams at a vegan artisanal bakery in Williamsburg that I've been *dying* to try. Where's the gallery you're going to?"

When I tell her it's in Bushwick, she offers to send me in a car. With pepper spray.

Psh. It can't be that bad. I guess Aunt Vee must have missed the trend piece about the "Man Buns of Bushwick." I reject the pepper spray but happily take the car.

The drive across the Williamsburg Bridge is so beautiful that I don't even mind the bumper-to-bumper traffic. As the car slowly traverses the East River, putting us somewhere between Manhattan and Brooklyn, I take in the best view of the New York City skyline that I've seen since arriving. Skyscrapers pierce the starless night and the top of the Empire State Building is illuminated with purple and yellow light.

No matter what filter I choose, none of the photos I take captures what's in front of me. Don't get me wrong, I still add one to my Snapchat Story, but it hardly replicates what I'm actually seeing and experiencing.

The people from Castalia High respond anyway. The first snap back is, oddly enough, from Bobby McKittrick. It's a selfie of himself holding up his shirt, exposing his chest. The text: "This view's better." Followed by an eggplant emoji.

Um, ew.

As if Kristina can read my mind that I'm about to text her how gross Bobby is, she Snapchats me a video from Bobby's backyard. Of course he's having a party tonight.

The panorama shot actually captures Bobby sending me his selfie, girls shouting "woo" and taking a shot, and some football player perched on top of a keg, growling at passersby as he drinks. "Bobby's brother taught people how to do a gargoyle keg stand," Kristina narrates. "So you aren't missing anything here. You'd better be taking your summer-flings pledge seriously at the fancy New York art party you're going to so that I can live vicariously through you."

It hits me: the blog. McKayla's orders.

Tonight has to be about more than just making friends.

• 14 •

I'M AT THE ADDRESS THAT GIGI TEXTED, BUT THERE are no signs of human life apart from two men smoking cigarettes outside the corner store across the street—which Ben taught me is called a bodega, famous for greasy breakfast sandwiches.

There are no crowds, no lights, no music, no man with a clipboard checking people into the art show. I examine the door's unmarked buzzers, debating which one in the long line of black buttons I should press that might lead me to Philistine Gallery. It doesn't look like a gallery. It looks like an abandoned warehouse. Its walls are marked up with graffiti and flyers. One is for a "Missed Connection":

> You were wearing a blue dress and walking your cat. I was
> in overalls and riding a skateboard. . . .

A plastic grocery bag rolls past my feet like a tumbleweed, propelled forward by a gloomy breeze.

Gigi hasn't answered my text, and panic sets in that maybe I'm in one of those stories you read about, maybe in *Shift*, where people are pranked to go to the middle of nowhere while everyone else is laughing.

Just when I'm about to text Gigi again, two girls in rompers pull up in a green cab. Without hesitation, one deftly presses the second-to-last doorbell and is quickly buzzed up. I slip through the door before it closes. These girls look like they know what they're doing. (So does Aunt Vee—she insisted I wear a romper too. Her wardrobe ranges from sixty-something going to a gala to adolescent on the prowl. She's very excited whenever one of her ensembles fits me perfectly. "I'm going to give my trainer an end-of-bikini-season bonus," she said when I fit into a snug pair of her jeans, my other option for the evening.)

Music pulses louder and louder as we climb a concrete staircase, which opens to the expanse that is Philistine Gallery, a mecca for modern art.

The gigantic loft is cordoned off into sections, each one displaying a different artist's work. Abstract sculptures are interspersed among colorful paintings and pencil drawings. Caterers uniformed in matching man buns offer appetizer trays of fried shitake mushroom risotto squares and dessert trays of miniature doughnuts with a hibiscus glaze to clusters of well-dressed art appreciators.

One of the well-dressed clusters is made up of some of the *Shift* Girls. Gigi, Brie, Sunny (frowning per usual), and Abigail are standing under a bright pink painting covered with disembodied Barbie doll parts. A head here. A torso there. Dozens of plastic doll shoes hanging from thin strings at the bottom left-hand corner. Its title: *Anatomically Incorrect and Whatever*.

I'll head over right after a necessary pit stop at the bar, which has a punch bowl that is billowing smoke. I'm not much of a big drinker. I typically nurse one foamy red party cup of beer per party. But I realize that alcohol isn't dubbed "liquid courage" and a "social lubricant" for nothing.

Praying that the bartender doesn't card, I ignore the mysterious smoking concoction and meekly ask for a glass of champagne. He acquiesces without question, so I order a second to be safe. Just in case the policy changes.

The first glass goes down smoothly. I'm no connoisseur, my alcohol consumption is usually restricted to one—maybe two—red party cups of watery beer, but I can tell that the champagne is good. Much better than whatever Bobby McKittrick buys in bulk for his New Year's Eve bashes.

I feel instantly lighter. Bubblier. I walk toward the *Shift* Girls with my second glass in hand.

When Gigi sees me approach, she waves me over and says what sounds like "bees bees" as she gives me an air-kiss on each cheek.

"It's short for *bisou*, which means 'kiss' in French," she explains.

"Cool," I say, fumbling through the air-kiss. "Thanks so much for inviting me. This place is amazing."

"Isn't it?" Gigi says.

Brie nods her head enthusiastically, big hair bouncing in agreement. "Even though it's totally sad to see all the decapitated Barbies. She was my icon!"

(None of us is surprised.)

"Well, the artist is a complete genius." Gigi's eyes scan the gallery. "I really want to find her and get an exclusive interview for the site. It would be perfect for *Shift*."

A caterer in a flannel shirt and bow tie comes over with a long tray of mini waffle ice-cream cones filled with guacamole.

"Where's Jamie?" I ask, grabbing one of the hors d'oeuvres. She's the only intern who isn't at the gallery.

"There are rumors that Kate Middleton might be pregnant again, so Jamie offered to stay home and write it up in case it's true," Abigail says. "It turns out that Jamie was right—she told me McKayla is considering her for the new viral reporter opening."

Abigail continues that McKayla has taken Jamie off intern duties and is putting her "on trial" to get a full-time job. If she does well, she'll be hired at the end of the summer. Every day is an audition.

"Good for Jamie!" I say.

"Good for us, too," Abigail says. "Now that she's a reporter-in-training and not an intern, she's not in the running to get the magazine feature."

Jamie is the only person so far who has been on the Leader Board. Now we all have a better chance of being the *Shift* Girl to Watch. I turn to see what Gigi makes of all this, but her attention is elsewhere. Her gaze is fixed on a very short woman whose hair is dyed in three horizontal chunks, brown to blond to pink, like Neapolitan ice cream.

"That's her! That's the artist!" Gigi says. "Be back. I *have* to get my exclusive!"

She pushes past the caterer and his tray.

Shift Girls are hungry, but not necessarily for food. They're hungry for stories. They're hungry to get noticed. Noticed by readers and, more importantly, by McKayla. *Shift* Girls want to make their mark.

So do I.

"Are you on the job tonight too?" Sunny asks. "Looking for a summer fling? I really liked your blog post. You're good."

"Wait, really?" I ask. Sunny, who always seems to be frowning in my direction, actually thinks that I'm good?

"Why do you sound so surprised?"

"Well"—I'm on champagne number three so am more loose-lipped than usual—"I always kind of thought you didn't like me. Actually, you always kind of get this grimace whenever I talk—"

Sunny actually breaks into the first smile that I've ever seen cross her lips.

"Well, don't take that *personally*," she says. "That's just because I have RBF."

"Is that a disease or something?" Brie asks, cocking her head to the side with concern, like a confused puppy.

"Yes. Incurable."

Now Brie looks like a puppy that just found out it's going to get neutered.

"No, it is *not*." Abigail corrects her with a huff. Always the Health intern. "Don't scare her like that, Sunny."

"Fine, it's not technically a disease," Sunny clarifies. "RBF means Resting Bitch Face. Basically, my neutral expression makes me look like I'm mildly annoyed on a good day and semimurderous on a bad one. So, no, I don't hate you. It's just my face."

Right.

This actually makes me feel better. Maybe everyone disliking me was just in my head. Maybe I'm the judgmental one.

"Does Gigi have Resting Bitch Face too?" Brie asks.

"No." Sunny shrugs. "I think she's just a bitch."

"I don't think that's a thing people have at UT." Brie tilts her head to the other side.

"At the University of Texas?" Sunny rolls her eyes. "No. RBF is less sorority girl, more fashion. Everyone at fashion school has it."

"Well, smiling gives you wrinkles, so I guess you'll beat us all in the long run!" Brie offers her beauty trivia with a smile.

"That and it's a chick magnet," Sunny says. "Cassie says that my smoldering is what drew her to me."

Hmm. My neutral tends to consist of nervous smiling followed by incoherent rambling, and that certainly hasn't made me a guy magnet. Maybe I should have Aspiring Bitch Face. It does seem very New York.

"Anyway, Harper, if you *are* looking for a fling tonight, I think that you should let us help you pick," Sunny says.

"Oh, please say yes!" Brie agrees. "My sisters choose guys for each other to go after at frat parties all the time."

If I'm going to survive as *Shift*'s dating blogger, I know that I need to up my flirting game from asking cute guys what time it is and running away. Fear of rejection sends me into fight-or-flight mode, and I don't know how to stop myself from always picking flight.

So maybe getting forced to flirt in front of my colleagues will actually be a good thing. Not only will the guy selection be out of my control, but I can't wuss out because . . . they will all be watching me.

Oh God.

I'm gonna need another drink. Luckily the server with the champagne tray is always circulating nearby. It's like he has a sixth sense regarding inebriation.

Brie smiles at the cute caterer while I take my drink. "There are tons of hot guys here."

"I won't let them pick any of the old creepers," Abigail says. "I won't be a part of the start of an unhealthy relationship. A wide age gap can cause tons of psychological trauma down the line."

"All right." I take my hundredth sip of champagne. "Fine."

Brie claps her hands and Sunny, going for a record, smiles again.

We scan the room for possible targets.

"What about that guy?" Brie asks, pointing to a man in skinny jeans standing alone in front of a canvas that's completely blank except for a glued-on plastic spork.

"He looks like he could be thirty!" Abigail says.

"So?" Brie asks.

"Ancient. Pass."

Good call, Abigail.

"Him?" Sunny nods her head in the direction of a hipster with a mustache that dramatically curls up at both ends like the bad guy who ties women up on train tracks in old Western movies.

"He has part of a risotto square stuck to the left tip of his mustache," Abigail overrules. "Unsanitary. Pass."

"Fine," Sunny says. "If you're just going to reject everyone, then you pick the 'healthy' choice!"

"Fine!" Abigail retorts. She takes a minute to assess her options. "Okay, him. He was a couple of years above me at school. His name's Carter. Kind of full of himself but relatively age appropriate and clean."

"And *gorgeous*!" Brie says.

I turn and it's him.

In all his green-eyed, Nietzsche-reading glory. The guy who was leaning against the Bosh Media Building the first day of my internship.

Leaning slightly to the right. Expression slightly smug.

I can feel an energy pulsing between the two of us. Like he knows I'm watching him. Like he knows that I know that he knows that I'm watching him. Wasn't that one of the pieces of advice in my blog? Let yourself get caught checking him out. Maybe I actually do know what I'm talking about. This time I don't turn away.

"Okay," I say. "I'm in."

"Also . . ." Abigail keeps talking, but I tune her out.

The champagne fizzes in my veins and the bubbles propel me forward, toward the exhibit that he's observing.

But how do I sell him on me?

Harper Anderson, Dating Blogger, would know these things. I need to figure them out. Right now.

The small section of the gallery where he's standing has art that's very different from the rest of what's on display. Rather than big paintings with bright splashes of color, everything in here is small and subtle. Black-and-white pencil sketches that are on pieces of paper no bigger than the pages of my notebook.

The series is called *The Ladies Who Give Zero Fucks*, and I'm immediately entranced by the intricately drawn tableau on each panel.

The first one shows a man and woman sitting across from one another on a date. The guy is wearing a jacket that says "Members Only." The woman is playing a dating app under the table on her phone.

The next sketch shows a barefoot woman in a party dress, holding her high heels in her hand. Too tired to walk, she's getting pushed around in a shopping cart by another fabulous friend. Lying back like a queen, swigging champagne straight out of the bottle.

I take one step to the right to get a closer look at the drawing. One step closer. The energy between us buzzes a little louder.

I am a *Shift* Girl.

I am unapologetic.

"So." I turn to face him head-on. I don't smile but instead try to smolder. "What do you think of ladies who give no fucks?"

There's an almost indecipherable shift in his body. Surprise, maybe? I don't think he expected me to say something first. I didn't expect me to say something first. I can sense I've thrown him off a little. And that he doesn't like to be thrown.

"The sketches." I take a slow sip of champagne. "That's the title of the sketch series."

He turns to meet my gaze. In heels, I'm almost exactly his height. His green eyes have small flecks of gold in them.

"I think the art is . . . okay." He's trying to stare me down. But my eyes don't falter. "But the concept is a lie."

"How so?"

"Every girl I've ever met has given a fuck."

I take a step closer. I'm playing a part, and this is what my character would do.

"Then you've been meeting the wrong girls."

And then I'm leaning forward.

And then our eyelashes are almost touching.

And then I'm kissing him.

And then he's kissing me back.

In an instant, I'm no longer watching from the sidelines. I am present. And this is real. We don't know each other at all, but as soon as our lips touch, a switch is flipped on. There's a jolt of electricity. I wouldn't be surprised if when I pull away, and I *have* to be the one who pulls away first, our hair is standing on end.

"Well," he says, hair still perfectly intact.

The rush of adrenaline and champagne is making me dizzy. What now? Oh God, what do I do next? I'm not sure if what I'm thinking is a flash of strategic brilliance or comes from a lame listicle, but here I go: The only way to follow a totally unexpected moment is with another unexpected moment. (The advantage of which is that I have no idea what would happen if I stayed. The advantage of which is that this satisfies my natural impulse to run.)

"Well. It was nice to meet you." I give him a quick *bisou* on the cheek and walk away.

My head is swimming.

"Wait, I don't get a name? A number?"

I feel like my head might explode.

"Maybe next time." I don't stop when I say this. I just keep moving forward. I have to escape.

Before I reach the stairs, I'm surrounded by a swarm of *Shift* Girls buzzing with questions.

Brie: "Did y'all just start kissing out of nowhere?"

Abigail: "Did you check for canker sores first?"

Sunny: "Did you actively steal my Resting Bitch Face? I *told* you it was effective."

And then Gigi returns, finished with her artist, and squeezes my arm.

"I would say that making out with a stranger at a chic art show is gauche if he weren't so damned attractive," Gigi says approvingly. "Well done."

"Thanks. See you all tomorrow."

"After that you're *leaving*?" Gigi asks. "I respect that. Bold."

Bold indeed.

I wave and make my way down the stairs, two steps at a time, to finally release myself into the night air. The chilly weather has turned into a summer storm, and fat drops of rain are falling from the sky. I don't have an umbrella, and I don't care. The water feels good against my skin, but it doesn't bring me down from my high.

• 15 •

"TINAAAAA," I SHOUT INTO MY PHONE FROM THE back of a taxi that's going to charge me a whole day of minimum wage work at *Shift* to take me from Bushwick back to the Upper East Side.

"Uh-oh, sounds like someone's a little drunky."

I only shorten her name when I'm tipsy and incapable of handling three-syllable words.

"I might have had a glass of champagne." I wring out my rain-drenched hair, leaving a small puddle on the cab's faux-leather seats.

I try to wipe it up as Kristina asks, "Just a glass?"

"Or four."

"But you're such a lightweight! *Four?* This is why I don't drink champagne. You just keep going."

Hearing her say the number makes me perk up.

"Speaking of four." I stop trying to dry the seat and announce with gravitas, "I have a new name to add to the list!"

She immediately knows what I'm talking about.

Kristina and I both have Word documents on our computers dedicated to chronicling the boys we've kissed. Kristina's, which is longer and far more salacious reading material, is surreptitiously saved as "Chemistry Study Guide." Mine has the even more covert name, "Rough Draft Spanish Paper." Just in case someone were to break into my files searching for double entendres.

My list comprises the following:

1. MATTHEW HOLLIDAY

It happened the summer before tenth grade. We were playing a game of spin the bottle on the second deck of a Carnival cruise ship, behind the state-of-the-art Twister Sister water slide. I was tagging along on what Kristina's dad called her "new family" vacation. ("More like my 'faux family' vacation," Kristina said. She told her dad that the only way she was going to not only meet but spend a whole week with her soon-to-be stepmom and stepbrother, Erik, was if she got to bring a friend.) Anyway, Matthew tasted like the late-night pizza buffet, but it was overall okay. After the game we talked about the *Hunger Games*, the books not the movies, but he didn't accept my friend request on Facebook.

2. D-BAG DULL MAN

You know the story. Junior year, homecoming. The kiss was great, but he was the worst. It should also be noted that his hand grazed my boob during our Dance Floor Make-Out.

3. BOBBY MCKITTRICK
My chin will never forget.

And now . . .

"Who is he?" Kristina's voice explodes out of the other line. "Tell me everything!"

I tell her that by some strange twist of fate, I ran into the cute guy she pointed out on FaceTime my first day of work.

"No. Way. That's absolutely insane. Who is he?"

"Well, his name is Carter. . . ."

"Carter what? I wanna Facebook stalk him."

"Um . . ."

I realize I don't know his last name and he knows . . . nothing about me except for the fact that I'm the girl who jumped him at a crowded party.

Kristina is in an excited tizzy and keeps the questions coming. "How did it happen? I want details. Do you like him? Are you going out?"

No. Because just like after you drink a Red Bull you get a spike of energy and then crash, I had a spike of confidence and then freaked out. And ran away. What if I never see him again? What if I *do* see him again since he's obviously connected to Bosh Media in some way and he thinks I'm a total crazy person?

Suddenly the champagne isn't sitting well. I don't say anything for a minute. There's no sound except for the French talk radio the cab driver's listening to.

"Harper, you're *killing* me. How did he do it?"

"I did it."

I give Kristina the blow-by-blow about how I came in from out of nowhere and essentially forced myself upon him without any warning. During pauses, Kristina says things like, "No way. No effing way!"

"Am I a slut?" I ask when I'm finished.

"Harper"—Kristina enunciates every word like I'm an idiot—"you *kissed* him."

Details.

"Fine, then, am I a *kissing* slut?"

"First of all, we do *not* use that word. We *never* use that word. It's pejorative and flat-out offensive. Second of all, even if we *did* use that word, you still wouldn't be a kissing slut. You're something way better. Something way more empowering."

"What am I, then?"

"You're a Make-Out Bandit."

"I kind of like the sound of that."

My first thought after Kristina and I hang up is, "I have a blog post."

My second thought is, "I have to throw up."

I really *am* a lightweight.

"Lothar warned me that you might have come down with 'food poisoning,'" Aunt Vee says from outside the bathroom door when she finally gets home from a late night with the Park Avenue Tulip Society. "Can you believe that dear doorman was trying to cover for you? As if I'd be disappointed that you finally went out and had some fun! Finally! I'll make you my famous hangover elixir before my aerial spin class tomorrow."

Between waves of nausea, I write different snippets of my night in my notebook.

The art.

The exhilaration.

The new, confident (until running away and hiding) me.

CONFESSIONS OF A MAKE-OUT BANDIT
No jail time involved.

This week I embraced a life of crime.

My victim was a cute guy at a party. I didn't steal his wallet or his watch. (I don't have the coloring to pull off an orange jumpsuit.) Rather, I stole a kiss and then disappeared without a trace.

This week I learned how to be a Make-Out Bandit.

I saw my target from across the room.

Just like a burglar cases a house before breaking in, to make sure the owners won't be sitting in the living room watching *Family Feud*, I cased my target. Making sure he was alone and unattached.

As I said in last week's blog, summer is about carefree flings. Sometimes, it's just about a carefree kiss and nothing more. Because you want to. On your terms. And there's no need to wait around twiddling your thumbs until a guy approaches.

I approached him very directly. I flirted a little and stole my kiss. His lips were very quick to meet mine and kiss me back. (Consensual banditry is key, ladies. Remember: orange jumpsuits.)

Then I left. Almost immediately. You steal a heart and escape unscathed.

He doesn't know my name. He doesn't know my number. Like any good bandit, I made sure my identity was never revealed. I wasn't going in to find my next boyfriend. I just wanted to kiss and run.

And I liked it.

And I'm still on the loose.

Carpe that Effing Diem!
Harper

• 16 •

MCKAYLA CALLS ME INTO HER OFFICE FIRST THING
Monday morning to discuss my blog, which took me longer to
write than the others. Maybe because I wasn't making it all up as I
went along this time.

When I walk in, I notice that McKayla's changed her nail art
again. She now has tiny Mona Lisas on her accent nails.

"I get bored easily," she says when I compliment the new look.
"Remember that, Harper, and don't bore me. Ever."

Her face is stoic. I can't tell if she loves my blog or detests it
and is kicking me out the door, with what I now recognize as Tory
Burch ankle boots, like she threatened to do on our first day. I don't
want to know . . . but I also *have* to know.

"And did I?" I pull the words out of my mouth. "Did the blog
bore you?"

She stares me down. I know it's impossible with Bosh Media's
climate-controlled air-conditioning system—the halls are so cold
that reporters sometimes walk around in "fashion snuggies," courtesy

of Dolce & Gabbana—but I feel the temperature rise twenty degrees.

"Surprisingly," she says, "no."

Yes!

"I actually thought it was . . . ," McKayla continues tentatively, "fun."

Yes, yes, yes!

"But is this an actual thing? A Make-Out Bandit? Is this a thing that your people call yourselves?"

I think "your people" translates to teens. Like I'm her phone line to "the kids these days." Staffers at *Shift* are often asking interns things like, "Is One Direction still cool? Do we still care about them?" It's pretty funny.

"Well, I'm not sure if there's a Wikipedia page definition of it," I reply, "but—"

"No matter." McKayla's dwindling interest applies even to the answers to questions that she herself has posed. "We can brand it as our own. Then if your blog post catches on, everyone will have to say Make-Out Banditry started at *Shift*."

Maybe it's Aunt Vee's rejuvenation elixir she's been feeding me ever since my drunk night out, maybe it's the utter shock that I'm actually succeeding at this whole blogging thing, but my excitement brims over and I start thanking her, saying how "absolutely awesome this is, McKayla. Like, so, so great. It's so great that I—"

McKayla cuts me off. Again.

"Didn't I tell you to work on the bumbling?" Her phone starts buzzing. "Okay, I have to go yell at the viral team."

I laugh nervously.

"I'm not joking. Their web traffic should be double what it is right now. Anyway, go tell a photo editor to put a picture of a sexy cat burglar or something in your Make-Out Bandit story, and then have the social team promote it on Facebook."

"Will do." Maybe I should warn Jamie about McKayla's impending wrath.

"Oh, and, Harper, for your next blog, instead of reading how much you enjoy making out with everyone in sight, I think it would be nice for you to write about going on an actual *date*. It is in your job title, after all."

Uh-oh.

Over the next few days, now that Jamie is out of the competition, the *Shift* Girls are reinvigorated in their attempt to make the Leader Board and prove we can write "clicky" stories when we aren't doing other intern tasks—like getting coffee and transcribing three-hour-long interviews. I'm less worried about clickiness than I am about my impending blog post of doom.

But, come Wednesday, the impossible actually happens.

After it goes up, my Make-Out Bandit blog post breaks the barrier and becomes the tenth most popular story on *Shift*.

I bask in the glow of the Leader Board, projected on the television screen above my head, and pray that Jamie doesn't write a viral post about Curmudgeon Cat that knocks my story down to number eleven.

"I totally want to make us shirts that say 'Make-Out Bandit'!" Brie says. I've learned a lot about sororities by looking through Brie's

Instagram, but one of my biggest takeaways is the fact that membership involves a lot of custom-made shirts. Or "rally gear," as Brie puts it.

"Make-Out Bandit," Gigi says, lingering on the words.

Out of habit, my body tenses up, preparing for offensive remarks. But they don't come. Ever since I stood up for her and then stood my ground when she questioned my motives, my relationship with Gigi has changed. We're even tiptoeing around the possibility of friendship.

"I love it," Gigi continues.

"I think it's pretty feminist," Brie adds. "Taking control of your sexuality."

I never thought about it that way.

"Wait, the sorority girl knows about feminism?" Sunny asks.

"Um, don't try to stereotype my sorority," Brie retorts. "What about living in a group of strong, supportive women with a three-point-six average GPA and a promise to combat the boys' club in the professional world after graduation makes me not a feminist?"

Sunny stares.

"Feminism is about believing in equality for everyone, period," Brie continues. "Chimamanda Ngozi Adichie wrote a book based off a speech she gave called *We Should All Be Feminists*. I'll e-mail y'all a link—we read it for sorority book club."

"I *love* that author," Gigi says. "She's Nigerian and a genius *and* she's quoted in 'Flawless.' She taught Beyoncé about feminism."

Whoa. When I first met Brie and Gigi, I assumed that they limited their reading material to features in *Icon*. I've definitely been misjudging people.

My computer dings with Brie's e-mail, and I promise her I'll order the book. Then I look through the rest of my surprisingly full inbox. Three weeks ago, the only e-mails I got were from *Shift* coworkers, mostly directed to the whole office about getting more #CleanEating options in the open kitchen. But now that my dating blog is making a blip in the Twitterverse, it's a whole different story. PR firms have put my e-mail on media lists related to just about anything I've mentioned in an article. I'm getting press releases about new Ben & Jerry's flavors (since I wrote about cute fro-yo guys), UV-protected clothing (since I'm a fan of sunscreen), breath mints (for make-out reasons?), and my personal favorite—books (since I advised girls to ask hot guys in bookstores for reading recommendations).

But one of my e-mails has nothing to do with press releases or appeals for more kombucha in the *Shift* kitchen.

FROM: carter@deviant.com
TO: Harper_Anderson@Shift.com
SUBJECT: Two questions

1) Am I the victim of a crime? 2) Is it problematic that I liked it?

Hi. I'm Carter. I believe you burgled my lips.

I have to read the e-mail three times to process it, and as soon as I do, my heart starts racing and my entire face turns beet red.

Oh my God.

He found me.

"How the hell did he find me?"

"What are you talking about?" Gigi asks, signaling to me that I'm speaking out loud and not to myself. "Who's 'he'?"

"Carter. From the gallery." My left arm feels tingly. Am I having a heart attack? No, that's ridiculous.

"No. Way. Mr. Make-Out Bandit?" Samples of eye shadows fall on the desk as Brie literally drops what she's doing (sorting makeup) to scurry over. "How *did* he find you?"

"Oh," Abigail says. "He Facebook messaged me to ask who you were after the art opening. Didn't I mention that?"

Umm, no. She most definitely did *not*. That I would have remembered.

"What do I say back?" I turn the *Shift* Girls into a focus group so I don't nervously babble via e-mail like I inevitably would in person. I try to summon cool-and-collected Harper in the formulation of my response.

FROM: Harper_Anderson@Shift.com
TO: carter@deviant.com
SUBJECT: Re: Two questions

1) Afraid so. 2) If that means I won't get a visit from the NYPD, I'm okay with that.
I'm Harper, and this isn't my usual MO.

FROM: carter@deviant.com
TO: Harper_Anderson@Shift.com
SUBJECT: Re: Two questions

And here I was hoping you'd be a repeat offender.

Don't worry, I get exploiting people for a good story. I'm interning at *deviant*. I'm a writer too. Here's a link to my author page if you want to read my stuff.

deviant is a Brooklyn-based online-only publication so edgy that it even eschews capital letters. The articles it publishes are smart, sarcastic, and completely unapologetic when making fun of something or someone. It's full of first-person essays (often involving sex and drugs, though lacking in the rock-and-roll department) and snarky social commentaries.

"*deviant*'s where all the cool kid Internet people work," Jamie says. "At media-intern events last summer, they wouldn't even talk to us."

Curious, I click on the link he included at the bottom of his e-mail.

"'A Day in the Life of a Scum-Sucking Online Troll,' by Carter Bosh," I read out loud.

"Wait," Jamie jumps in before I get to the first sentence. "Did you say *Bosh*?"

"Oh yeah, didn't I mention that?" Abigail asks. "He's Trenton Bosh's son."

"No, Abigail, you really didn't mention that!" I say, acutely aware that I'm currently sitting in a building that has his last name on it. That explains why he was waiting outside the building on my first day of work.

Soon I'm in the throes of full-fledged e-mail flirtation. Carter goes to Columbia, which happens to be my dream school. He drops the Dad Card pretty quickly. I bring up the fact that my mom's an English professor, and that's why she named me after Harper Lee—just so he knows I'm a reader too. He tells me that Mom should have named me Truman, since the writer's next-door neighbor, aka Truman Capote, "100 percent wrote *To Kill a Mockingbird*." Under other circumstances, I would consider those fighting words. But even though I immediately feel defensive and tell him that his claim is "100 percent incorrect" (discussion of the Capote conspiracy theory is banned from the Anderson household because it makes my mom so mad), it's kind of exciting to be talking about books and authorship with an extremely attractive and debatably interested member of the opposite sex.

"I think I actually like this guy," I say after a few more rounds of e-mails. And, in a strange twist of fate, I think this guy might actually like me.

"How would Bobby feel about this?" Brie asks, back at her computer.

"Bobby . . . ?"

"McKittrick. He just posted on your wall. There's a picture of you two making out."

"What?"

"I was a victim!" Bobby writes, linking to my Make-Out Bandit article.

Gross. I do not need the world to know that I made out with Bobby McKittrick. I'm about to delete it from my wall when a new comment appears.

A comment from Adam Lockler. "Great story, Harper," he writes.

I click on Adam's profile and realize that he doesn't look half as cute as I remembered. But that doesn't diminish how satisfying it feels that he read my article. Actually, as I keep getting new Facebook notifications, I realize that lots of people from Castalia are reading my blog. I'm getting comment after comment.

When I look up, I see that I've moved up to eighth place on the Leader Board.

And as if my day couldn't get any better, it does.

FROM: carter@deviant.com

TO: Harper_Anderson@Shift.com

SUBJECT: Re: Two questions

So, I have another question. What are you up to this weekend?

," I nod my head in the direction of the couple at the table
right, lean in, and confess with glee, "They're having the best
first date ever. He's making her fist bump whenever they have
ething in common. It's happened, like, ten times."

As if on command, the guy sitting next to us loudly declares,
No way! I've seen Kanye in concert too. Pound it!" He holds his
st in front of his date's reddening face for an awkwardly long time
until she meekly bumps it, just to make it go away.

"And boom goes the dynamite!" Bad Date Guy exclaims.

Ben bursts out laughing, which causes the fist bumpers to look
at him like he's a crazy person. I quickly grab my notebook and
fully jump out of my seat this time, dashing to the door. I am the
anti-possum. I don't freeze; I run.

"I can't believe you got us caught!" I hit him in the chest when
he joins me outside in the humid air. "The first rule of listening in
is to *never* get caught!"

"Not to point fingers, but you running away might have been
the real tip-off that we were eavesdropping. We could have passed
it off like you'd told a funny joke." He ruffles my hair like I'm a
little kid, and I slap his hand away, laughing. "Anyway, sorry I was
so late. I thought I'd be done sooner."

I fight my inner grammar freak from correcting "done" to "finished," something that has gotten me in trouble with jocks before,
and instead ask him what he was doing.

"I was at a Bark Mitzvah," he says, like that's a totally normal
event.

• 17 •

I HAVE A SHADY FAVOR TO ASK YOU. . . .

This is how I start my first-ever text-message conversation
with Ben. Maybe I should have led with a "Hey" or a "How's
your Saturday?" or "Princess made it to her food bowl and back
to my room without panting!" but *Shift* has taught me that you
have to grab readers' attention from the get-go. (We've learned this
important journalistic lesson through repetition, after overhear-
ing McKayla's "Boring! Boring! Boring! This is me clicking away
because I'm so *bored*!" tirades echo through the office halls. Jamie
was recently on the receiving end of a public freak-out after she
wrote a short post McKayla said "would have gone viral if your
headline and lead weren't so damn dull.")

Also, I'm desperate and don't have time for formalities.

After a series of extreme e-mail flirting (each one of my messages was written as a group with the other *Shift* Girls), Carter
asked for my number and invited me ("plus whoever") to a dive
bar in the Lower East Side tonight. But while the other *Shift* Girls,

apart from Abigail, seem to have fake IDs tucked between their Sephora Insiders and Metro Cards ("The older girls at my sorority 'will' them down to the freshmen after they graduate. It's like sorority law," Brie said.), I don't. After hours of Googling "where to get fake ID New York" led nowhere reliable, I decided to possibly abuse the fact that Ben gave me his number to beg his help.

I nervously watch *Gossip Girl* (ever since seeing the steps of the Met, I've been binge watching the series in my free time) while I wait for Ben to respond.

Apparently he's into shock-tactic rhetoric, too.

Ben: Drugs, guns, and other potential felonies?

Harper: Revision: I have a borderline shady favor to ask you. Zero drugs. Zero guns.

Ben: Shoot.

Harper: Zero shooting of any kind.

Ben: Shoot = ask. lol

I hold my breath as I type: Do you know where I can get a driver's license that would magically make me twenty-one by tonight?

I decide to add a prayer hands emoji since I can use all the help I can get.

Nothing.

Followed by nothing.

Followed by more nothing.

I stop holding my breath becau[...] out oxygen for only so long, and se[...] text just to make sure it goes through an[...] order. (It is.)

An episode later, when Blair Waldorf descen[...] panic attack (Will she get into Yale? Will she be[...] attending a different Ivy League college?), my phone[...] most beautiful four-letter word I could ever hope to see:

He texts again: "We have to go to St. Mark's. Meet [...] Starbucks by the Astor Place subway stop. Be there in an hr.[...]

My squeal wakes Princess from her late-morning nap, wh[...] Aunt Vee has warned me is the pug's second most importan[...] respite of the day, before her early-afternoon siesta and after her late-afternoon nod.

I apologize to Princess and close my computer so quickly that it takes a few seconds for Netflix to realize that it can stop streaming. Blair's lament serves as brief background noise through my closed MacBook while I throw on a sundress and bound out of the apartment toward downtown.

When Ben plops down across from me at Starbucks, I'm so startled that I almost jump out of my seat. He laughs and reaches out to steady my iced coffee.

"I waved to you through the window too, but you were busy concentrating," he motions to my open notebook. "Working on your next article?"

"Pause, rewind, explain?" I ask, as we walk up 4th Avenue. "Bark Mitzvah, like a bar mitzvah but for a dog?"

"I told you my clients are intense."

Apparently being the employee of helicopter dog parents comes with its strange perks, including high-society pet parties. So that the owners can take advantage of the bar, Ben sometimes gets hired to chaperone soirees like mastiff birthday parties, Chihuahua Cinco de Mayo fiestas in the park, and apparently "Bark Mitzvahs" in Chelsea to celebrate when a Shiba Inu puppy becomes a dog.

"Should I feel slighted that Princess wasn't invited to this?" I say as we turn onto St. Mark's Place, which it turns out is a street and not a, um, place.

"Probably. It was pretty sick."

Ben hands me his phone and lets me scroll through his photos while we walk to our undisclosed, shady location. And they're actually pretty good. No, scratch that.

"Ben, these are *really* good." His pictures capture in-between moments at the party. I pause on an image of a man in a patterned shirt trying to pin a yarmulke onto the Shiba Inu's fluffy head. Even on the small iPhone screen, the details are vivid.

"Nah, the pictures basically take themselves," Ben replies as we walk past cheap sushi bar after cheap sushi bar. Lined with three-star Yelp restaurants, sunglass stands, karaoke spots, and stores displaying bongs of all shapes and sizes in their big glass windows, St. Mark's Place is a broke summer intern's dream.

"Not buying it. These details, these moments"—I zoom in on

a teacup poodle with his head stuck in a kiddush cup. I wish I could capture moments with words as well as he does with pictures. "Ben, have you ever thought of doing this, like, professionally? You shouldn't just chaperone your next Bark Mitzvah or whatever. You should be the photographer!"

"I dunno."

"This *can't* be the first time you're hearing this. I mean, your Instagrams are all awesome. Even just the ones of Delilah playing soccer—and I'm not even into sports!"

"Delilah thinks I Instagram *way* too much." Ben slows his pace. "She'd give me so much shit if I were pimping myself out to be a dog photographer."

"Why?"

"Stop worrying about it. I'm good doing what I'm doing. I'm ready for a simple senior year."

I've been surprised by how unsimple Ben is, and now he's selling himself short. But before I can say anything, Ben stops walking and announces, "We're here."

I almost forgot the whole point of this journey. The ID.

"'Ice Cream and Ink'?" I read the sign in front of the store.

"Looks can be deceiving," Ben says as he pushes open the door to reveal a joint ice-cream/tattoo parlor, with one side relegated to soft-serve machines and the other for the inking of skulls, Chinese symbols, and intricately drawn designs. The back room secretly caters to a different vice altogether. Fake IDs.

A man with sleeves of tattoos approaches and gives preppy Ben a fist pound. Tattoo Guy is a Saint Agnes alum and has been serving his underage high school community with fake driver's licenses for years—a fun factoid I imagine has never made it to the alumni newsletter. I leave the mismatched pair alone to catch up and slink over to the ice cream, catching my reflection in the shiny label for the salted caramel machine. I smooth down my brown hair and twist it up into a bun, trying to figure out if I look more mature with my hair up or down. Before I have time to send a Snapchat to the *Shift* Girls to ask which one looks more "twenty-one" to them, Tattoo Guy calls me over to go to the back room to take my picture.

He doesn't ask for my name or the name I'd like to have on the fake. And when I inquire about the address that's going to be on the ID so I can start memorizing, he just shrugs and takes the picture. There is no "say cheese" warning.

"I think I blinked. Can I redo?"

He shakes his head. "Come back in a few hours."

This might not be the DMV, but it definitely has the same dedication to good customer service. I can't complain, though. This has all been suspiciously easy. So easy that it should be illegal. . . . Which it is. God, I hope I don't get in trouble for this.

And then my phone buzzes and it all seems worth it. It's a text message from Carter asking if I'm coming tonight. I am *so* coming tonight but remember Kristina's dating guru advice and respond with a cool, "Think so. I'll keep you posted."

He replies without even waiting the "I have to seem busy and desirable, so I'm not texting back for a few minutes" window. Never one to have a poker face, I walk out of the back room blushing.

"Why are you all smiley?" Ben shouts across the multipurpose parlor.

"Nothing, just a text." I click off my phone, as if Ben were going to run over and comb through my unscandalous text messages.

"Is it from whatever guy you're planning on using this ID with?" he asks.

"Dude, we don't discuss the merchandise!" Tattoo Guy chimes in. "We *never* discuss the merchandise!"

"Who said there was a guy?" I ask.

"The Make-Out Bandit guy."

I shrug.

I don't know why I don't tell Ben about Carter or my group excursion tonight. Carter did say to invite friends. But for some reason, I want to keep Ben in a separate box from my *Shift* life. With him, I can be my clueless self. With the others, I can't. Besides, I don't think Ben and his uniform of Saint Agnes sports shirts and flip-flops ("I absolutely *detest* man sandals, and if I were straight, they'd be my deal breaker," Sunny says.) would mix with the chic new world I've landed in.

Things are starting to get complicated.

· 18 ·

SHARON SMITH.

My name is Sharon Smith, and I'm from 111 Main Street in Salt Lake City, Utah.

The name sounds faker than fake. The address sounds faker than fake. The ID *looks* faker than fake. But hey, at least the tattooed forger made Sharon Smith an organ donor. Maybe I'll get lucky and bouncers will only notice "my" posthumous generosity and overlook all the other questionable details.

Still, I go over and over my new identity's birthday, zip code, and astrological sign on my way to dinner with Gigi, Brie, and Sunny at a new restaurant in Tribeca before we go out to Carter's dive bar. Abigail doesn't have an ID ("And I don't want one!") and Jamie has to work.

"Ah, to be young again," Aunt Vee said as I pregamed my 9:15 dinner with french fries I picked up on my way home from picking up my ID from Ice Cream & Ink. (My stomach leans toward the early-bird special rather than trendy late-night reservations.)

"Just don't marry the first Saudi prince you meet out at a club," she warns. "I don't care how big he says his yacht is."

Aunt Vee got married very young to a prince she met through Andy Warhol's personal assistant at Studio 54.

And then she got married (only slightly young) again.

And then again and again.

The only evidence of her string of marriages that I've found is a neat row of framed pictures on the bookshelf in her study that display images of her and her husbands at each of their respective weddings, in chronological order.

Don't worry, Aunt Vee. Sharon Smith will stay away from all princes.

Sharon Smith, whose driver's license number is NQ311452J. On second thought, it would probably be more suspicious to a bouncer if I volunteered my driver's license number by heart, wouldn't it? Probably.

"Should we go over the names on our fake IDs?" I ask the girls at dinner. The restaurant's so loud that we have to lean in really close to hear each other speak.

I had suggested we go to Serendipity—Kristina and I have wanted to try its frozen hot chocolate dessert ever since seeing it in a *Gossip Girl* episode—but Gigi nixed the idea on the grounds that it was (1) too touristy and (2) all the way in the Upper East Side. Instead, she made us a reservation at a popular new restaurant downtown that specializes in updated versions of 1960s classics. Deconstructed pot roasts and retro chic gelatin desserts. *Mad Men* meals for the modern man. Or if Alice from *The Brady*

Bunch took a master cooking class in molecular gastronomy.

"Why would we do that?" Gigi asks.

"So that we know what to call each other in front of the bouncer," I respond, offering, "I'm Sharon Smith!"

I get blank looks.

"No one cares, Harper," Gigi says.

We're interrupted by the arrival of our appetizer. Our waitress sets down a plate of deviled eggs. I wouldn't expect that a hard-boiled egg counts as "fine dining"—you can get that at any diner in Castalia—but the waitress said we had to try it. According to the menu, it's the restaurant's signature appetizer, spiced with smoked Spanish paprika and topped with a black truffle puree. We each pick up an egg half and clink them together in the middle of the table as if they were champagne flutes.

"Wait, that would make a really cute Instagram. Do it again!" Sunny forbids us to take a bite and pulls out her phone.

We fake "cheers!" our hard-boiled eggs three more times to get the perfect camera angle and then weigh in (with very strong aesthetic opinions) about which filter best highlights the yolk.

"Good thing we don't have to worry about these getting cold," I say. The deviled eggs have yet to be consumed.

When I bite in, the flavors explode in my mouth. Okay, you definitely couldn't get this in a diner in Castalia. Our main courses are delicious in a simple but surprising way, too. But everyone is insisting on Instagramming the meal, so the dinner crawls on at a lethargic pace, which makes me antsy. It's getting late, and I want to get going and see Carter.

"We should probably head over soon," I say, after the girls surprise me by opting to share the mandarin orange Jell-O mold with four spoons for dessert. "Carter texted to see what our deal is."

Lie.

I'm the one who texted Carter to make sure he was still at the bar. But they don't need to know that. Gigi has very strong opinions that the boy should be the aggressor in this kind of situation. Especially considering how strongly I came on at the gallery.

"We'll head over soon," Gigi says. "I put on my dive bar outfit and everything."

She's wearing espadrilles, frayed denim cutoffs, a loose-fitting, white button-up tank, and a pair of big, gold hoop earrings.

"Where are we going?" Sunny asks. "Pianos? Spitzer's? Welcome to the Johnsons?"

I've never heard of any of those places.

"It's called Maverick," I say. "Have you been?"

"Oh, *ew*. No one told me we were going to *Maverick*," Sunny squawks. "One of Cassie's friends had his twenty-first birthday there last year. Male sock model. I don't care if *Thrillist* says it's 'grungy chic,' the place is unsanitary. Hard pass."

My stomach free-falls. No. Carter's eyes. Carter's lips. We *have* to go to Maverick.

"Unsanitary?" Gigi pokes her spoon at the jiggling Jell-O but doesn't take a bite. She grimaces. "Now you're sounding exactly like an Abigail clone."

"This isn't Abigail-standard gross." Sunny shows us Instagrams that were recently posted at Maverick to offer proof. "It's gross by any normal standard of decency. Look."

I hate to admit it, but Maverick, named after the main character in *Top Gun*, does look pretty icky. Not only is there a Tom Cruise shrine over the urinals in the men's bathroom, but other Instagrams show hundreds of bras hang from the ceiling like a chandelier.

"I sincerely hope those are brand-new bras they got shipped to them in bulk and girls didn't take off their underwear in the bar!" a horrified Gigi stutters.

"It reminds me of Sigma Chi's basement," Brie says, although it's unclear whether she's referencing the frat boy décor as a good thing or a bad thing.

"As I said," a triumphant Sunny continues, "as much as I'd love to get gonorrhea from sitting on a bar stool. *Pass.* Sorry, Harper."

"No!" I say a little too loudly, a little too invested. "I mean, it's just, I already told him we would meet him there and I don't want to be rude."

But it seems like they've already reached a decision, consensus be damned. They're already working on finding an alternate option for the night, heads down and mass texting their "going-out friends."

"Stop freaking, Harp," Gigi says, not looking up from speed texting. "He'll like you even more if you're hard to get. Think of this as a *good* thing."

My head spins with options. I don't care if the bar is disgusting. I really want to see Carter. See what happens. But the thought of going alone sounds terrifying. Besides, I don't want to rock the boat with the *Shift* Girls. Last week I would have killed to be out with them. To have Gigi call me "Harp." I don't want to go back to how it was before.

I text Carter, "Bad news . . ."

Carter: ?

Harper: Hard to sell Maverick to friends. Bra decorations and everything.

I see him type and stop. And type and stop. And finally type and send.

Carter: Might mobilize troops soon anyway to go to house party in Crown Heights.

I can't tell if he's asking me to go to the party with him or is just sharing information. I also can't tell if I'm blowing it with him.

"What if we go to Crown Heights instead?" I offer the group, not knowing where that is, let alone if we're even invited.

"Brooklyn? I am *not* in the mood for borough hopping tonight," Sunny, our self-proclaimed New York nightlife expert says. "Besides, I found us a winner. A promoter took Cassie and some of the models from her agency to Mode in the Meatpacking District, and it's cool to crash their VIP table."

Brie's impeccably smoky-eyed eyes widen. "No way. Jenni Grace tweets about Mode all the time!"

"Shit." Gigi's hands sweep over her outfit. "I dressed for 'upscale dive bar,' not 'hottest club in the city'! And I'm not the only one."

Gigi gives me a look.

"Me?" But I'm wearing a cute floral sundress!

Gigi's eyes flick down to my feet. "And your shoes."

"What's wrong with them?" My feet have been killing me from weeks of wearing stilettos to work, so I'm wearing Aunt Vee's Chanel ballet flats. She said that if I insisted on forgoing heels, then I'd better make up for it with the designer.

"Unless you're a six-foot-tall model, bouncers won't let you in without heels," Gigi says. "It's, like, the first rule of going out in the Meatpacking District."

"And even the six-foot-tall models are wearing heels," model expert Sunny adds.

"If we're dressed incorrectly, we *could* just stick with the original plan," I offer.

"No way." Gigi's eyes sparkle mischievously, like she's a little kid who's certain she's about to get away with something. "I have an idea. And it's brilliant."

• 19 •

WE TELL THE BOSH MEDIA NIGHT DOORMAN THAT
we have to go upstairs because Brie left her work phone at her desk.

"I'm *such* an airhead!" Brie says a little too convincingly, twirl-
ing a finger in her hair and leaning forward to provide a not-so-
subtle peek of cleavage to further enhance her case.

But it's all a lie.

We're at *Shift* to retrieve something far more exciting than a
work iPhone from two upgrades ago.

"Just so you know, if I'm going down for this, I'm taking all of
you bitches down with me," Sunny warns. She then leads us to the
back right corner of the *Shift* office and types the top-secret six-
digit code into the wall. And so opens the door to one of the most
envy-inducing places in the entire city: the coveted *Shift* fashion
closet.

Even Sunny isn't supposed to know the combination, which
changes every month with the close of each magazine issue. It was
entrusted to her after a model's Jimmy Choo shoe broke during a

Kristina warned me that boys would be able to tell that it was cushioned when I got to second base. ("Don't you mean 'if' I get to second base?" "I mean 'when.' Stop being so fatalistic!")

"I happen to be just fine with what I've got!" I declare, and carefully hand the dress to Sunny so that she can hang it up in its proper place.

Sunny doesn't need to change. She came club-ready in a black razorback.

Wait.

"Is it going to be weird if we all roll in wearing matching little black dresses even though it's the middle of summer? Like we're trying too hard? Like we're in a uniform?"

"Of course we're in a uniform," Gigi says, totally unconcerned. "An LBD is a crucial staple. It's New York. It's chic."

Sunny nods. She's always in a Little Black Dress, and she always looks fantastic.

"It's like what my fashion sensei Karl Lagerfeld says," Sunny recites by heart, "'One is never overdressed or underdressed with a Little Black Dress.'"

I'm going to write this in my notebook as soon as I go to the bathroom, where I sometimes go to jot down notes.

"My favorite Karl Lagerfeld quote's, 'Trendy is the last stage before tacky,'" Brie pipes in.

"Thank you for your input, Brie," Gigi says, taking off her cutoff shorts, "but really not relevant at the moment."

"Whoops!" Brie tries on dress number three.

"Quiet!"

"I said whoops!"

"No, quiet because I think I hear someone! I think someone's coming!" Gigi might not be wearing bottoms, but she is wearing a look of pure terror.

"Hide!" Sunny grabs me and Brie, each in different stages of undress, and pulls us behind the cherry blossom decorative changing screen. Gigi dives behind a stack of shoe boxes wearing only a bra and underwear.

It's one thing to come upstairs after-hours to supposedly pick up Brie's work phone. But getting caught trying on designer dresses in the fashion closet would be a serious problem.

"Oh my God, we're all going to get arrested," I whisper.

"In our underwear," Brie responds.

"Or worse," Sunny says. "We're all going to get fired!"

"Shh!" The stack of shoe boxes across the room angrily hushes.

The door opens and no one breathes. No one even thinks of breathing. We just concentrate on not moving and praying that the flashlight doesn't illuminate our discarded clothes on the floor.

It might last for only fifteen seconds, but it feels like a lifetime. It feels like I lost at least a year of my life.

Even after the door closes, we stay still for a few minutes. It must have just been a routine midnight security check. We're in the clear.

My phone breaks the silence.

Kristina.

"Turn that thing off!" Gigi snatches my phone and silences it.

"Oh my lord, that was scary," Brie whispers.

"Should we leave?" I ask.

"No way," Gigi says. "We've come this far. We're not leaving until we've got our wardrobe change!"

• 20 •

WE ARRIVE IN A ROW OF LITTLE BLACK DRESSES.

(And with a shopping bag crammed full of our discarded outfits to leave at coat check.)

The line to get into Mode wraps around the block, and the number of people trying to cut the line is debatably larger than the crowd politely queuing up.

"I swear my friends are inside," a guy tells a bouncer with a clipboard.

"Yeah, you and everyone else," the bouncer replies, arms crossed over pecs so large that I think his tight black T-shirt is at risk of bursting open. "If your name's not on the list, you wait like the rest of 'em."

I go over the information again as I finger the ballerina-chic tulle skirt of my dress: Sharon Smith. 111 Main Street. Born November 21, the very last day of Scorpio, thanks for asking!

"Come *on*, Harper." Gigi snaps her finger at me as I walk toward the back of the queue.

"It's *Sharon*," I hiss.

She rolls her eyes and says, "Whatever."

The *Shift* Girls ignore the crowd completely and confidently strut directly to the bouncer. I teeter behind.

Sharon Smith. Blue eyes. Five feet two inches.

Sunny stops just shy of the velvet rope and starts talking to a baby-faced man who must be in his thirties. (Abigail would not approve.) His hair is slicked back into a ponytail, and a gold chain necklace is tucked inside his red silk shirt, which is just one button too unbuttoned.

"Marco?" she asks.

"And you must be the other half of 'Hashtag Sussie' that I've heard so much about," Marco says, using air quotes. He gives Sunny a kiss on her cheek, and then turns to inspect our group. Marco looks at us head to toe, nods approvingly, and motions for us to come forward.

"Who's that?" I ask Gigi.

"A promoter. Quick, look cool and give him your ID."

I actively calm every facial muscle and try to look bored. Like I've done this a million times. Like I go to the club every weekend *and* on Mondays, which Aunt Vee has prescribed as the best going-out night of the week.

Sharon Smith. Zip code 84101.

We pass our fakes to Marco and he fans them out like a deck of cards. He waves them abstractly in the bouncer's direction and says, "Four girls, Ernie. They're with me."

I brace myself to get quizzed as Sharon.

But as quickly as the gigantic bouncer turned the other guy away, Ernie unhooks the rope and lets us in. He doesn't even look at our licenses. He doesn't even care. The inside of my right wrist is stamped with the word "Mode," and Sharon Smith is tucked back safely into my clutch in less than a minute.

I guess Ernie will never know that I'm an organ donor.

"I can't believe it was that easy!" I whisper to Gigi with a squeal, and erupt into a wide, toothy smile.

"Marco's *job* is to get cute girls into clubs," she responds coolly. "Not check our IDs. That way rich guys will come and buy us drinks. Lots of drinks. It's a win-win for everyone; you just have to know the right people."

I don't even care how sleazy that sounds. This *so* beats the parties back home. This is a completely foreign beast.

Electronic dance music pulses as Marco leads us down a staircase into the underground bunker that is Mode. The dance floor is thick with people. Overhead, women in sparkling bustiers contort their bodies and wrap around streamers of long silk fabric hanging from the ceiling like at Cirque du Soleil.

Brie grabs Sunny's hand, I grab Brie's hand, and Gigi grabs mine and gives it a little squeeze. We lift our arms high in the air and snake through the dance floor in an unbreakable chain. Brie bobs her head and shakes her butt to the music as we slide toward our intended destination. The VIP section.

Sunny's the first to break free, and she runs toward a table full of models. And I don't mean that in an "oh, you could totally be a model" way, but in a "congratulations on booking that three-page spread in *Icon* magazine, you literal model, you" way.

We all watch as Cassie, instantly recognizable from #Sussie pictures, stands up in all of her five-eleven glory and wraps the tiny-by-comparison Sunny up in a hug. Any remnants of RBF are erased from Sunny's face. She looks totally happy, and it's infectious.

"Aww," Brie coos to me, before taking a picture of the surprisingly not annoying #Sussie PDA. "I know you're all about the hooking up, but I want *that*."

My throat gets a little tight. I don't know if I actually want a series of summer flings. I want what Sunny has too. But it's better to focus on the small accomplishments—a kiss, *maybe* a date— rather than a relationship, which seems totally out of my reach.

I automatically look at Carter's most recent Instagram activity. He posted a picture one hour ago at Maverick, surrounded by a group of friends, laughing and cheers-ing with cans of PBR, the hipster's choice of beer. The caption reads: "'Is life not a thousand times too short for us to bore ourselves?'—Friedrich Nietzsche."

He quotes Nietzsche? I think that the pros of intellectualism definitely outweigh the cons of Maverick. I think I made a mistake.

"Dance," I announce abruptly, somewhat shocking myself. "Now. Let's dance!"

Let's dance and deflect.

Not even allowing Brie and Gigi to get a drink from the table's bottomless supply of vodka and cranberry juice, I pull them with me toward the DJ booth. The bass booms, we put our arms in the air, and just totally let loose. Even Gigi. She starts out modestly but intensely moving her hips but soon incorporates the rest of her body, flipping her thick hair to emphasize a song's beat.

At home I keep to the sidelines. I take calls or, if there's a discreet place to do it, take notes. But not now. A space opens up on a platform and we hop up, visible to the whole crowd.

Even though it's packed, we manage to carve out room for ourselves to execute big, high-energy dance moves. We incorporate each other into our swivels and turns, and whenever a guy approaches we just shake our heads (among other things) and one of us shouts, "Girls' night!"

"Our bigs gave my entire pledge class matching shirts that say 'Forget Guys, I Just Wanna Dance,'" Brie says, moving her body like she's in a music video. "I should have brought mine with me to New York."

We keep dancing through the early hours of morning.

• 21 •

I WAKE UP THE NEXT DAY TO THE SHRILL BEEP OF A
text message.

When I manage to lift my pounding, heavy head from the pillow, I see that last night's eye makeup has left an abstract work
of art in the form of disjointed black streaks on the expensive
cream-colored fabric.

I sit up and pull my hair into a topknot.

Why is it sticky? And why does it smell like overripe fruit?

Oh yeah. The champagne shower.

Late last night, or, rather, early this morning, some bro thought
it would be fun to make it "rain" Dom Pérignon in the VIP section.

"My hair!" literally everyone, male and female, shrieked as
champagne sprayed down from on high.

"Where does this asshole think he is? We aren't at 'da club' in
Atlantic City," Gigi shouted, trying to protect her dress with her
hands, mortally offended that someone would make such a messy
disturbance at what is clearly *le club*. "We aren't wearing trashy

dresses made out of gross material that doesn't even absorb liquid. This is silk!"

Sunny preempted our freak-out over potentially ruined LBDs by assuring us that she knows a good dry cleaner who owes her a favor. "He can get out stains in twelve hours or less—plenty of time before I sneak them back in the *Shift* fashion closet Monday morning."

My phone beeps again.

Dammit. There's nothing from Carter. I was really hoping he'd text. Mode was fun. Really fun. And bonding with Gigi, Brie, and Sunny was essential. But I'm worried that I totally blew it with my one potential summer love interest.

A quick sweep through social media shows snippets of Carter's night. On top of the Maverick picture I already saw and restrained myself from liking, he's also been tagged in a group shot on Facebook by some (very pretty) girl where he and the same attractive group huddled together in someone's concrete backyard over a man-made fire pit. "How we do s'mores in the city ;)" she wrote.

This must be the Crown Heights party.

After I've exhausted my social media stalking expedition, I go back to my phone to see who actually tried to contact me. A couple of messages from Kristina that I'll answer later. ("I'm bored!" "Did you just Snapchat from a CLUB? I want to hear EVERYTHING!")

And a text from Ben.

> **Ben:** Since you were still passed out when I picked up Princess, I take it the ID worked out?

Damn. It's one p.m. When Ben and I parted ways at Ice Cream and Ink yesterday, he noticed that I wasn't being my chatty self, so I agreed to crash Princess's prelunch walk and give him a debrief of my night.

> **Harper:** So good I forgot to set an alarm. I'm the worst!
>
> **Ben:** No worries. I'm sure I can read about ur night and the guy u were meeting in ur next blog.

I wish. No Carter. No dating material for my column that's due tomorrow.

> **Ben:** Or u can just tell me. Heading back to the apt w Princess.

While waiting, I plop down on the plush, eggplant-colored living room couch in my Castalia High sweatshirt and ducky pajama bottoms and watch a rerun of Jenni Grace's TV show. Her character has just found out that she isn't the only shape-shifter in town when Ben drags a panting Princess through the door, with a plastic to-go bag in hand.

"Hangover cure," he says, unhooking Princess's leash from her bedazzled collar. Princess doesn't notice. She's already fallen asleep, right in the middle of the entryway.

"What is it?" I lift my head from the plush couch, intrigued.

"Lemon-lime Gatorade to replenish your electrolytes." Ben pulls out a radioactive-colored beverage from the bag. "Our lacrosse coach is all about the importance of keeping our electrolytes in check."

Green, but kale/spirulina/wheatgrass-free. I'll take it.

"And, of course, the most important part of the goody bag: Everything bagel with lox, low-fat cream cheese, tomato, and cucumber sliced *extra thin* from Hot & Crusty."

"You remembered my order!"

Even though Hot & Crusty is quite possibly the least appetizing name for a bakery in the history of named bakeries, the food is still pretty satisfying. Ben and I stop there on 86th Street and Lexington sometimes on Princess's walks, depending on the day's route. ("Just wait, the best is yet to come," Ben says, promising we'll go to Absolute Bagels on the Upper West Side once Princess has built up the stamina to survive a walk across the park and back. "Any day now!")

I could hug him—which we haven't done since my total meltdown that first time we more formally met—but it would mean getting off the couch, which seems out of the realm of possibility at the moment.

"You're seriously my savior. I was dying. Aunt Vee doesn't believe in keeping carbohydrates in the house. Controlled substances, no problem. Baked goods, on the other hand, are grounds for eviction."

"The sad thing is, I can't even tell if you're joking."

I'm not.

"How a woman that weight obsessed ended up with a dog that fat, I'll never know."

"Shhhh," Ben says. "Princess can *hear* you."

Princess snorts upon hearing her name.

"Fine. Big boned?"

"Harper! An attitude like that, and I'm going to give the dog the bagel."

"I'm kidding! You know I love Princess. She's, like, my best friend here"—probably accurate—"other than you, maybe. Did I forget to mention you're my savior?"

"I appreciate your sarcasm, but it's always a treat to see the sweet side peek out from underneath the snark." Ben holds out the bag. "Come and get it."

I put on my most convincing puppy-dog eyes.

Ben responds well to puppies.

"Could you maybe"—I pout out my lips—"*bring* it to me?"

Ben rolls his eyes. But he also walks over.

"Bless you!"

"Here you go, your royal highness."

"They will write songs about your goodness."

"Who's they?"

"Details!" I dismiss his question, take a chug of Gatorade, and start tearing into the bagel. It tastes like happiness.

"You are seriously my hero!" I reiterate, mouth full.

The front door clicks open and Aunt Vee walks in, sweaty from her Zen Warrior Xtreme Boot Camp.

"Oh, I know I am, dear," she says.

"Not you, Vee," I respond. "Love you, but this morning Ben's my hero."

"Oh good, Benjamin's here!" Aunt Vee gracefully hops over Princess, who is also prostrate. We have a lot of things in common.

"I was hoping that I didn't miss you," Aunt Vee continues. "I have something to show you!"

She dashes off to her bedroom and returns waving something very purple, very taffeta, and very small. Now *there's* a fabric so synthetic that the champagne droplets would never stick.

"It's Princess's prom dress." She waves it even more excitedly. "Won't she look glam?"

"Wait, the pugs have *proms* here?"

Ben and Aunt Vee look at each other and shake their heads as if *I'm* the crazy one for not knowing about the Third Annual Pug Prom, which is considered the crème de la crème of Manhattan pup culture.

"It's like Corgi Con," Ben explains. "Only with flower arrangements, a DJ, and mandatory formal attire."

"Exactly!" Aunt Vee says, again waving the miniature ball gown. "So when I saw this exquisite number in the window at Ruff and Ruffles on Fifty-Ninth Street, I *had* to buy it."

Princess flouncing around in a party dress is something I have to see. Although from the size of it, it looks like getting her into the gown will be a very difficult, if not impossible, task.

"Aunt Vee, is she going to fit into that?"

"The salesperson was very rude. Going on about how they don't carry clothing for full-figured dogs."

great his cheekbones are. Or that apparently I have a thing for guys with great cheekbones.

"What does 'Oh, he went to Holland Prep' mean?"

"That he's really rich and probably pretentious." Ben doesn't have defined cheekbones. His face is rounder. Softer.

"My friend Abigail went to Holland Prep and she isn't pretentious," I say, leaping to the school's defense. "Also, don't you go to a rich and pretentious prep school?"

"Even Saint Agnes is more low-key than Holland Prep," Ben says, like that's as obvious as the fact that pugs have proms. "Besides, I'm on scholarship. This guy definitely wasn't."

I decide against pointing out that Carter's father owns some of the biggest magazines in the world. Including mine.

"Are all his Instagram captions Nietzsche quotes?"

I take back my phone and start scrolling.

"There." A recent picture of Carter and his coworkers at the *deviant* office late. "That caption's Kafka."

"I take it back," Ben says. "Play all the games with this guy that you want."

"That's ridiculous!" I say, incensed on Princess's behalf. "You should boycott that place."

"It was too fabulous *not* to buy. Besides, I always get dresses a size smaller to motivate me to get down to my target weight! Benjamin, do you think Princess will be able to fit into it by the beginning of August so that she can wear this to prom?"

Is this real life?

"In three weeks?" Ben takes the dress, holds it over Princess's sleeping (and snoring) body, and starts crunching the numbers. "She *has* been losing weight on our walks, so it's possible. But if she does, it's going to be for health reasons, not fashion."

"Whatever you have to tell yourself, Benjamin."

Looks like Ben's everyone's hero today.

With that settled, Aunt Vee disappears into the master bathroom for a post-workout steam and shower.

"So the pug prom," I say, when we have the room to ourselves. "Are you going to take my advice? Will you try to photograph the party too?"

"Come on, Harper. Why are you pushing this?"

"Someone should!"

I wish I could let it lie, but I can't. Ben's lack of ambition gnaws away at me. It's just such a waste.

"I could branch out too," I offer. "Ditch the dating blog and pitch a dog fashion article for *Shift*. Give Yves Saint Bernard the exposure he deserves."

"Or Ruff Lauren." Ben sinks into the other end of the couch. "For the all-American dog."

"Barc Jacobs!"

"I think I'm out of designer names. In case you couldn't tell."

He's wearing Vans, khaki shorts, and instead of his lacrosse shirt, a Saint Agnes wrestling tee. How many teams is he on?

"So, can I crash the pug prom?" I ask.

"Seriously?" Ben looks at me cautiously.

"Um, yeah." I wipe my mouth to make sure I don't have a cream-cheese mustache. "It sounds awesome."

"I've been trying to get Delilah to go with me for weeks. It's right after she gets back from soccer camp. I even told her I'd get her a corsage and everything."

"Right," I say. "Of course. Obviously you're going to take your girlfriend as your date."

Obviously.

"No, I'm not!" Ben says. "She doesn't want to go. She thinks those kinds of things are lame. You should definitely come."

I totally want to, but to Ben I say, "I don't want to force myself in. Or make things strange with you and Delilah."

"I *want* you to," he says, but I don't know if I believe him. "After all, dogs are boring conversationalists."

There's a grunt from the corner of the room.

"Sorry, Princess!" Ben shouts.

Shift Girls don't say sorry. Or feel sorry about themselves. So to feel less awkward about basically forcing myself upon Ben, too nice to say no, as his pug prom date, I decide to tell him about Carter.

"You were right the other day," I say. "I was meeting up with the Make-Out Bandit guy last night. And I think I actually like him."

I start my signature blabbering about Carter, our e-mail flirtation, and how I'm afraid I've messed it up before anything really started by backing out of meeting up with him last night. Ben gets a weird look on his face when I go on and on, probably because I'm making him OD on girl talk.

"Gigi said that the mystery would keep him interested. That no one likes anyone who's too available." I'm talking a million miles a minute. "But I think it might have been a mistake."

Ben hides his face in his hands. "I hate games."

"So you think it's over? That he'll be done with me?"

"No. I didn't say that. It probably *will* pique his interest. Girls can be *such* emotional terrorists."

"But, *effective* emotional terrorists?"

"You're evil." Ben sticks out his hand. "But, all right, give me your phone. Show me this poor sucker."

I go to Instagram and pick out one of my favorite Carter pictures. It's from last summer, and he's sitting on a beach somewhere in jeans and a modest V-neck white shirt, reading something called *The Love Affairs of Nathaniel P.* I haven't read it but put it on my Goodreads to-read list. I can't wait to casually drop it into conversation when I see him next. If I see him next.

Ben quickly goes past the picture I carefully selected and starts going through the rest of them.

"Oh." He stops at a picture from two years ago where Carter is wearing a cap and gown. "He went to Holland Prep."

I lean into Ben's shoulder to take a closer look at the photo. It must be before Carter started wearing glasses. I never noticed how

7 SIGNS YOU'VE SPENT TOO MUCH TIME SOCIAL MEDIA STALKING YOUR CRUSH

The first step of recovery is admitting you have a problem, right?

I tell McKayla that this week's blog post is service journalism. It's a way to teach our impressionable *Shift* readers about when they've descended into the realm of borderline creepy. What not to do.

I find no compelling reason to tell her that over the course of the past twenty-four hours—while I waited futilely for Carter to make some form of contact (although why would he, since I totally ditched him?)—I've committed every single social media stalking faux pas on this list. Including:

1. You know his middle name.

(Emerson.)

2. You also know the names of his parents, siblings, and childhood pet.

(RIP Meowy the cat.)

3. You know what he was for Halloween last year.

(A shark.)

4. And the year before.

(Trick question: He didn't wear a costume.)

5. You know that the girl in his fourth most recent profile picture is his sister.

(Bianca Bosh. She goes to Yale.)

6. You accidentally favorited one of his ex's Instagrams . . . from 97 weeks ago. And then proceeded to have a panic attack.

(But I think I unfavorited it before anyone noticed?)

7. You know his jersey number from his basketball team.

(This one is a test for in case Carter reads the article. He didn't play sports in high school.)

But Carter doesn't read the article. No one does.

"What do you think?" I ask McKayla when she's finished the listicle.

"What I think is that it's not what I asked for." McKayla puts down her tablet and gives me a death glare. "Because what I *asked* for was action. A date. Because you're the *dating* blogger."

Damn. She did. And it wasn't a suggestion. McKayla doesn't suggest; she orders.

"Well, I was supposed to meet up with a guy this weekend, but it kind of fell through," I confess, nervously looking down at her desk. "So I pivoted directions. The stalking post is kind of funny though, right?"

"I don't care if this one's funny. Write the blog I want. Your date fell through? Find another one! I'll even be generous and let you go on it during the workday so I can have the story by Wednesday morning."

As if it's so easy to just pick up a random guy off the street. Contrary to what I've written, I know that it's anything but. Not wanting to break my ubercool desirable-to-all cover, I pose a different concern.

"What if, on such short notice and all, I can only find a boring date? Something uninteresting and unblogworthy?"

McKayla stands and walks toward her window to get a view of the Hudson River, letting me stew in the silence. Then she turns.

"Journalists don't allow themselves to have mediocre dates. If you're even a little competent—which I'm now questioning—you'll find a way to make it interesting. Ask questions. Push his boundaries. Juice the date for everything it's worth. *Why aren't you writing this down?*"

I pull out my yellow notebook and start writing. Maybe I should reconsider my goal for this internship. Change it from starring in the "Teen Journalist to Watch" feature to simply not getting fired before the end of the week.

"Personally, I think that the only acceptable ways for my dates to end is in flames or in bed." McKayla pauses. "How old are you, again? Maybe cross out that 'in bed' part."

I cross it out.

"I think I prefer a date going up in flames anyway," she says. "Bad dates are way more fun to tweet about."

"You live tweet your dates?"

"Who doesn't?" McKayla asks, genuinely perplexed. "In fact, if I'm on a 'meh' date, I'll just find one of his weird quirks and exploit it for the story."

To avoid looking horrified, I bend my head toward my notebook. "So," I scribble, "bad dates are better."

"Actually"—McKayla presses her pointer fingers together—"they're mandatory. I'm in the mood to read about a really good *bad* date."

Oh no.

"But what if it isn't?" This hypothetical date I'll be going on in the next, what, day and a half?

"Have you not been listening? *Make* it bad. Just don't make it depressing like your homecoming sob story. I want snark. Read some articles on the *deviant* site—mean does really well on the Internet."

"I think I can do that," I say through gritted teeth.

"Don't think. Do. This is your job, Harper, not some sort of optional high school extra credit assignment. Did I make a mistake hiring you?"

She doesn't let me answer the rhetorical question, and kicks me out of her office to take a call.

What am I supposed to do?

Since I know Kristina is in the middle of a Skinny B's shift, and since I suspect she'll be ever-so-slightly pissed that I never got around to returning her calls over the weekend between the IDs and the going out and the subsequent hangover, I turn to the closest thing to a real confidante that I have here.

I call Ben from the open kitchen during an emergency Diet Coke break. He barely lets me finish asking if he'll please, please, *please* set me up on a date by tomorrow before he says a resolute "no."

"Why not? Are you worried I'd embarrass you or something in front of your lacrosse bros?"

"It's not that." His voice trails off.

"Then what is it?" My stomach is in knots. "I *need* you."

Silence.

"What about that pretentious guy? Why don't you ask him?"

Carter.

"He's *not* pretentious." I bristle. "Besides, I don't want to go on a bad date with him."

"Wait, it has to be a bad date?"

Ugh! I wasn't going to say that. Now he'll never set me up with one of his friends.

Maybe I should just go back to Union Square and find that cult guy. I'm sure that would be a disaster.

But Ben surprises me. "I think I know someone who would be perfect. Give me a little time to see if he's free."

An hour later I get the following text.

Ben: 1:30 tomorrow. Meet by the Alice in Wonderland statue in Central Park. Get ready to meet the most hypocritical guy at Saint Agnes.

· 2 3 ·

IT'S A BEAUTIFUL DAY FOR A HORRIBLE DATE.

The colors in Central Park pop so vividly that if I were to post a #nofilter photo of it, people would comment that I was lying. The grass is never really that green and the sky is never really that blue.

But this is real life. And as I approach the bronze Alice in Wonderland statue, I go over different ways I can torpedo this date in case it's going well. God forbid.

I finally call Kristina on my way from the office to the park, knowing that she's in between swim and her Skinny B's shift.

Luckily she doesn't seem too pissed at me for being MIA over the weekend. Since we aren't FaceTiming, I can't see any of her tell signs of lying, so I'm just assuming that she's telling me the truth.

"I don't think I'm a good source of advice on this one, Harper. Usually I aim to have *good* dates. What do you know about the guy?"

"Basically nothing. Dog Walker"—which is how I refer to Ben with Kristina—"only sent me his yearbook picture. He said that he knew what he was doing but wanted to keep the mystery alive. I just know his name is Anthony."

"If things aren't going sour, you can always bring up a no-no first date topic."

"Like?"

"Ask about his ex-girlfriends?"

Children are running around the sculpture, dripping ice cream from a nearby stand, and climbing all over Alice, the White Rabbit, and, my personal favorite, the Mad Hatter. As I approach, however, I make out my date looking down at his smartphone screen, leaning against a metallic mushroom.

Poor guy has no idea what he's signed himself up for. He looks normal and totally inoffensive from here. He isn't even wearing a Saint Agnes–related athletics shirt, which, after hanging out with Ben and seeing his friends on Instagram, I worried was the unofficial summer uniform of every guy who goes there. He's wearing a dark blue polo shirt and is actually pretty well dressed, even if he is preppy. I really hope Ben knows what he's doing in blindly setting me up on a bad date.

"Hey," I say, careful not to startle him on his phone. "You must be Ben's friend, Anthony."

He looks up.

"You're Harper?" he asks. "Sweet. I was worried you were going to be ugly. Since Ben said you were so desperate for a date and all."

"Ben said *what*?"

"But you're hot!"

"Um, thanks?"

This is not off to a great start.

Instead of going directly into bad-date mode, I ask him if he wants to grab an ice cream since it's so hot.

"Nah, I can't," he replies. "I'm a freegan."

"Well, the Popsicles shouldn't have dairy."

"No," he says. "I said *freegan* not vegan. I don't believe in buying stuff. Ever. My money isn't going to the capitalist machine."

Ben, you freaking genius. This I can work with.

I start asking Anthony questions immediately, both because it's my job and also because I'm curious as hell. The freegan scavenges for things like food (that his parents don't pay for) and other necessities.

His new edition iPhone?

"Found it in a bathroom."

I think that's called stealing, but I let it go. For now.

"And, no offense, but aren't you wearing a Burberry shirt?" He definitely is. I can see the check print, familiar from shirts in Aunt Vee's closet, lining the inside of his collar. "Isn't that really expensive and against your code of ethics?"

"It would be if my mom hadn't bought it for me. It's okay because I never touched the money, so I'm clean."

I might need to Wikipedia freeganism later, but I'm pretty sure that's not how it's supposed to work.

"If you want to treat *me* to ice cream though," he adds, "then that's cool."

Yeah, this is definitely less ideological opposition to corporate America and more opportunistic cheapskatism.

I already have enough material for a blog post, but I remember what McKayla said about pushing the limits. Turning a neutral date to bad, and a bad date to atrocious. As obnoxious as he is, I need to up the stakes.

I have a plan.

"I would get us both ice creams, but I don't have any cash on me," I lie, "and I doubt the little cart accepts Visa. I am really hungry though." (Another lie. I grabbed leftover sushi in the open kitchen before I left.)

"What would you do for food right now if I weren't here?" I ask.

He looks over at a little kid dropping his SpongeBob SquarePants Popsicle on the ground. The child picks it up and then, good citizen that he is, throws it in the garbage.

Freegan raises an eyebrow.

No!

I ask, "Is there another option?"

NO, FORAGING FOR ROOTS DOES NOT COUNT AS A LUNCH DATE

I'd never met a salad bar I didn't like. Until I did.

When it comes to the early stages of romance, a lunch date is generally considered a safe bet. It's a step up from a casual coffee but doesn't have the same pressure as going out to dinner. Not to mention the fact that if a guy wants to hang out in daylight hours, he probably wants to get to know you intellectually rather than just biblically.

This week, however, I found myself on an outing so bizarre, so entirely unappetizing, that not only has it turned me off lunch dates, but it also might have turned me off lunch as a whole.

It all began in Central Park.

Might we be having a picnic? I wondered, anticipating a spread of seedless grapes, French bread, and hard cheeses.

If only.

It turns out that my date, a setup through a soon-to-be-disowned friend, was a freegan. That means he has turned his back on consumerism and has decided to scavenge for food and clothes rather than buy them.

He eats out of garbage cans, is what I'm trying to say. Not because he's impoverished, which would be tragic and not the stuff that dating posts are made of. But because reaching his arm—decorated by a Rolex his mom bought for him—into a bag of fly-infested refuse so as not to have to pay for his own ice cream is his thing.

After I made it clear that I wouldn't be participating in Dumpster diving, the freegan offered our alternative: "We're going foraging!"

Now, the only foraging that I've ever participated in involved foraging through Netflix to find a good show to binge watch. My guess that that wasn't what he had in mind turned out to be right.

 "No, we're foraging in the park for food," he clarified. "It's like apple picking, but with roots!"

Let me tell you, apple picking it is not. Because apple

picking is a carefree, minimally difficult activity that always yields sweet, delicious rewards that are lethal only if you've pissed off the wrong Disney villain. Foraging is the polar opposite.

Crouched in the brambles of Central Park, I ruined a pair of shorts, got dirt under my nails, and succumbed to tasting a bitter root that my date then momentarily worried he'd misidentified as nonpoisonous.

The Folly Forager spent a lot of the time whining about how the really good edible weeds only come out at the end of the summer. Pokeweed, jumpseed, and Japanese knotweed will grow in the shadows, hiding from the sweltering August heat. I doubt they taste any better.

While dandelions make for great flower necklaces, they leave something to be desired in the raw snack department.

In the future, I think I'll stick with the more traditional salad bar.

Don't Carpe that Effing Freegan!
Harper

Ben: U aren't mad at me r u?

Harper: No! Why?

Ben: U said u were set up by a soon-to-be-disowned friend.

Harper: That was just for dramatic flair. Creative liberties and whatnot. I love you for that setup.

Harper: I mean, not love you love you

Why am I so awkward? I try to refocus the conversation with a triple text.

Harper: It was just a good bad date. Don't think we'll be double-dating w you and Delilah tho.

At the end of the date, it was the Folly Forager who ended up rejecting me, saying we had philosophical differences that couldn't be overlooked: Not only did I refuse to eat a suspicious-looking mushroom for fear of inadvertent poisoning but I bought a water bottle from a hot-dog vendor to wash down the roots' bitter taste. ("I thought you had no money," he said, catching me in my lie from before. "That's so wasteful when you could have gone to a water fountain. But if you *were* going to buy a Dasani anyway, the polite thing would have been to offer to get me one too.")

> **Kristina:** You tore him apart.
>
> **Harper:** I know! It went exactly as planned.
>
> **Kristina:** You don't think it was a little harsh?
>
> **Harper:** Um . . . no.

Actually, I think this conversation is kind of harsh.

> **Harper:** Aren't you the one always BEGGING me
> to mock your conquests to you?

The only thing I see as being different this time is the fact that instead of making fun of her dates, I'm making fun of my own.

> **Kristina:** Yeah, but that's just to me. This is to the
> whole world.

Kristina's not the only one who gets to know I'm funny anymore. At first I was a little worried about snarking so hard about a guy that I actually went out with. Playing it up for laughs. But when I got going, I found out that McKayla was right—it was fun. (Not to mention the fact that, on the date, the forager made it clear that he was *not* the "chick-lit" *Shift* demographic, so I think the chances of him reading the story are slim.)

> **Harper:** Whatever. I gtg.
>
> **Kristina:** I didn't mean to be negative.
>
> **Kristina:** Srsly I'm sorry. It was good!

I put my phone in my bag, push Kristina's underwhelmed reaction out of my mind, lean back in my chair, and watch my story inch up the Leader Board. McKayla was right about that, too: Bad dates are clicky. Right now my blog is the seventh most popular story on the site.

There's only a month of the internship left, a month until McKayla decides which of us *Shift* Girls gets to be immortalized in the magazine, and it's a pretty even race. We've all been on the Leader Board at this point, but sometimes what does and doesn't do well seems like a roll of the dice. ("Why did no one click on my amazing artist interview, but *everyone* clicked on my article about how Miley Cyrus's knee looks like Seth Rogen's face in some pictures?" Gigi lamented.)

But I think I have a shot. My blogs have started to get a following—"A very *small* following," McKayla pointed out, but a following, nonetheless. I'm getting way more Twitter followers and some readers are even e-mailing me their dating stories.

The person who isn't e-mailing me is Carter.

As the day wears on, staring at my inbox gets more depressing. No, PR person, I do not want to try "MatchBook Teen! A revolutionary dating app for the younger set!" I don't want to meet total strangers on my phone. (Creepy much?) I want the quasi stranger I already know is a damn good kisser.

And so I succumb to my obsession. I give in and e-mail him first.

I could write him a novella, packed with hidden references to the things I already know he likes based on my extensive . . . let's call it "research." But I manage to wrestle away my bad, long-winded impulses and maybe overcorrect. I just send him one word. No capital letters. No punctuation:

FROM: Harper_Anderson@Shift.com
TO: carter@deviant.com
SUBJECT: (No Subject)

hey

He writes almost immediately. Like he was waiting for me.

FROM: carter@deviant.com
TO: Harper_Anderson@Shift.com
SUBJECT: Re: (No Subject)

Please tell me you didn't ditch me this weekend
for the freegan. I could have provided much
better story fodder.

"What do you guys think?" I ask Gigi and Sunny. Jamie's in
her own world, Abigail's in a health meeting, and Brie is off very
pragmatically rearranging the lipsticks in *Shift*'s beauty closet based
on shade. She's even using a color wheel.

"No!" Gigi says in horror. "Oh, Harper, no. You e-mailed
him first?"

"It's fine," Sunny assures. "Sometimes you need to be aggressive. And he also made the tactical error of responding two minutes
later. You're even."

The three of us huddle together to discuss my response strategy.

FROM: Harper_Anderson@Shift.com
TO: carter@deviant.com
SUBJECT: Re: (No Subject)

I don't know if I should be offended that you
didn't like my article or intrigued as to what
better fodder than foraging you possibly could
have provided.

Even though our office e-mail automatically updates every
twenty seconds, I keep refreshing my inbox.

FROM: carter@deviant.com
TO: Harper_Anderson@Shift.com
SUBJECT: Re: (No Subject)

I didn't say I didn't like your article. It had lots of bite. You'll learn that I like biting. But that's why you should have come to Maverick on Saturday. It was a *Paris Review* editor's birthday. As a serious writer (I think?), I thought you'd be interested in the connection for when you're ready to move on from Teen-M-Z.

"*Paris Review*?" I say longingly. He thinks that one day I could maybe write for the *Paris Review*? My mom has subscribed to the quarterly literary journal since forever.

"Maybe we should have gone to Maverick after all," Gigi says.

"I can't believe you two!" Sunny's voice gets high-pitched. "You're focusing on entirely the wrong part of his e-mail."

"So what should we be focusing on?" I scan Carter's message again.

Sunny reads the sentence slowly. "'You'll learn that I like *biting*'?" Gigi and I don't register.

"He's basically saying he wants to have sex with you!" Sunny shouts, a little too loudly. Jamie looks in our direction, and Sunny lowers her voice back down to a whisper. "He definitely wants to have sex with you."

I still don't say anything, not because I still fail to register, but because each one of my synapses has exploded and now burned out. I feel comatose.

Other than Bobby McKittrick, no one has wanted to have sex with me before. (And Bobby would have sex with literally anybody.)

"Are you sure?" Gigi asks.

"What should I do?" The synapses are working again.

"Aren't you supposed to be the dating expert?" Sunny says. Gigi raises her eyebrow. Just the one. I feel as if I'm half an inch away from being exposed, a contingency I probably should have come prepared to deal with. Oh God.

"Umm, I might lose objectivity when I'm actually interested," I say. Sunny and Gigi look skeptical. "As opposed to when I'm just, you know, fooling around."

Sunny sighs. "I say ignore it. But definitely let him know you're down. Subtly. Actually"—Sunny, surprisingly strong for her size, pushes my rolling chair away from my computer and takes my place at the keypad—"I've got it. Just let me do it."

FROM: Harper_Anderson@Shift.com
TO: carter@deviant.com
SUBJECT: Re: (No Subject)

Maybe we can get together with the *Paris Review* people this weekend. Or just with each other.

I can't believe that I just said that to him. Or that someone pretending to be me said to him on my behalf. Am I more nervous that he'll say no or yes?

Carter doesn't make me wait for long.

FROM: carter@deviant.com
TO: Harper_Anderson@Shift.com
SUBJECT: Re: (No Subject)

No can do. I'm going to the Hamptons this weekend. Maybe when I'm back.

"I'm going to the Hamptons this weekend, too, with some boarding school friends," Gigi says, reading over my shoulder. Then, as an afterthought, she adds, "Care to join?"

Oh my God, Gigi is inviting me to the *Hamptons*! That's one of the fanciest places where the fanciest New Yorkers go to get out of the city on hot summer weekends. There are beaches, pools, gigantic mansions . . . and me?

"Seriously?" I ask. Gigi and I have started hanging out after work in groups, but joining her on a trip for a whole weekend in the *Hamptons* is a whole new step in our relationship. "Are you sure it would be okay?"

"No. I'm lying to you," she says, deadpan. "Yes, obviously it's fine. They probably wouldn't even notice an extra person. The house is huge."

I spring out of my seat and give her a hug.

"Don't make me uninvite you." Gigi wriggles her way out of my arms as soon as they wrap around her. "You can come too, Sunny. Save me from overdosing on Harper."

"I can't," Sunny says. "It's Cassie's and my twenty-second month-a-versary."

"Gag me," Gigi replies with a scowl.

There's just one last thing to figure out. I look back to the *Shift* Girls and ask, "Do I tell Carter I'm going to be there too?"

"No," Sunny says. "You should surprise him."

Who doesn't love a good surprise?

· 25 ·

GIGI INSTRUCTS ME TO MEET HER AT PENN STATION
Saturday morning to catch the 9:35 train heading for East Hampton.

"Maybe we'll beat the rush," she says.

Considering that people in Manhattan think that three p.m. is an appropriate time for brunch, I think that Gigi's prediction is plausible. But as soon as the escalator begins its descent into the depths of the underground train station, which entirely lacks both the gravitas and the elegance of Grand Central, it becomes painfully clear that we definitely haven't beaten the crowds.

People with carry-on bags are packed in like sardines, sullenly waiting in long lines around ticket machines.

"Pray for me :/," I tweet, along with a picture of the teeming hordes of weekenders.

Gigi, who you can always count on to regularly scan all the necessary social media channels, quickly texts me her location.

> **Gigi:**   Standing in front of the departures
> board. I'm wearing a hat.

Unfortunately, that isn't going to help me identify her. Hipster fedoras and oversize sun hats so big that you'd think one of the trains is going to a Royal Wedding fill the waiting area. Their brims tilted slightly upward toward the board, anticipating the announcement of what track they will be leaving from.

(Note: Apparently a hat is a staple piece of the weekender's wardrobe.)

After searching through bronze-legged, lanky girls in immaculate outfits, I find Gigi hidden among the Lilly Pulitzer sundresses. She's wearing a straw blue-and-white-striped boater's hat and the same all-white ensemble she wore on our first day at *Shift*.

We have come quite a long way.

Gigi catches my squinting eyes probing the area where remnants of the soda stain would be.

"Thank God for dry cleaning," she says. "Otherwise I don't think you'd be here with me right now. Actually, you might be dead."

I laugh like it's a joke. Gigi doesn't.

Suddenly there's a change in the atmosphere. Without warning, the people around us, once still and staring hungrily at the departures board, erupt into scrambling chaos.

"What's happening?" I ask Gigi, as someone elbows me in the side to move.

"They announced the track number for the Hamptons train."

She throws her weekend bag over her shoulder. "Quick, let's go."

Apparently everyone here is going to the exact same place. And since there's a limited number of seats on the train, which will be a three-hour journey, there's a mad rush to the platform.

"It's like the running of the bulls in Pamplona," Gigi says as the crowd surges toward track 14, bottlenecking at the escalator down.

"Or," I reply, "like when Walmart opens its doors early on Black Friday."

Given that two Castalia Day moms were hospitalized (and later arrested) last Black Friday after breaking into a brawl over a discounted PlayStation, I'm worried that we're at risk of getting pummeled by someone's golf clubs on our quest to nab an elusive seat on the train.

Gigi's behavior quickly makes it clear that if anyone's doing the pummeling, it's going to be her. While I try to dart between empty spaces in the crowd, Gigi runs in a straight line, swinging her massive weekend bag to part the masses with violent determination.

We swoop in and grab two seats—"Facing forward because I get nauseated," Gigi says—from two girls whose bikinis are fully visible through their sheer tank tops. They fan themselves angrily with fashion magazines.

"I wouldn't have hit them as hard if they were carrying *Shift*," Gigi says very matter-of-factly. I must look shocked, because she says, "Joking, Harper."

Our prize seats are upholstered in a plastic material that sticks to my bare legs whenever I readjust. It makes a snapping sound when I reach into my overnight bag for my bagel (I leave the Diet Coke carefully tucked inside for now), and Gigi pulls out a container with mango slices.

Others on the train appear to be partaking in a liquid diet. Even though it's not even ten in the morning yet, beer cans are cracked and paper Dixie cups of rosé, or as the loud group of guys wearing Ralph Lauren boat shoes sitting next to us loudly refer to it again and again, brosé, are clinked.

For the young Hamptons-bound, apparently the party starts before the train even leaves the station.

"Are we the only sober people here?" I ask.

"I hate the Saturday morning train to the Hamptons," she replies. "It's far too early to deal with loud, binge-drinking miscreants. We could have come last night. We should have. But. I was supposed to meet up with this guy who went to my boarding school. He goes to NYU and I'm going to apply early." She looks out the window, and I barely hear her say, "But it fell through."

"That's annoying."

"It's typical," she says in a tone that makes me think there's more to the story. Even though Gigi and I have gotten closer than I ever would have imagined when I first started at *Shift*, I realize that the love life conversations have been extremely one sided.

"Was this just some college counseling, or maybe more," I ask, "like a date?"

Gigi throws her arms in the air. "It was nothing because he canceled on me last minute. In fact—"

I'm excited to hear Gigi open up to me, but she doesn't get a chance to elaborate. One of the brosé bros leans across the aisle, two Dixie cups in hand, and smugly asks if us "girlies" want to play a drinking game.

"No. Us 'girlies' want to continue our conversation you so rudely interrupted." Gigi snaps her head to the side and gives him a stare that would make Medusa proud.

Feeling the glare's full impact, the bro nervously retracts his cups and offers them to the bikini girls, who are sitting on their bags on the floor of the packed train. They are far more amenable.

"That was awesome. I thought your stare was going to turn those guys into stone," I say, waiting for Gigi to continue her story. But she doesn't. Instead she is silently looking down at her white leather short-shorts I once marred.

"You know," I say, "this weekend doesn't just have to be about me meeting up with Carter. If there's someone *you're* interested in . . ."

"Stop with doing the love guru thing or I'll turn *you* to stone," Gigi says, popping another mango slice into her mouth and resolutely slamming the door shut on our previous conversation.

My phone rings and I see that Kristina's calling me on the drive to her Skinny B's early shift.

"Ignore it," Gigi says at the second ring, putting away her mango slices. "I forgot that I have something to show you!"

Harper: Talk later? On the train so can't be loud.

I realize that this isn't exactly true. As I press send, the bros next to us are in the midst of a very loud disagreement over the rules of their complex drinking game, which seems to be comprised of pointing and making animal noises.

Kristina: Kk. Call later tho?

"Helloooo," Gigi says. "Attention, please!"

"Done." I put my phone down in my lap and try to tune out the bros, who are now flapping their arms and clucking. "What did you want to show me?"

She's holding up a white tank top in front of her torso that reads in block-print black letters:

Don't Worry Be Yoncé

"Oh my God, Gigi, that's perfection!"

"I know." She shrugs. "I got it at this great boutique in Soho. And, just so you don't die of jealousy, I got one for you, too. Only with a different message, since I don't want us to be like little girl twins."

She holds up a second tank that says:

Fries Before Guys

"No. Way."

She tosses it over along with one of two gold lamé bandeau bras so that we don't expose epic amounts of side boob in the shirts' deep armholes.

"I remember you saying that to Sunny," she says. I did. When I thought Gigi hated me.

"This is really thoughtful, Gigi. Thank you."

As if on cue, my phone alerts me that the one guy I would deem worthy of forgoing fries for this weekend—thank God this is just a hypothetical—has replied to my tweet. Publicly. For the entire Twitterverse to see.

From @CBosh:

@HarperAnderson Hell is Penn Station. Where are you going?

Yes. This weekend is already going according to plan.

· 26 ·

IF BARBIE GREW UP, CHANGED HER NAME TO BABS, ditched Malibu for Park Avenue, and married a Waspy investment banker named Kenneth Jr., then this would be her East Hampton dream house. I have never seen anything quite like this.

The property is massive, with a sweeping lawn, Olympic-size pool, home movie theater, fully stocked kitchen, and prints with numbers on them so you know just how rare they are. The only perplexing detail is the human-size statue of the Pillsbury Doughboy in the backyard. ("People get weird when you ask about him, so just don't," Gigi advises.)

The house belongs to the father of one of Gigi's boarding school friends, who didn't want to give it up when he was relocated from the Upper East to the Middle East. So on summer weekends when he's not in town from Abu Dhabi, the mansion is occupied by a rotating group of ten to twenty of his daughter's friends.

Gigi and I are assigned to sleep in a closet.

No, not a room so small that I'm likening it to a closet.

A literal closet. (That's actually pretty big, considering.)

"There aren't enough real rooms for everybody, unless you want to cram three people to a bed." Gigi tosses her bag onto our air mattress. "Thankfully, this is a walk-in."

When we go to the backyard, it smells like summer. Hamburgers on the grill and coconut-scented suntan lotion. Gigi rushes up to her mishmash of boarding school friends lying on lounge chairs. At Castalia High, a jet-setting lifestyle usually means something like driving into San Francisco regularly to see plays and shop at H&M. For Gigi's friends, jet-setting involves jets, which is how I'm guessing they got here from their assortment of home countries. I'm worried that they won't even show me the time of day, but Gigi brings me into the cluster with ease. She's not warm and fuzzy, but I'm starting to think that we're actually friends.

As the sun beats down and the afternoon wears on, more people emerge from the house to discuss our game plan for the day. ("Late nights, late starts," says an English guy.)

"Sloppy Tuna?" someone suggests.

"Tell me there isn't a real place called Sloppy Tuna," I say to Gigi.

"Oh, but there is, and it's just as sloppy as you'd expect it to be. Where's the Bosh heir?" Gigi asks, using her new favorite way to refer to Carter. She knows the mission of this journey and has promised to travel with me to wherever my love interest may be, even if it does have cheap lingerie hanging from the ceiling. ("I can't take another week of you moping around the office about your missed connection," she said.)

"I've actually resisted contact. I didn't even respond to his tweet asking where I was going!" I say triumphantly. I hope that pretending I'm uninterested will have its intended effect of making Carter incredibly interested.

"I'm all for playing hard to get," Gigi says, "but how will you know where to find him if you don't contact him?"

"You underestimate my stalking capabilities."

Twenty minutes ago Carter tweeted to complain that his nine-passenger taxi charged each individual fifteen dollars for the five-minute ride from his family's house to a bar. ("Hamptons-cab cronyism at its worst!") Then, a mere five minutes ago, Carter added video on his Snapchat Story of some guy walking around the back of some bar wearing a donkey mask, braying. (Could it be the bros from the train? Why is animal impersonation suddenly such a thing?) Corroborating Instagram evidence places both him and the donkey at someplace called Cecil's Surf Shack, which according to the geotag locator map, isn't too far away. If writing doesn't work out, I'm considering joining the CIA.

"You're crazy. I love it." Gigi jumps onto her lounge chair to get everyone's attention. "Everyone, we're going to Cecil's. End of discussion."

It turns out that Cecil's Surf Shack is the place to be. Boarding school cliques and investment banking interns pile out of minivan taxis as if they were clown cars.

I don't have a game plan, other than to casually bump into Carter in an "Oh, *you're* here? What a surprise!" kind of way. I feel nervous, but mostly excited. As if the past few weeks of e-mail flirting has been leading toward this moment. Gigi and I first inspect the front area, which is blasting throwbacks out of giant speakers. Lots of guys. No Carter.

We move our search party to the actual party area out back.

"Follow that donkey!" I squeal to Gigi, pointing to a familiar-looking guy in a mask walking donkey ears above the crowd.

"And why would I do such a thing?" She crosses her arms, covering the "Don't Worry" portion of her tank.

But Donkey Head answers the question for me when he sits down with a group of lost hipsters at a picnic table.

"Oh, I see." A devilish smile cracks on Gigi's lips. "Shall we?"

And as we're staring across the crowd of boarding school cliques talking in closed-off circles, Carter Bosh stares back. I've been spotted. And I'm *not* sad about it.

"We *definitely* shall," I respond. Fake the confidence until you feel it. Until you are it. I take slow, tempered breaths with each step through the crowd. I haven't seen Carter since that one night in the gallery. In person, that is. But I feel like I have. I feel like I know him. His taste in literature, the fact that he *calls* it literature, his writing, and the fact that he thinks of me as a real writer. No question. No hesitation.

Carter reveals a thin half smile as I come closer.

"Harper, Harper, Harper," he says smoothly. "We finally meet again."

That buzzing sensation that reverberated between our bodies at the gallery is still there, maybe even amplified.

"Yeah, I decided to escape the city with a friend last minute,"

I reply, trying to play it supercool. Like my being here is totally by chance, rather than very carefully orchestrated.

We don't say anything for a second. He's gotten a haircut since the gallery. His hair is brushed back and shorter on the sides than in the middle. His signature glasses are the same. Carter breaks eye contact first. "Are you the friend?" he asks Gigi, who isn't used to being ignored.

"*C'est moi.* Just the friend. No name necessary."

Carter walks toward me.

And then past me.

"You should join me and my friends, No Name." He puts his hand on the small of her back and leads her to his table. She doesn't resist. Then, as if as an afterthought he adds, "You too, Harper. Nice shirt."

What. The. Hell.

Have I been making up our flirtation? I get it in the sense that Gigi has a good seven inches on me and is show-stoppingly beautiful. But I really thought that things would be different. I'm used to playing sidekick. I want a new role.

I can't just stand a yard to the side of the table, analyzing if I've misread every interaction leading up to this moment, so I dejectedly drag my espadrilles and follow behind. Carter is already sitting next to Gigi, who gives me a little shrug (good) but then angles her body back in his direction (bad). I can't tell if this is betrayal or just normal human behavior. Technically, Gigi isn't doing anything wrong. What is she supposed to do? Ignore the guy? She's just talking to him and taking his lead.

I sit myself across from them and actively try not to notice the fact that his left pinkie finger is resting on the table, a hair away from touching Gigi's right thumb.

I feel another body plop down next to me, sandwiching me tightly on the bench. I'm barely looking, though. Still focusing on those fingers.

"You look like you could use a Mango Tango," the body next to me says with a muffled voice. "We got a ton extra."

I raise my head and can't help but smile to see the guy in the donkey mask offering me what I'm told is Cecil's signature drink.

"Thanks." I accept the cup and take a sip, hoping that the frozen drink will lower my body temperature and cool my burning cheeks. The Mango Tango tastes sweet, delicious, and totally nonalcoholic. Which probably means that it's very alcoholic. Kristina and I learned this lesson on her faux family (plus Harper) cruise, when her cute, soon-to-be stepbrother, Erik, "accidentally" switched the "kids' table" pitcher of virgin strawberry daiquiris with the adults' spiked one. ("How else are we going to survive this?" he asked Kristina, nodding at their parents, who were getting way too handsy at the other table.) While I nervously took a few sips of the sweet concoction, terrified of getting caught, Kristina and Erik egged each other on, drinking glass after glass. Their parents didn't notice the mistake until Kristina drunkenly started giggling so hard at Erik's jokes that she fell off her chair and onto the floor. (Erik blamed the beverage mix-up on the waiter.)

Donkey Mask pulls me out of the memory Kristina asked me to forget—"We don't talk about them again, or think about them even," she told me after her dad's disastrous wedding; her bonding with Erik was short-lived.

"Wait, do I know you?" Donkey Mask asks. "I think I recognize you from somewhere. "

"I'm not sure. What with the . . ." I motion toward his hidden face.

"Whoops, forgot I was wearing that." He fumbles with the full-head mask to reveal an oval face with wide-set eyes that I don't recognize. "Ta-da!"

I shake my head. Definitely don't know him.

"No? Are you a writer, too? Maybe I recognize you from your Twitter picture."

Wait a second. Stop yourself from shaking your head again, Harper. Sit up tall and drink from your Mango Tango proudly as you announce that you are, in fact, a writer.

"I'm the summer dating blogger at *Shift*!"

"That's it! You're pretty funny. Harper something?"

Oh my God. Donkey Head knows who I am. I want to burst out a "Thank you!" but realize that that isn't a sensical response. Instead I nod excitedly and take another sip of Mango Tango. Carter be damned. I should focus less on being noticed by boys (even though I suppose that Donkey Head does qualify in that department) and more about getting recognized as a writer.

"I'm Davie. I intern at *deviant* with Bosh." He gives a little wave. "Are you staying at his place, too?"

Davie tells me that Carter—who is either harmlessly talking or shamelessly flirting with Gigi right now—has invited some *deviant* interns and other journalism friends to camp out at his dad's compound for the weekend. Get out of the city. Breathe normal air. Buy groceries you don't have to carry up five flights of stairs, cook meals in an actual rather than dollhouse-size kitchen, and eat the food in rooms big enough to hold more than five people at a time. (Not exactly my experience of living in Manhattan with Aunt Vee, but I get it.)

"I've realized that city people only go to the Hamptons so that they can have the basic experience of being in a house," Davie says. "I could have done this at home in Topeka!"

"But in Topeka, can you casually go into a bar pretending that you're Nick Bottom?" I ask, pointing at the donkey mask.

Most of the people at Castalia High would give me a confused look in response to my reference to Nick Bottom's head turning into a donkey's head in *A Midsummer Night's Dream*, even though we all had to read the play sophomore year. But my nerdy Shakespeare joke isn't lost on Davie. Maybe I'm finding my people.

"This donkey head wasn't forced on me by an elf, though. My boss made me wear it."

"Um, why?"

Davie shrugs. "He thought it would be funny to make one of the interns wear it for an entire weekend and then write an article about what it felt like to be an ass."

"Again . . . why?"

"Because my boss loves torturing me?"

"Davie's the *deviant* whipping boy," Carter interjects. His pinkie is no longer close to Gigi's. "His beat is shit."

"I'm sure it's not that bad," I say sympathetically, still looking at Davie, whose mouth is now drooping grimly. Two can play at this game, Carter.

"No," Davie admits. "It is. I write about literal shit."

"Come again?"

"Human feces," Carter boasts as Davie squirms.

My face scrunches up as Davie describes what writing *deviant*'s "Turd of the Day" column entails. Readers tweet in tips about where there's stray poop around Manhattan, and Davie is tasked with going out, photographing it, confirming that it is indeed human, and then waxing poetically about its state.

"An editor joked about making interns do it last summer whenever we messed something up as, like, a fake punishment. As a joke," Carter explains. "But then, this year, he realized that a 'Turd of the Day' column could actually be hilarious. Maybe get a cult following. I'm just glad I don't have to do it. No offense, Davie."

"That's disgusting," Gigi says, frowning as she takes a Mango Tango of her own. I can't tell if she's talking about the fact that Carter's attention has shifted or the fact that Davie lives a life full of real-life poop emojis.

"Tell me about it." Dejectedly, Davie puts his donkey mask back on. "I should probably go back out there."

Davie gets up to mingle. Gigi and I are introduced to the rest of the table, also made up of *deviant* interns. I'm acutely aware of the fact that Gigi and I are the youngest in the group, so when we reach the point in the small talk when someone asks me where I go to school, I just say "Castalia." It's not my fault if they think I'm referring to Cal State Castalia instead of Castalia High.

"Gigi, you should meet Luanne. She also covers the arts, probably less pop culture news than *Shift* has you do, but still." Carter lets the sentence taper off before seamlessly beginning a new one, directed at me: "And, Harper, it looks like you could use a refill. Come with me to the bar?"

"Sure." I slam down my glass, which has a small melted pool of syrupy mango juice at the bottom, and get up quickly. Making sure to avoid eye contact. Because once our eyes catch, I don't know if I'll be able to pull myself out. My heartbeat quickens and I worry that I'm about to go into babbling overdrive. Because I don't really know what it will be like to be alone with Carter. The only time it happened was brief and mostly consisted of me grabbing on to his face and kissing it. Tempting as that is—as his hand now touches the small of *my* back when we go to the bar, making every nerve ending of mine explode like fireworks over the East River—I think that I should probably hold off. For now. And actually talk. You know, talk outside of all the hypothetical conversations we've had in my head, outside of my very carefully crafted e-mails that have been analyzed for everything from extraneous punctuation (Is an exclamation point too obvious?) to appropriate sign-offs ("From Harper"? "Yours, H"? No name at all?)

"So, do you like the Hamptons?" I feel the jolt when Carter breaks the ice.

"It's . . ." I search for a good way to capture the essence of this cool new setting, but instead land on the safe answer. "Nice."

"Just nice?" He stops walking and turns me toward him. "Come on, something tells me there's more in that mean little mind of yours."

"I'm not mean."

"I've *read* your blogs. Why so defensive? It's not a bad thing." The green in his eyes glints. "It's one of the reasons why I like you. Who wants vanilla? What do you really think?"

What I really think is that the Hamptons are like the most luxurious parts of Manhattan without any of its grit. No hot dog carts or trash smell fermenting in the summer heat. And it feels exhilarating. Like everyone is at an exclusive playground. And once you have been invited, you're taken in with open arms. Because while I was a little nervous when I was riding the train into town, so far everyone has been extremely nice.

But that's not what Carter wants to hear. Like McKayla, he wants the edge. He wants the flash judgments I write in my notebook, which are just part of me but not the whole me. But maybe that's a part I should be embracing more and more.

"Let's put it this way," I say, close to his ear, "when I walked in, I saw a guy wearing a Reagan-Bush '80 bro tank walk by at the exact second the song 'Gold Digger' started blasting from the speakers. If a bomb went off right now, Goldman Sachs would lose an entire generation of its junior management."

It's a mean observation I'd write in my notebook but not necessarily say out loud. Carter claps his hands.

"And there it is. That's why I can't stop thinking about you."

You know the thing that I said about getting stuck in his eyes? Well, I'm drowning in them.

Don't lose your cool, Harper. He says he likes the edge. Be difficult.

"I mean, you stopped thinking of me for a little. Earlier with Gigi. The hand on the back and whatnot. The flirting."

"Come *on*." He stretches out the word like it's a piece of salt-water toffee. "You know that wasn't me flirting with your friend."

"Then what was it?"

"That was me flirting with you." Carter inches closer. "The hot and cold and hard to get. Kissing me, then canceling on me. Ignoring my tweet. You play the game, I play the game."

The way he says it makes it sound like poetry. Our moment is almost wrecked by a loud group of people who bump into us as they pass, but Carter grabs my elbow as I stumble and doesn't let go. Once I'm stabilized, his pointer finger traces a slow line up my bare arm. Then, in a swift movement, he scoops the part where my scalp curves up from the base of my neck in his hands and pulls me in.

The tension immediately melts away and we are no longer in this crowded bar with sticky floors. It's just us. Our lips. Our breath.

Carter's kisses are confident. Purposeful. He switches up the tempo and dynamics like he's playing an instrument. Fast and slow. Hard and soft. And I, the girl who's always thinking, just get to turn off my brain and be.

Just as his finger traveled up my arm, Carter's lips make their way to my earlobe, a body part that until this moment I didn't realize served any purpose except as the canvas for earrings, and bites it. Light enough so that it doesn't hurt, but hard enough so that it wakes something up inside of me.

"I told you I liked biting," he whispers.

I don't respond. Words aren't working for me right now. Coherency is totally out of the question.

"You should come back to my place." He gives my ear another nip. "See what else I like."

And suddenly I'm thinking again.

Does he mean sex? Sunny would say he's talking about sex. And Sunny would *know*.

If anything, my virginity has been situational rather than purposeful. I'm not opposed to . . . I'm not saving myself for . . . but . . . I don't know how to finish that sentence. That thought. So instead my mind hopscotches to easier, more logistical questions. Would Gigi come to his house, too? Would we both have to spend the night?

"I'm here with my friend," I reply. There. Not an answer, exactly. Not a yes or no. Just the simple statement of a fact.

"A ton of people are staying at the house. Two more won't be a problem."

"I don't know."

He kisses the side of my neck.

"Okay," I say. "Maybe. Let's go back to the group. I'll talk to Gigi and . . . see?"

"Of course. No pressure." He gives my hand a squeeze and I feel lighter again. "But I know you want to."

We come back to the table with armfuls of Mango Tangos, giving way too many details about how long the wait was. Gigi, who has a few empty glasses in front of her already, raises an eyebrow and informs me that my lipstick is smeared. I squeeze in next to her on the picnic table's bench. I want to pull her to the bathroom and gush about what just happened, but it turns out that Cecil's makes all the prepsters use Porta Potties lined up outside, and there's no way that Gigi would want to be dragged there. Besides, she has adopted Sunny's Resting Bitch Face since I left. I just apologize for having disappeared for so long. She rolls her eyes.

Now that we have a new round of drinks, a girl with short hair and a septum piercing suggests we play a game. Specifically, Never Have I Ever.

I try not to look as relieved as I am when Gigi protests loudly, declaring the game "gauche."

I very purposely haven't played Never Have I Ever since Trisha Atwood's slumber party in the eighth grade. I can still remember how I felt when I had to keep all ten of my fingers fanned out for the entire game while my friends proudly dropped theirs one by one, passionately debating what differentiated a make-out from a plain old kiss. ("It's a make-out if your lips touch for more than five seconds," Kristina explained with certainty.)

But Gigi's request to nix Never Have I Ever goes ignored.

"I haven't played that since I was a *child*," I say.

"It's so much better older," Carter says. "There's so much more juicy shit you can call people out on."

Or not. Considering that Never Have I Ever done half the things I've claimed to have done as *Shift*'s teen dating blogger, this is so not the game I want to be playing right now. But it starts anyway.

Never have I ever smoked pot. (I have never tried Bobby McKittrick or anyone else's pot. But I'm in the minority. Everyone except me, Gigi, and the girl who said it puts down their first fingers.)

Never have I ever had sex on the beach. (I decide to put my finger down for that one. Even though I've never had sex. Even though Castalia is absolutely nowhere near the beach.)

Never have I ever plagiarized.

"Now that's the only thing I'll judge people for doing in this game," Carter says. The interns around him nod their heads solemnly, myself included. Passing off someone's work as your own is a cardinal sin in the journalism world. Who would do that?

Uh, possibly someone who "borrowed" her best friend's life to get an internship. Possibly me when I misappropriated Kristina's hookup story in my application for *Shift*.

I reassure myself that that wasn't plagiarism. That was fictional redistribution. And I wrote every single word. But why didn't I pick some other damned story to redistribute?

Good job, Harper. It wasn't plagiarism. It was worse.

But you don't get to mull things over for long in Never Have I Ever. Because the game continues.

Never have I ever been in love. Never have I ever hooked up with two people in one night . . . two people in twelve hours . . . two people in two hours.

But when it gets to be Gigi's turn, she gets a weird look on her face and abruptly stands up and announces that she has to pee.

"Me too," I say. "Gigi, wait up."

Gigi doesn't respond when I call after her, and it takes a bit for me to catch up. As was demonstrated in Penn Station, we have different tactics and levels of success when it comes to cutting through crowds. When there's finally a clearing, I run around Gigi to physically stand in the middle of her path. I expect to be met with a typically Gigi surly mood. I expect an annoyed eye roll for whatever indiscernible reason. But what I don't expect is the running eye makeup.

"Whoa. Are you *crying*?" Clearly I'm not winning a prize tonight for sensitivity or observational skills. "What just happened?"

Gigi covers her face with the palms of her hands. Her body stiffens when I touch her shoulder and ask, in my very gentlest voice, "What's up?"

"You wouldn't understand." She wipes under her eye.

"Try me."

"No, really you wouldn't. It's stupid. The game—it was my turn at the game and I just blanked."

This is about a silly game? I don't understand, but Gigi, whom I've never seen as anything other than composed, even when she's seething, seems genuinely upset. So I pretend. "It's not a big deal," I tell her. "If you can't think of something you haven't done, you can just say something stupid. Like never have I ever been to Canada."

"I've been to Canada."

"Of course. Um, Uruguay?"

"I've *been* to Uruguay. Travel is the only kind of thing I *have* done. The other stuff . . . I haven't done any of the *other* stuff. Do you understand what I'm saying?"

Oh.

Gigi cuts ahead of the Porta Potty line to grab toilet paper to blow her nose and then returns. "This is so humiliating. I go to boarding school in Europe for God's sake! We're supposed to be sexually liberated."

"But didn't you put your finger down for sex on the beach?"

"Yeah, because I'm a fraud. I'm a total liar," Gigi chokes through her tears.

"You're not a liar; it's just a tiny white lie. We all tell them," I assure her, although maybe I'm reassuring myself a little bit, too.

"Everything is *so* easy for you. I wasn't just being bitchy by letting Carter flirt with me, I was being bitchy and an idiot because he was so obviously doing it to get your attention. I'm such an *idiot*! And apparently a bad friend now, too."

I want to tell her everything.

In that moment, I want to tell her that really, I'm a fraud, too. Nothing is easy. I'm pretending to be someone I'm not, and for some bizarre reason, people believe me. I'm letting them believe me.

I want to bond with her over inexperience and perception, but I can't.

Gigi is a completely different person from who I thought she was. But in a good way. And I suddenly feel protective of her.

"Look," I say, "why don't we Uber back to the house, make some of the popcorn I saw in the kitchen, go to our closet, and binge watch *Gossip Girl* on Netflix?"

Gigi gives a small sniffle and asks, "But what about Carter? I can't sabotage you twice in one night."

"Don't worry"—I sweep my hands dramatically over her torso—"Beyoncé."

"That makes zero sense."

"Just shut up and let's go back," I say.

Gigi sniffles again. "Okay. But only if you're sure you don't mind."

On my way back to the table to grab our bags, break the news to Carter (I hope he meant it when he said he liked the chase), and request an Uber, I see a new text . . . make that texts . . . from Kristina.

> **Kristina:** I've texted you a million times.
>
> **Kristina:** Call me?
>
> **Harper:** Later. Friend's having a crisis.
>
> **Kristina:** Oh.
>
> **Kristina:** Ok I guess . . .

She obviously wants me to respond, but I just can't. I haven't been the best about texting her back, I know it, but I can't turn my back on a crying Gigi right now.

"Our Uber will be here in five." I throw Gigi her purse, and she quickly takes out her compact mirror to assess the damage.

"Thank God," Gigi says, dabbing the last black streak from under her eye. "Because I really do have to pee, and I was not looking forward to using that Porta Potty."

"Luckily your friend's place has better bathroom accommodations," I say. "But when we get back, you have to help me come up with a dating blog to hand in Monday."

"Oh please," Gigi says. "I'm sure you'll find a date on the bus."

We walk out of Cecil's, arm in arm.

MY THREE-HOUR RELATIONSHIP

That's one way to kill time on a bus ride.

Sometimes being a good friend means putting your love life on hold. So my salacious Hamptons weekend became all about LITERALLY Netflix and chilling with a girlfriend in need rather than euphemistically "Netflix and chilling" (aka hooking up) with a cute boy I'd been talking to.

But a *Shift* Girl can balance all of her relationships. So, not wanting the weekend to be a total romantic bust, I managed to fit in not only a date, but an entire relationship—complete with a beginning, middle, and end—into the three-and-a-half hour fancy bus ride (called the Jitney) back into Manhattan.

The relationship started by chance. I was stretching my legs in the aisle of the bus when the driver took a sharp turn, causing me to stumble into the lap of an adorable stranger—who just so happened to have an empty seat next to him.

By hour one, we were already sharing ear buds as we streamed a movie on his laptop. And like a true gentleman, he comforted me during the scary parts.

By hour two, we'd had our first romantic meal together, sharing a bag of Doritos Cool Ranch.

By hour three, we had inside jokes and plans for him to visit when I go back to California in August. He couldn't wait to meet my friends, and I had already plotted our road trip up Route 1 when he came to visit. We were going to make this long distance thing work!

But when the bus pulled into Manhattan, things went tragically downhill.

When the driver made another sharp turn, the book I was reading (that I highly recommend) called *We Should All Be Feminists* fell out of my bag.

"Oh no," my new bus boyfriend said, grimacing at the title. "You aren't one of those are you? Feminism is just so . . . gay."

Alas, the love was gone. After three hours of bonding, we were torn asunder by one sentence that revealed our major irreconcilable differences.

I gave him a fake number . . . but we'll always have the Jitney.

Carpe that Effing Diem!
Harper

· 27 ·

"relationship" also included an hour-long nap in the middle that I didn't mention—goes up on Wednesday and works its way up to the Leader Board. But the exciting new traffic comes with a dark side I wasn't expecting: the comments section. So. Many. Comments. And tweets. Wow, people are mean on Twitter. Apparently antifeminist jerks who use "gay" as a pejorative have some rather vocal supporters out there. @PGoods99's tweet declaring "Well, that guy dodged a bullet. She's a loser #bitch" was one of the nice ones.

The other *Shift* Girls tell me not to fixate on the haters and insist that getting mean comments is just part of being a writer. I know that's true, but it still sucks. They pry me away from refreshing the comments on my computer and drag me to an outdoor movie screening of a nineties classic in Bryant Park.

Once I recharge my deader-than-dead phone back at Aunt Vee's apartment, the iPhone springs back to life with a series of terse texts from Kristina sent over the course of the night.

Kristina: Remember me?

Kristina: So glad you have time to have an entire relationship but not to text me back.

Kristina: "Being a good friend means putting your love life on hold?" Ironic much? PLEASE

Oh no. I never got back to Kristina.

Harper: Didn't see these until now!! Was watching Clueless after work w friends. It's been a crazy week, but didn't you see I called back Monday?

I feel terrible. I didn't call her, but I'm hoping that since Kristina's phone is always malfunctioning, she'll think it just didn't record my fake missed call.

Kristina: You know I hate that movie.

Harper: Shit. I wasn't thinking.

Clueless is Kristina's kryptonite. Especially considering her relationship with her ridiculously cute, ridiculously awful stepbrother.

Kristina: How could u forget something like that? Altho u seem to be forgetting a lot of things lately.

Harper: Well, we're talking now. Things have just been really crazy. You know having a love life is new for me. What's up?

Kristina: Nothing. Just my stepbrother got off the wait list at Stanford and now I have to find a new school to swim for.

Harper: What?!?

This is serious. I snap back into best friend mode. I call her instantly.

It goes to voice mail after only one ring. Is she screening my calls?

Harper: ???

Harper: Do you wanna talk about it?

Kristina: gtg going on a date.

I can't tell if she's mad or hurt mad or fake mad or actually just on a date.

I pick Princess up for more moral support and plop us down onto my bed, sinking extra deep into the feather-down mattress. She rests her head on my lap and lets me pet her ears while I stare at my phone, willing Kristina to write more.

As if by my will, the phone vibrates in my hand. But the text isn't from Kristina.

Carter: It didn't take long for you to forget all about me.

My brief stint as a dating blogger has given enough insight to make me certain that Carter's text isn't angry, it's flirty. Since when do I get guys better than I get my best friend?

I stop myself from texting that I actually didn't forget about him. I texted Carter from the jitney to ask how the rest of his night went and he never responded, even though he was tweeting during my whole bus ride back. I guess this blog post got his attention.

Harper: I take my job very seriously.

Carter: Maybe I should give you a date to blog about.

I freak out silently under a slumbering Princess.

Harper: Gigi gave me her unwanted tickets to *Phantom of the Opera* this weekend. Wanna go with me?

The fact that there could be such a thing as an unwanted *Phantom* ticket is impossible for me to understand. But when a PR person sent a pair to the Arts & Culture editor, she gave it to a reporter who gave it to Gigi who gave it to me.

Carter: There's a reason those tickets are
unwanted. You'll be surrounded by
tourists, the geriatric and the pediatric.

I won't be the one to remind him that I am a tourist. Or tell
him that I love that show. Kristina and I didn't just have a *Phantom*
phase when we were little, we had a full-blown obsession. After
the movie came out, we would incorporate opera house story lines
into all our games, in spite of the fact that we're both tone deaf.
("Maybe sing with your indoor voices, girls," Mr. Jefferson would
say in music class.)

And now I'm going to see it on freaking Broadway. My first-
ever Broadway show. I just won't be seeing it with Carter.

Carter: I'm going out of town for a week for a
story, but my parents are having a party
the first Monday in August. Wanna
come?

I loudly squeal "YES" under a no-longer-slumbering Princess.

Harper: That can be arranged.

"What's going on in here? I heard yelling." Aunt Vee pushes
through my doorway wearing a fabulous gown for the Park Avenue
Tulip Society gala she just got back from.

Since I can't gush about it to Kristina, I decide to tell Aunt Vee
everything. That I just got asked out by an incredible guy.

"His name is Carter Bosh."

When I say his name, Aunt Vee's jaw drops. Her excitement rivals Brie's when the beauty editor told her she could take her pick of makeup from the summer collection, since in magazine world, we are well into shooting for fall issues.

"His mother and I are on the board of the Park Avenue Tulip Society. I *just* saw her," she says. "I'm not one to brag, but Kiki and I were entirely responsible for the tulips' color scheme this year." She takes out her phone to show me pictures of flowers lining the Upper East Side sidewalks.

Aunt Vee goes on to tell me that the party I've been invited to is one of the most exclusive events of the summer season. It's the Boshes' thirtieth wedding anniversary party.

"The Bosh family is a very good one to be connected to. Kiki tried to set me up with her divorced brother a few years back, but I was unfortunately considering reconciling with my fourth husband at the time. What a waste that was. If you think Princess's snoring is bad . . ."

My cheeks heat up from all the Bosh conversation. I can't talk about Carter anymore right now. It makes me too nervous. So I change the subject instead.

"Have you noticed that since she started taking her walks, Princess has been snoring less?" I ask. "I think that the exercise is finally helping her sleep apnea."

"And she's getting closer to her prom dress size," an easily distracted Aunt Vee says. "Benjamin is melting away those adorable fat rolls one by one. I wonder if he trains humans, too."

"You should ask him." I can totally picture Aunt Vee in her neon spandex running circles around Atticus in the park. They'd probably make fantastic workout buddies.

"I will as soon as he's back."

"Back from where?" I've been out every night this week with the *Shift* Girls so have been skipping our walks.

"New Hampshire with that athletic girlfriend of his," Aunt Vee says. "Thank God he'll be back by the weekend. Princess hasn't taken to his temporary replacement. It's all very inconvenient."

"Wait, he's visiting Delilah?" I've gotten a sad series of text messages every time she's canceled one of his trips to New Hampshire at the very last minute. ("The car was even packed!") So I wonder why he didn't send me dancing girl emojis and fireworks to tell me that he was finally making the trip. We need a serious debrief—and I know the perfect place. Ben wouldn't make fun of me for my musical-theater proclivities.

> **Harper:** Question, when do you get back in town?

He responds quickly.

> **Ben:** I haven't been out of town.

Wait, what? Before I ask, Ben texts again.

Ben: Why? Do u need more drugs, guns, and other potential felonies?

I ignore his ominous implications and ask if he has any interest at all in being my plus one to *Phantom of the Opera* Saturday night. He doesn't respond, so I add:

Harper: Please? We need to catch up.

Ben: Ur right. We do. I've been staying off my computer and phone for a few days. But Phantom sounds great! I can pick you up at your place at 7?

Harper: It's a date.

I regret it as soon as I hit send because obviously it's not a date. That's so awkward.

Harper: Not really.

Harper: You know. Just an expression.

Harper: Friend.

Yup, I've officially made it more awkward. It's, like, a gift.

Ben: U can stop now, BUD. I got it. See u 2morrow.

Maybe I can squeeze a blog post out of it: the importance of the platonic guy friend. The surrogate boyfriend.

· 28 ·

EVEN THOUGH BEN HAS A KEY TO AUNT VEE'S apartment for dog-walking purposes, he rings the doorbell on Saturday night.

Princess comes running as soon as she sees him walk through the door.

"Actually, I'm here for this one today." Ben nods in my direction as he scratches her ears. Princess harrumphs.

"You look different," I say, looking over Ben's ensemble choice. He's ditched the Saint Agnes sports tee and gym shorts in favor of pressed jeans and an ironed, short-sleeved, pale blue collared shirt. I think he even put gel in his typically poofy hair. He shifts uncomfortably in his dress shoes.

"Don't you two make a pretty picture," Aunt Vee says, entering the living room.

"Don't get any ideas, Aunt Vee."

We give Princess a dog treat to distract her so that we can leave the apartment without her.

"So, New Hampshire," I say, when we go underground in the sweltering subway station. "How was finally seeing Delilah?"

"Um . . ."

Ben looks flushed.

"Are you okay?" I ask. "You're wearing jeans and it's like a hundred degrees?"

"Yeah." He tugs on his collar. "It's just hot down here. New Hampshire was interesting. Let's talk about it after the show. Are *you* okay? I read some of the comments on your blog."

Apparently calling yourself a feminist and saying you don't want to date someone who tells "that's so gay" jokes puts a big target on your back for Internet trolls. I'm still getting angry messages about how I'm an "ugly femi-nazi who should take any date she can get."

"Ugh, I had to stop reading them," I say as we exit the subway at Times Square. "They're the worst."

Ben tells me that he spent the better part of this afternoon on Twitter, responding to some of my hate tweets.

"You didn't!" We break apart to go around a group of tourists who have inexplicably stopped in the middle of the sidewalk, and come back together again. "You're supposed to ignore them! Don't feed the trolls!"

"The only food I was offering was a knuckle sandwich." The severity with which he says it, completely unironically, makes me burst into a fit of giggles.

"You did *not* just say that! That's so corny."

Ben lets the laughter roll off his white button-up shirt's back, which is starting to freckle with perspiration.

"Corny?" He smiles in a way that activates his dimple. "Says the girl making me see *Phantom of the Opera*?"

"Touché."

"And *that's* why I'm risking heatstroke, by the way," he says. "I knew I couldn't show up in Nike gear and my Saint Agnes shirt. You invited me somewhere nice. Thanks, by the way."

We turn the corner and see the image of the phantom's white mask glowing in the marquee of the Majestic Theatre.

"Air-conditioning!" Ben lets out a groan and folds at the waist, with his hands on his knees, after we're engulfed in the cold lobby's air.

"Thanks for coming," I say, and we head to our seats.

Screw highbrow New York theater society. *Phantom of the Opera* is freaking incredible. I tune out all the crinkling candy wrappers around me and am transfixed by what is happening on the stage. The crash of the chandelier, the smoky boat ride to the phantom's lair, those high notes. . . . I become a little girl again, and by the final scene I'm bawling like a baby and reaching for Ben's hand. His entire body stiffens, and I realize that this probably isn't acceptable behavior. I quickly pull my hand back but can see that he's facing me and not the stage as the cast transitions into the curtain call. I just clap enthusiastically and pretend that nothing happened. Ben pretends right along with me, suggesting that we wait outside the theater's back exit to see if the cast will come out and sign our programs.

"We might as well do this right," he says.

"I can't believe I've been in New York for almost two months and it's taken me this long to see a show on Broadway. What have I been doing?" I ask Ben, in the middle of a crowd eagerly waiting for the performers to take off their makeup and greet their fans. "You're so lucky you live here. You must see these all the time."

"Not really." He's using his program as a fan and then waves some air in my direction.

"Not even with Delilah?"

"She's not the musical type," he says. "Neither am I, really."

"So why did you agree to come with me?"

"Because you asked me." Ben's face softens. "You wanted me to. And I actually liked it. It's nice to be asked to try new things."

The crowd around us bursts into applause as the backstage door swings open to reveal a smiling and waving cast. I start to push up toward the front to get an autograph, but Ben grabs my hand and keeps me back.

"Why'd you invite me, Harper? Why not the Nietzsche guy?"

Ben's eyes probe my face for an answer. This is because I texted "date," isn't it? Because I held his hand. I quickly assure him that I asked Carter, of course I did, but he was busy. So I thought it would be good to go with a friend.

"Actually, I'm thinking of writing about this for my next blog," I say, talking really quickly. "About the perks of having a surrogate boyfriend. You know, a guy friend who you'd never be romantic with but you can count on for, like, emotional support and going on platonic dates to events and places you've been wanting to check out."

"Surrogate boyfriend?" Ben pulls a Brie and cocks his head to the side. This would be when his floppy hair would flop if it weren't gelled into submission.

"It's just a phrase," I say as the actress who played Christine signs my program. "I could call it something else if you think it would weird Delilah out. Basically it just means that I feel comfortable asking you to do dorky things with me that I couldn't ask Carter to. Like go to cheesy musicals or eat at Serendipity!"

As soon as my program is done being signed, I brush against tourists in fanny packs to get back to the subway at Times Square.

"Slow down," Ben calls from behind. I stop on the crowded corner of 44th Street and Broadway, in the middle of a swarm of people dressed up as off-brand Disney characters and superheroes pandering for tips. An adult-human-size Elmo swathed in faded red fabric waves in my direction.

"What if I don't want to be your surrogate boyfriend at Serendipity?" Ben asks.

"What does everyone have against Serendipity? I've seen pictures and that frozen hot chocolate looks amazing."

"No, Harper, you're not hearing me." Ben takes a step closer. "I want to eat frozen hot chocolate with you. But . . . not as your *surrogate* boyfriend."

No, I'm hearing him, but maybe I'm not fully getting him. Why is he looking at me like that?

"I wasn't in New Hampshire this week," he says.

This is news. "Well, where were you?"

"Okay, so I went up there, but I left after an hour." He takes a long pause. Oh no. Did Delilah break up with him? But before I can ask, he says, "I ended things with Delilah. I wanted to do it in person."

"But her soccer camp was almost over! I thought you were *so* excited for her to come back!"

"It was inevitable." He looks so miserable and uncomfortable talking about this, so I take his arm. "In the beginning of the summer, I was really bummed that she didn't want me visiting her. That she didn't have time to take my calls. But then I realized that when she *did* pick up, we didn't have a lot to talk about. I didn't miss her as much as a boyfriend should miss a girlfriend. I didn't miss her as much as I miss you between walks."

"Oh," I say, head swirling. *Oh*. I miss Ben, too, but like you'd miss a friend, right? Things are finally starting to work out with Carter. Maybe I should tell him that we're finally going on a date, before he says something he regrets, but I stop myself. What if I'm overinterpreting what Ben's saying? So instead I just ask, "How'd she take it?"

"Not well. She said that we'd outgrown each other anyway. And since this is the school year when she has to impress college coaches, she probably should only surround herself with serious athletes anyway. She said I'm just a fun distraction, but I'm not a *serious* anything."

I'd be such a mess if someone said that to me. I want to comfort Ben, but I also don't want to make things any more weird or ambiguous.

"You have to know that's not true, right?" I shake my head,

horrified by how harsh and flat-out wrong Delilah was. "Anyone who thinks that about you is just, I don't know, stupid. When did this happen?"

"Exactly a week ago."

A whole week?

"Ugh, that sucks," I say. Elmo starts break dancing in front of a crowd for tips. Ben is staring at Elmo so intently that's it's like he's memorizing his moves. "You could have told me. I'm your *friend*; I would have been there for you."

"I know you're my friend, and that's one of the reasons why I couldn't be with you right then." Ben's lips form into a half smile. "Because I needed to make sure that I was actually feeling what I was feeling. That I wasn't about to do anything rash."

"Like what?" I look up at Ben's face, my eyes squinting because of the bright lights of Times Square. He gently puts one hand on each of my arms and before I fully realize what's happening, he begins lowering himself down so his lips can meet my lips.

"Ben!" I exclaim, as I step backward toward the dancing Elmo to avoid the kiss. How did I miss this? I'm an idiot!

Ben stumbles back, startled. His eyes wide in what looks a lot like terror. "Oh no. Harper, I'm sorry. I'm so, so sorry. I misread the signs. I thought—"

"It's just," I say quickly, trying to explain, "I like Carter . . . but . . . I love our *friendship*."

His shoulders droop and he lets out a sigh.

"I didn't mean for that to come out as lame as it sounded," I whisper. "But it's true. I do love it."

"I thought it wasn't serious with that guy. You go out with other people," Ben says.

"That's my *job*." I inch back toward him, patting his arm sympathetically but making sure I don't linger. How can I make this easier? Because I really *do* like Ben. But Carter . . .

"Think about it," I say. "Think. We're so incompatible. We're into totally different things. You know I'm not your type. You don't like me. Not really."

God, I'm not making this better.

Ben bristles. "Don't tell me how I feel. You get me and maybe even make me *better*. You're the person I want to tell exciting things to. Like, the pug prom, I decided—"

Pug prom. I was so looking forward to it. But all I foresee is a whole lot of awkwardness and making Ben miserable in front of a bunch of dogs in formal wear.

"Maybe I shouldn't go to pug prom?" I leave it as a question. I so want to go, I so want things not to be weird between us, but I feel like he should be the one to decide.

Ben's face looks like he dropped all the leashes and the dogs are running in all different directions. He's trying to wrangle them in but isn't sure where to start.

"Maybe you shouldn't," he replies, not even looking me in the eyes. "Maybe we shouldn't hang out for a while. I should go."

"Ben—" I start to speak, but he's already lost in the crowd.

I don't feel like a confident, above-it-all *Shift* Girl right now. In the land of the hypothetical, my favorite mental vacation spot, I always assumed that having the opportunity to reject a guy would feel empowering. But now that it's actually happened, it kind of just sucks. A part of me wishes that Ben hadn't felt what he felt in the first place, so I wouldn't be in this position. But then I just feel guilty for feeling that.

Kristina always knows what to do, but for the first time in a long time, her phone is off when I call her for late-night counsel.

· 29 ·

I SLEEPWALK OUT OF BED MONDAY MORNING AND can't even blame my restless night on Princess, who is now snore-free.

I'm scared to go into work today without a blog post. There's no way I can write about surrogate boyfriends and platonic dates now. Ben reads my articles. It would be wrong.

"You're half an hour late!" Jamie, who looks like she could use a nap and a hairbrush, reprimands when I get to the office.

"Don't worry, I covered for you," Brie says with a smile before lowering her voice to a whisper and adding, "I said you were in the bathroom fixing an eyeliner emergency. McKayla understood."

Before I can thank Brie, a very frazzled Jamie cuts her off. "No one should be making excuses for you." She turns to face me. "It's the end of the month, which means we have traffic goals to meet. You should be writing, not rolling in late. You can't just expect other people to pick up your slack!"

Whoa.

What the hell have I just walked into? The atmosphere is completely tense.

"Didn't mean to cause any issues, Jamie," I say.

Jamie takes a deep breath. "Didn't mean to explode like that," she says, giving us a glimmer of the saner Jamie from the beginning of the summer. "I'm just stressed because I have to meet my click quota."

"A click quota?" I ask. "What does that even mean?"

"Everyone on the viral team has to write enough 'clicky' stories that we meet our monthly traffic goals," Jamie says. "But McKayla said we *all* have to do more. Including you guys."

The *Shift* staff has noticeably thinned since the beginning of the summer, either because people have cracked under the pressure and quit, or because they've cracked under the pressure and been kicked down to the thirteenth floor so that Skirt Suit in HR could fire them on McKayla's orders.

And there's no question of who's on the verge of cracking next. Jamie has been working beyond overtime to get hired. And it shows. She was intense before, but in the beginning of the summer she seemed happy. Mostly nice. Now she's always jittery and on edge. Everyone has noticed. Abigail wants to stage an intervention for Jamie's espresso dependency. ("She got busy writing a string of stories last Friday and started getting the shakes when she hadn't had caffeine in ninety minutes. Classic symptom of withdrawal.") Brie's concern mainly lies in her tired eyes. ("Just give me five minutes with her in the makeup station, and I'll get rid of those bags immediately. It's not even a favor. Her tired serial killer look is freaking me out.")

I wonder how I'll look when I'm done telling McKayla that I don't have a story ready.

But when I walk into her office, McKayla takes over before I even open my mouth.

"I don't care what you were planning to write about this week," she says. "I'm canning it."

There is a God.

"I downloaded MatchBook this weekend and I'm *obsessed*. I don't know why I was holding out for so long to get on a dating app."

McKayla holds up her iPhone and shows me Scott, 29, smiling at the camera.

"Not only is he on partner track at his law firm, but he also has a CrossFit bod." McKayla scrolls to a picture of Scott at the gym. "I mean, how cute is he?"

"Cute!" I reply, eager to please.

But McKayla quickly reveals that she isn't showing me her dating prospects for bonding purposes. "You are writing about dating apps this week. MatchBook has such great blog-material potential."

I look up from McKayla's iPhone screen. "But, isn't MatchBook for old people?"

McKayla's eyes widen. "*I* use MatchBook. Am *I* old?"

"No! Of course not!"

Backtrack, backtrack, must backtrack.

"But, is it safe for people my age?" I ask.

"Look at this press release. MatchBook Teen: It's *for* people your age; no one over eighteen can be on it. Brand new and crying out for a blog post. My only question is why aren't you telling me about it? Your job is to know about these things."

"I don't know," I say. "Dating apps seem kind of—"

"I TOLD YOU YOU'RE WRITING ABOUT IT, SO WRITE ABOUT IT!" she shouts. "Be edgy. Be bold. And close the door on your way out."

It's not like I have a better alternative for this week, anyway.

I bribe the other *Shift* Girls with the promise of buying them Ladurée macarons ("They're gluten-free!" I tell Gigi.) to download MatchBook Teen with me and check it out after work.

Gigi agrees happily, saying she's in need of other entertainment after spending most of the weekend binge watching *Gossip Girl*. "I'm obsessed. I'm already in season two. But it's weird, I don't even know if I'm having fun watching it anymore, I've gone through so many episodes. But I'm incapable of stopping."

"That's what I call purge-watching," I say. "It's not about enjoyment anymore. You just have to finish and get it out of your system."

"I love that," Gigi says. "I'm definitely stealing it."

Everyone joins us on our dating expedition except for Jamie. We decide to explore the app in Battery Park, by the water.

"That way I can get a good Instagram of the sunset over the Hudson River," Sunny says.

"Gross," Gigi squeals, interrupting our conversation on where we think we'll get the best view of the sunset. Obviously she's not talking about the night sky.

She raises her phone and shows me the picture of Albert, 17, making a kiss face at a bathroom mirror—toilet *visible*—while he lifts up his ribbed white tank top to expose a nipple piercing. His description area reads: "Say hello to my little friend."

We immediately explode with laughter. Of the snorting variety. People are turning around and staring.

"Bathroom mirror selfie? That *is* gross!" I say, in between gasps for air because I'm laughing so hard.

"Definitely swiping no," Gigi says. A lit match appears when she touches the screen and it follows her finger. As she swipes to the left to reject Albert, 17, and his "little friend," the flame extinguishes. When she finishes the swipe, "BURNOUT" spans across the screen. (If you swipe right for yes, graphics make it look like the match has lit the entire screen on fire under the declaration "HOT HOT HOT." Once you're paired in a couple, the app encourages you to send a message and thus, "KEEP THE FLAME ALIVE!") It doesn't take us long to become completely consumed with MatchBook's ever-updating stream of guys.

This one's first picture is of him taking a hike, to show he's outdoorsy.

That one's on a private jet to Monte Carlo to show he's richer than you.

And here is yet another shirtless, bathroom mirror selfie. Why do guys think girls like this?

It's a fascinating character study, and we find ourselves way more excited to go through profiles than to get a match. Sure, the positive affirmation of mutual attraction is nice, but we're not here to date as much as we are to play.

This is a game.

I have my blog.

MATCHBOOK BINGO: THE BEST GAME ON YOUR PHONE IS ACTUALLY A DATING APP

I downloaded a new teen dating app, but I didn't use it for dating.

I've always thought of app dating as a thing only old people do. But after MatchBook launched its teen-only edition, I decided to check it out. In order to stay #relevant, I convinced my fellow *Shift* interns (and fellow dating app virgins) to download it and see what all the fuss is about.

What I found were bathroom mirror selfies and a whole lot of really creepy messages—don't worry, I won't subject you to the visuals.

Okay, so maybe not everyone was terrible. But we were way more interested in looking at how guys represent themselves on dating apps than dating strangers we met on our phones.

So to make MatchBook Teen more enjoyable, we started turning all the app dating clichés we kept seeing into a game.

May I introduce MatchBook Bingo.

Whoever makes a row (or blacks out) the bingo board first by matching with guys who fit the below descriptions wins. And, remember, a match is only made when a guy likes you back, so work on that duck-face selfie.

All's fair in love and app dating. Let the games begin.

Carpe that Effing Bingo!
Harper

IS PICTURED PLAYING A MUSICAL INSTRUMENT (Bonus points if he's closing his eyes.)	MESSAGES YOU SOMETHING THAT'S ACTUALLY FUNNY (Rare.)	LOOKS LIKE HE WOULDN'T GET LET INTO PG-13 MOVIES (Hope you like Pixar.)	IS PICTURED PLAYING SPORTS (Jock, jock, jock.)	IS PICTURED WITH A PET (Actually, this is okay.)
IS PICTURED WITH A BABY (Not ready to be a mom, sorry.)	SPEAKS ONLY IN EMOJIS 🙁	IS PICTURED SURROUNDED BY MEMBERS OF THE OPPOSITE SEX (We get it. Ladies love you.)	HAS A THREE-LETTER FIRST NAME (It's rarer than you'd think.)	MESSAGES YOU A REALLY BAD PICK-UP LINE (No, I didn't fall from heaven.)
IS PICTURED WITH A CELEBRITY (Real or Photoshopped.)	POSTS A BATHROOM MIRROR SELFIE (Way, *way* too common.)	FREE SPACE	IS PICTURED AT A SHOOTING RANGE. (I don't look good in camo?)	IS PICTURED IN A BLACK & WHITE PHOTO (So artsy!)
IS PICTURED IN AN AMBIGUOUS GROUP PICTURE (Who *is* he?)	IS PICTURED WITH HIS GRANDPARENT (To let you know he's *so* sensitive.)	IS PICTURED READING A BOOK (To let you know he's *so* deep.)	WANTS YOU TO ADD HIM ON SNAPCHAT (Trust me, you don't want those photos.)	TOTAL HIPSTER (Hello, skinny jeans.)
SENDS A CREEPY MESSAGE (AKA, everyone.)	IS PICTURED WITH HIS PROM DATE (Um, aren't you here to date *me*?)	WANTS YOU TO ADD HIM ON INSTAGRAM (Too IRL for me.)	HAS TWO TYPOS IN HIS PROFILE (Your SAT score must be this high to ride.)	POSTS A SELFIE WITH A CAR (But is it *his* car?)

• 30 •

"BONUS POINTS IF HE'S CLOSING HIS EYES WHILE playing a musical instrument?" McKayla reads from my blog post. "This is hilarious. Good job, Harper."

This is the nicest McKayla has been to me after setting one of my articles live. Things are starting to look up.

"You're smiling?" Gigi says when I walk back to the intern area. "That must mean McKayla's in a good mood. I'd better tell her a story idea I have now, before it passes."

McKayla has always been emotionally erratic, but with the website end-of-month traffic goals looming, her mood swings have been amplified by a thousand. One second she's praising a reporter for her "Genius! Genius! Genius!" story idea. The next, she's making her cry for not executing it to perfection. Publicly.

Gigi sprints to McKayla's office so quickly that even Treadmill Desk looks up.

All the other interns are furiously typing away. Sunny and Brie, who are usually in the fashion and makeup closets or running

247

errands for their editors, are looking for stories to write up to help *Shift* meet its traffic goals.

"What should we do for lunch?" Sunny asks. "Sushi?"

"Salmonella outbreak," Abigail warns.

"Do you have an off button?" Sunny responds. "Kidding. Kind of."

"Well, if there's nothing good in the open kitchen, I just e-mailed y'all the menu of a new salad place," Brie says. We have spent a lot of hours of this internship scouting out lunch spots.

I take a break searching through a paparazzi photo database for pictures of actors making out in public—I was assigned to compile a photo slide show about celebrity PDA—and check my e-mail.

Sandwiched between Brie's message about lunch and a bunch of spam from PR people is an e-mail from Carter, sent only a couple of minutes ago.

It's four simple words and a link: "Congratulations. You've been aggregated."

"What does 'aggregated' mean?" I ask the *Shift* Girls.

"It's when one website basically rewrites another website's article," Jamie says. "Like if I got an exclusive about Curmudgeon cat"—she gets a look of ecstasy at the thought—"and then a bunch of other websites write about my exclusive, to piggyback on my clickiness."

I click the link in Carter's e-mail, which takes me to *deviant*'s website. And there, spanning across the screen, is a headline that reads: "This Girl's Turning Your Crappy Dating App Profiles Into a Game."

Below the headline is a big picture of me wearing my "Fries Over Guys" shirt next to Carter in the Hamptons.

Below that picture is a copy of my MatchBook Bingo board and a link to my article.

Holy shit.

"Helloooooo, earth to Harper." Brie is waving her right hand in my direction. "I asked what you want to order."

"What's going on?" Gigi says, back from her meeting with McKayla.

I continue to stare at my screen.

Gigi looks over my shoulder, sees the article, and lights up. "You guys, *deviant* wrote up Harper's blog. You're famous!"

Sure, people have tweeted about some of my stories before, they've talked about them in the article's comment section, but that's been the extent of my blog's notoriety. None of my blog posts have ever been picked up by another publication before.

At first I'm too nervous to read the article. After all, *deviant* isn't known for being especially nice. Whenever the *New York Times* writes a trend piece on something that *deviant* thinks isn't really trendy, they completely tear it to shreds in a vicious but deliciously entertaining way. But this isn't a takedown piece—they actually liked my blog. And it's exhilarating. I feel like I just drank three Diet Cokes in a row.

FROM: Harper_Anderson@Shift.com
TO: carter@deviant.com
SUBJECT: Re: Congratulations

!!!

I know I should have a more eloquent reaction, but so far the best I can do is punctuation. I feel honored that *deviant* thinks my bingo game is funny . . . I know how brutal you guys can be. Thanks for not being mean.

Also—how's your reporting trip??

FROM: carter@deviant.com
TO: Harper_Anderson@Shift.com
SUBJECT: Re: Congratulations

Oh, we were being plenty mean . . . just with you and not to you.

Reporting trip was good.

FROM: Harper_Anderson@Shift.com
TO: carter@deviant.com
SUBJECT: Re: Congratulations

My blog wasn't mean. It was tongue in cheek!

FROM: carter@deviant.com
TO: Harper_Anderson@Shift.com
SUBJECT: Re: Congratulations

Ha. Keep telling yourself that. I told you, your snark is one of your greater assets.

Also, I know we're meeting for my parents' next week, but wanna join in on a group brunch Sunday? My friend is having a thing at Bacchanal. On him. Bring whomever.

I light up brighter than my computer screen. I flash back to D-Bag Dull Man telling Kristina that I wasn't one of "them." It wasn't exactly rocket science to figure out that I didn't fit. But Carter is telling me just the opposite. He thinks I'm talented. He thinks I'm worthy. Carter is picking me, specifically. I imagine sitting next to him in a booth at brunch, in front of all his friends, sharing a stack of pancakes. I imagine him putting his hand in the small of my back and guiding me through a swanky party to meet his parents. And then I can't help but imagine him telling me that he doesn't want this to end when I finish the internship. That he can't, because just like I've been waiting for someone like him, he's been waiting for someone like me. I can't turn off my internal narrative.

I feel powerful. Like I can do anything.

My story is fourth on the Leader Board.

The *Shift* Girls and I stay on the lookout to see if other websites have picked up my blog too.

"Once one site starts to write something, they all do," Abigail says authoritatively. "No one wants to miss a trending story, right, Jamie?"

Jamie responds only by furrowing her brow. She puts on her earphones dramatically and turns the volume of her music up so loud that we can hear it.

"She's just bitter that your story is doing better than any of hers today," Gigi says, shooting Jamie a pointed side eye. "She is the viral expert, after all."

Viral.

I've always hoped one of my blogs would go viral, but now that it actually might happen, I realize that I don't know what that actually means.

After half an hour of searching, when nothing else comes up, we take a break from looking. We pick up salads. We get back to work. I resume my assigned search for pictures of celebrities making out in Starbucks. But Brie interrupts my flow.

"I'm glad you've grown out your hair," Brie tells me. "I don't really like it shoulder length."

"Um, thanks?" I download a picture of Beyoncé and Jay Z kissing at a basketball game. "But I haven't had short hair in, like, two years."

"Non sequitur much?" Gigi asks.

"Not really," Brie says, beaming. "Because in the picture that BuzzSnap posted of Harper, her hair is short."

Everyone stops what she's doing. Even Jamie. The only noise to be heard comes from someone yelling at a PR person on the phone from across the office. And then we go from complete silence to every single one of us talking at the same time, our words traveling over and under and in between one another's as our bodies rush over to see Brie's computer screen. We're making such a commotion that reporters and editors who never acknowledge the interns' existence, unless they're ordering us to run an errand, come over to see what all the fuss is about.

BuzzSnap has not only written about me creating the game but it's copied my bingo board and is asking readers to tweet screenshots of the worst dating app profile pictures they've seen using the hashtag #MatchBookBingo. They're creating a master bingo board of shame.

I look up at the Leader Board. My story has ascended above a think piece about Kim Kardashian and a video post about Curmudgeon Cat meeting a baby duckling. (Curmudgeon Cat is less than enthusiastic.) When it reaches the number one spot, McKayla comes out of her office.

Our gut reaction is to brace ourselves. Usually when McKayla deigns to enter the main office, it's to humiliate someone in front of a crowd. If there were ever a campaign to bring back public hangings, we know where she'd stand. But now McKayla is at her most effervescent.

"This is how it's done, ladies," McKayla says, arm outstretched toward the Leader Board television screen. "One story, by a freaking intern, and we meet our July goals one day early. I think we might even make a record. I'm always saying, it's not about writing a million stupid articles about things that have already gone viral online. It's about finding one good story that can make it on its own."

Out of the corner of my eye, I see Jamie look around helplessly. "That's not what she says *ever*," she whispers, loud enough for only interns in close proximity to hear. It's true. McKayla is always telling people to write more, more, more, and faster, faster, faster.

But whatever. Don't dwell on that. Don't diminish your success. I worked hard. I wrote well. I earned this.

McKayla continues her grandstanding. "It's too bad *you* aren't graduating from college early," she says to me. Like sharks taste blood in the water, like dogs sense fear, McKayla has a knack for spotting insecurity and then exploiting it. Jamie's a goner. "You're the only one here who would make any sense to keep on next year. Maybe we'll have to extend your column and you'll write it remotely."

"I would love that!" I don't know if McKayla means it or is just saying that to push Jamie's buttons. (If so, it's working. Jamie starts snapping the hair tie on her wrist and taking slow, long breaths through her nose.) But if I could keep writing during the school year, that would be incredible.

As a reward, McKayla tells me that I can go home a few hours early, after I round up some #MatchBookBingo tweets for a follow-up post. "We want to milk this for all the clicks we can get," she says.

I start going through Twitter and rounding up tweets.

At 3:10, @LadyLana tweets, "Say no to bathroom mirror selfies #MatchBookBingo."

At 3:15, @manicpixiedreamgirl99 tweets, "'your' instead of 'you're' #hardpass #MatchBookBingo."

At 3:16, @jetsfan22 tweets, "We aren't here for your amusement @harperanderson #shallow #MatchBookBingo."

At 3:16, @MRA4life tweets, "@harperanderson is a dumb slut #MatchBookBingo."

Wait, what?

No matter how many times I read it, the angry message stays the same. My stomach drops. I click on my mentions to see if maybe it's just a fluke, but it isn't. There aren't a lot, but there are certainly enough. And they're meaner, and way more personal, than the bus-back-from-the-Hamptons blog tweets.

"Um, McKayla?" I get her attention before she goes back into her office. "This might not be a big deal"—please don't let this be a big deal—"but a few guys are really mad about the post. They're saying that I'm objectifying men."

"They're saying a lot more than that!" Gigi laughs. "What losers."

McKayla comes over to my computer to investigate, and starts clicking on the profiles of some of the angry tweeters. "Oh, this is nothing," she says. "Men are so touchy."

"But I didn't mean to objectify them!" I say. I really didn't. Even though, as I think about it, I kind of sort of did.

"I cannot handle this negative energy," McKayla says, and I realize that she's talking about me, not the angry men. "Just go home and have a drink—er, virgin, of course. If this were actually a problem *Shift* needed to be worried about, you'd know it."

It doesn't take long to find out how right she is.

· 31 ·

WHEN I GET OFF THE SUBWAY BY AUNT VEE'S apartment, my phone buzzes with texts from Kristina.

> **Kristina:** Are you doing okay?
>
> **Kristina:** Don't listen to these assholes!
>
> **Kristina:** I'm sorry we got in a fight. Love you. Call me.

Then I check my Twitter.

By the time I'm back at Aunt Vee's, it's safe to say that the shit has officially hit the fan. Internet outrage is flying at me from all directions, and the comforter that I've pulled up right under my eyes (so I can still read what people are saying) isn't enough to shield me from the vitriol.

My blog has definitely gone viral. And while some articles reacting to the piece are positive, quoting funny lines from the blog, the tide has definitely turned.

A men's rights activist blog inserted some of my Facebook pictures into a manifesto about how "Harper Anderson is everything that's wrong with teenage girls today." Not only do they think I'm exploiting boys on MatchBook, but they think I'm exploiting them in real life, too. Using my Make-Out Bandit blog post as Exhibit A ("Did Harper Anderson get consent?"), my Forager Date as Exhibit B ("If her dates refuse to buy her expensive meals, she makes fun of them."), and my Three-Hour Relationship as Exhibit C ("I'm sick and tired of the man-hating, feminist, PC agenda.").

Another site is accusing me of compromising privacy by telling girls to tweet real guys' profiles, putting vulnerable teenage boys at risk.

"That wasn't me!" I defend myself to Princess, who looks as lost as I do. "I just told girls to play Bingo! BuzzSnap's the one asking for real profile pictures."

I start to get really worried when not just fringe blogs, but more mainstream news sites also start to criticize me, "controversial teen dating blogger Harper Anderson," and *Shift* magazine for other offenses.

Bigger news outlets start to pick it up and pick it apart. All the criticism, the poking and prodding at every little detail, weighs me down. A blogger for the *Good Morning America*'s website is freaking out that a teen magazine is "practically begging underage girls to subject themselves to predators on unsafe dating apps."

An opinion piece on CNN has a different critique. It says that MatchBook Bingo is "obviously a thinly veiled drinking game." For proof, the article includes screen grabs from my and some of the other *Shift* Girls' public social media posts. And while I could argue that my tweet saying "Drink if you see a MatchBook bro posing with his grandma" was a joke, I don't think that anyone would believe me.

Princess nuzzles me with her nose. She understands.

According to Fox: "Not only is this encouraging *Shift*'s twelve-to-nineteen-year-old demographic to binge-drink, but the interns are all teenagers themselves. *Shift* should be taken to task for endangerment, and their promotion of underage drinking should be stopped, through legal channels if necessary."

As McKayla said, it's really easy to tell when things have gotten bad.

I don't know how to control this.

My phone buzzes again.

The *Shift* Girls tell me to "hang in there." Carter asks if he should be jealous of all the attention I'm getting. (*Jealous?*) Ben is still radio silent since our last awkward encounter. Bobby Snapchatted me a picture of his new MatchBook Teen profile. My parents say to call them back. Kristina says to call her back. She's already warned her manager that she's going to need a break.

I pick Kristina.

I miss Kristina.

As soon as the FaceTime connects, I realize that this is the first time I've actually seen her in weeks. (We've texted. Kind of. But I've been busy.) The summer sun has lightened her hair and darkened her skin. She has the look on her face that she usually reserves for her own rare personal crises.

"Is everything okay?" I ask.

"You're asking *me* if everything's okay? Harper, I wanted you to call me to talk about *you*. How are you holding up? I saw some stuff on Facebook and it's looking pretty brutal."

As soon as we make virtual eye contact, mine start to water. I don't want them to, but it's not up to me.

"Am I a horrible person?"

"Oh my God, are you being serious? Harper! Sure, I thought that you might have been a little unfair to the forager dude, sure, I wish that you had called me back, but this is ridiculous. You're a good person and a funny writer."

"But what if my other blogs were kind of mean, too?"

"Stop it," Kristina says. "They were funny. You're not mean, you're my best friend. People love kicking you when you're down. It will pass as soon as Curmudgeon Cat sneezes adorably in a new YouTube video."

Between the clubs and the dates and the Hamptons and the boys, I've forgotten that I might need my best friend. "I wish you were here."

"Really?"

"Of course I do!"

"You haven't said that in a while." She settles into a smile. I missed her smile. "I have to go back to work soon, but call me later. Also call your parents! They're freaking a little."

"You've talked to them?"

"*Obviously*. You aren't the only Anderson in my life. Hang in there."

By the time I get off the phone with my parents, who don't agree that I'm "everything wrong with teenage girls today"—although maybe I should tone down the snark—I feel like every bit of energy has been sapped from my body. And it isn't even dark out yet.

I drag one foot in front of the other to the balcony off Aunt Vee's master bedroom, so that I have a front row seat for the sun's final descent over the park. No matter how bad a day I've had, I can at least enjoy this. There aren't enough adjectives to describe New York's summer sunsets. The outlines of skyscrapers are stenciled into the electric pinks and purples of the transforming sky, and the entire city becomes magical.

"Isn't that sight something?" Aunt Vee slides open the balcony door. She waits until the sun disappears to ask about the blog.

"You saw it too?"

"I don't understand what all the fuss is about," she says. "I was doing much worse than playing bingo at your age. Much, *much* worse."

"Yeah?" I ask.

"I could tell you a story or two about objectifying men." She smiles fondly at memories that I think would be emotionally scarring to hear.

Aunt Vee sits down by my feet at the end of the lounge chair and gives me a serious look. "Do you think you're in trouble at *Shift*?"

"I don't know."

"How are you going to handle things tomorrow?"

I just raise my shoulders and sink lower into the chair.

Aunt Vee pats me on the foot. "You'll think of something. They won't do anything drastic, I don't care what the petition says."

Petition?

I grab my phone and see that there's an online petition saying that "*Shift's* dangerous teen dating blog should be canceled," I should be fired, the internship program should be disbanded, and basically that Bosh Media should be burned to the ground. A lot of people have signed, offering to dance on the ashes in the comments section.

I also have a new e-mail from McKayla.

"Come to my office first thing in the morning."

That doesn't sound good.

I might not have to figure out how to handle things at all. McKayla might handle them for me.

· 3 2 ·

WHAT DO YOU WEAR TO WORK ON THE DAY THAT
you're probably going to get fired?

I follow the advice of Sunny's fashion guru Karl Lagerfeld and
opt for a little black dress. It's a simple, jersey A-line I got shopping
at Forever 21 rather than shopping in Aunt Vee's closet.

Princess makes an uncharacteristic, early-morning venture across
the bedroom to rub her head against my calf as I stand in front of the
full-length mirror. At first I think it's her way to comfort me while
I carefully put on my eyeliner, my declaration to the universe that I
will not cry today. But when I hear the jangle of chains outside my
door, scurrying paws and little yips in the living room, I realize that
Princess isn't being affectionate. She wants to go for a walk.

But then my stomach drops. If dogs are here waiting to be
walked, that means Ben must be here too.

Ben.

I haven't seen him since the weekend. Ever since *Phantom*, he's
been picking Princess up before I've gotten home from work. And

I get it. But now he's here earlier than usual, and I wonder if it's because he saw everything that happened with my blog post, all the "I Hate Harper" fan clubs popping up all over Facebook, and he came over to help me through it.

I leave my room mideyeliner, still holding the pencil in my hand, and say, "Ben, I'm so glad you're here. You won't believe the shit storm I've been in since I went viral—"

I stop abruptly when I realize that while the dogs look familiar, the walker does not. Atticus is chewing on the shoelace of a complete stranger in a Saint Agnes Mathletes T-shirt.

"I'm not Ben?" He says it like it's a question. And like I don't have eyes. "I'm walking dogs for him for a few days?"

"Oh." Ben sent a replacement. I watch the younger, shorter dog walker as he tries to untangle himself from the leashes. "I'll just leave you to it then."

"But, uh, I hope you get better soon," he says, unwrapping Pepe's blue leash from around his head.

"What?"

He lowers his voice to a whisper. "Your . . . *viral* situation."

"Oh, no! It's"—Not-Ben gives me a pitying look—"not worth explaining. Never mind."

I try not to catastrophize on the subway to work. I'm used to waiting forever for a train, but today is one of those rare days when the express train rushes into the station right when I get to the platform with an exhilarating whoosh that makes my dress balloon like Marilyn Monroe's, hair fall out of place, and heart skip a beat.

Is a perfectly timed train a good omen?

I get to work early and go to the open kitchen to grab food to fuel up for the day ahead in the hope I won't be out of an internship and escorted out of the building before I have time to eat it. Two editors are huddled by the espresso machine, and when they see me come in the room, the volume of their conversation lowers to a whisper. But my eavesdropping skills have been fine-tuned for these kinds of situations, and I inch closer to inspect a basket of minimuffins on the counter. I can't make out what the editors are saying in terms of full sentences. But the words I parse out are scary enough to make me drop the blueberry muffin. "Intern." "She has to go."

Bad omen.

Absolutely terrible, horrible omen.

Come to think of it, not even an omen. A direct message from above. I am totally about to get fired.

I don't bother picking the minimuffin back up. Instead I head directly for McKayla's office, going over the list of defenses I spouted off to my parents that I can regurgitate to my boss.

I push through McKayla's glass doors without even knocking. "Before you fire me—"

"Trenton, I'm going to have to call you back. It appears that one of my interns is having a psychotic break." McKayla waits a beat before continuing. "No, a different one. I'll tell BuzzSnap we'll have a statement for them by noon."

If McKayla is fielding calls from reporters and has to bring Trenton Bosh in for damage control, then things are worse than I thought. If that's even possible.

"Now, what the hell are you blubbering on about?" McKayla asks.

I can't even look her in the eyes, and stare intensely at my wedge sandals. If looks could crack toenail polish . . .

"Listen, McKayla, I understand if you want to fire me, but I truly didn't realize—"

"Fire you? Harper, I'm not allowed to tell you this, but you're practically a shoo-in for the intern magazine feature."

My eyes snap up from my feet to her face so quickly that I get whiplash.

"What?" I'm searching her expression to see if she's being serious. "But everyone wants me fired or arrested. Or worse."

"Oh my God, Harper." She slaps her forehead with the palm of her hand and makes an are-you-clueless face. "What have I been saying since day one? Any click is a good click! People might hate your article, but they sure as hell are reading it. Now that you have an audience, I think you should push the limit even more. Take advantage of a good thing."

"Oh."

McKayla rolls her eyes. "Yeah, oh."

"So editors saying I was getting fired in the kitchen, and your phone call with—"

"Harper, *why* are we still having this conversation?" She stands up and makes scooting gestures to get me out of her office. "Get back to work! Think of something for next week's blog that will *really* get people's panties in a twist. All buzz is good buzz. All clicks are good clicks. All scandal is . . . well, *almost* all scandal is . . ."

Her phone starts to buzz, and McKayla allows her tangent to trail off. She nods at the door as she reaches for her phone.

I take my cue and go.

Still employed.

MatchBook Bingo doesn't budge from the number one spot on the Leader Board for the rest of the day.

"I'll bet Jamie doesn't even really have a summer cold," Gigi says. "I'll bet she just called in sick because she's jealous."

Jamie is always the first of the interns to arrive and the last to leave, so it's strange not seeing her at her desk. I don't know if I should feel guilty that she's so upset or annoyed that she's so bitter. Just like I don't know if I should be freaked out by the fact that hundreds of strangers hate me, or proud that McKayla doesn't.

I know you aren't supposed to read comments or listen to trolls, but I can't help going through my inbox and reading the hate mail. But not all my messages are bad. Like the e-mail from my dad.

FROM: eddie.anderson@aol.com
TO: Harper_Anderson@Shift.com; HarpAnd32@gmail.com
SUBJECT: Checking in

Hey, kiddo:
Sending something over to Aunt Vee's to help you feel better. It should be there on Friday when you get back from work. Love you, HunBun.

Brie passes me her Clinique concealer when I get in Friday morning. "For the bags under your eyes."

"It looks like someone had a fun last night," Gigi says. "What did you do and why weren't we invited?"

"Reading the hate mail." It's still coming in, and I can't stop reading it. McKayla says it's a good thing. Carter thinks it's funny and that people with thin skin don't belong in journalism. Even though Ben and I still haven't talked, I can see on Twitter that he is defending me against the trolls.

"I feel sick." I put my head down on my desk.

Abigail pushes her roller chair away from her desk in panic. "You don't have what Jamie has, do you?"

"Harper's probably just hungover. Wouldn't be the first time," Sunny says, before asking advice on which cowl-neck sweater she should buy online. Cowl-necks are going to be everything next season.

"I'm not hungover." Although the fact that my head is still facedown on my desk isn't helping my case.

"See!" Abigail stretches her arm out as far as it goes so that she can open her desk drawer without moving her body closer in my direction. "Here, take this."

Something lands next to my right cheek. I lift my head and see it's a blue medical mask. The kind you see on dentists when they are filling cavities or germophobic tourists on the subway.

"You keep those in your desk?" Gigi asks.

"Doesn't everyone?"

"No."

"Well, everyone *should*." She puts another mask on her own face instead to escape my nonexistent germs. "If disease is spreading around the office, you can count me out, thank you very much."

Before Abigail can start in on her familiar rant about how the end of the world won't be caused by nuclear fallout or global warming but by uncontrolled contagion, someone approaches our desk cluster. Skirt Suit from our first day heads our way, an empty cardboard box in hand.

"Is this Jamie Sullivan's?" She motions the box toward the only empty seat at our electric-blue table.

"Is she okay?" Abigail asks in a muffled voice. Skirt Suit starts dumping everything in Jamie's drawers into the box. "Oh my God, has that all been contaminated?"

"It's against policy to discuss why I'm here," Skirt Suit says, before placing spirals of reporters' notebooks into the crate. "But you're safe taking off the mask."

"You guys," Brie says, "this reminds me of what happens on *The Bachelor* when someone goes on a one-on-one date and doesn't get a rose."

"Come again?" asks Sunny.

Brie explains like we're idiots. "A contestant has to pack her bags before a one-on-one so if the bachelor doesn't ask her to stay, producers can go back to the bachelor mansion to remove her bags and send them back to Arkansas or wherever she's from so she can't make a scene. It's all very dramatic."

"And I'm lost," Sunny says.

"Wait." I'm now sitting up ballerina-straight. "Is Skirt Suit a producer in this scenario? Are you saying that Jamie is getting sent home?"

McKayla's assistant brings our speculation to a halt. "Didn't you see the e-mail?" she asks. "All-hands meeting. Now."

Reporters are getting up from their seats and heading to the conference room.

I catch Gigi's gaze. We *never* have all-hands meetings on Fridays. We walk over as a unit and go to our usual standing room only spots in the back of the conference room.

"No, no, girls," McKayla says, holding court. "Interns up front."

We *never* sit at the long table. That's reserved for permanent staff only, and they're more territorial than Atticus when he finds an abandoned water bottle on a walk. (Do not get in between him and a Dasani bottle.)

But lo and behold, there are five empty chairs.

"You're probably wondering why we've called you here." McKayla remains standing over us all, towering above in her red-bottomed Louboutins. She passes the baton to a gray-haired (due to age rather than fashion) woman in a pantsuit who introduces herself as Ms. DeMille from the fiftieth floor. One of the "dinosaurs from upstairs," I presume. From the business end of things. The lawyer end.

"It has come to our attention that one of *Shift*'s now-former interns has been guilty of plagiarism."

There's a sudden atmospheric shift in the room. The air becomes thinner. It's harder to breathe. A low hum of whispers erupts into hushed pandemonium. A few people reach for their phones.

McKayla slams her fists on the table. "Shut up and phones

down. There will be no tweeting, no texting, no talking about this whatsoever."

The only sound is the clatter of iPhones falling back down on the table.

"The only reason we're addressing this in person rather than via e-mail is because e-mails get leaked. And you don't know how many favors I had to call in to stop this from turning into a story."

McKayla gives a brief rundown about what happened. Two days ago, a BuzzSnap reporter was reading one of Jamie's stories about Curmudgeon Cat's new Disney Channel original series when he recognized a familiar sentence. Familiar because he had just written it in his own piece about Curmudgeon Cat's six-figure "Got Milk?" endorsement deal.

A sweep through Jamie's author page led the reporter to another cut-and-paste job in Jamie's article about a Jumbotron proposal gone wrong. Red flags waving, the reporter ran a bunch of Jamie's articles through scanning software Castalia High keeps threatening to buy whenever a teacher gets handed an essay copied from SparkNotes. He found twelve instances of plagiarism from various other news sources.

My stomach pitches like I'm on the Castalia County Fair's famous pirate-ship ride, which swings from side to side in a dizzying arc. I never would have suspected that the BuzzSnap statement and the editor gossip was about Jamie.

"I appealed to their compassion for an intern whose career would be ruined if this became a permanent part of her Google history." But then McKayla's voice lowers to a scary tremor. "If anyone's going to ruin her career, it's going to be me. An article about plagiarism or Jamie's boo-hoo sob story about how she was over-whelmed and under pressure would have done irrevocable harm to *Shift*'s digital progress. And to me. This was lazy, unacceptable, and un-freaking-believable. I will destroy any of you—"

Ms. DeMille cuts McKayla off before she has the chance to threaten us with bodily harm and informs us that for the rest of the day, we'll be having refresher courses on ethical standards and prac-tices. I think we skipped that bit during our orientation sessions about how to write quickly for clicks.

"What a shit show," Sunny says when we're released for a coffee break. "I can't believe Jamie would be that stupid."

"You saw how she was acting the past few weeks," Abigail says. "People under pressure do crazy things."

"She deserves what she gets for passing off someone else's work as her own," Gigi declares.

The pirate-ship ride swings to the left. I didn't plagiarize. I tell myself that Jamie's situation is a completely different beast from mine. I would never plagiarize. It's the biggest writing sin there is. I yell that loudly inside, overpowering any nagging "but."

"Do you wanna grab dinner with her tonight to hear about what went down?" Brie is looking at her phone.

"I mean, obviously," Gigi says. "Just because I think she deserves it doesn't mean that I don't want the gossip."

"Cool. How many people should I make a reservation for?"

"I don't think I can," I say. "My dad sent me something I have to pick up at my aunt's after work."

"That's probably for the best," Sunny says midtext. "Jamie's bitching to me about how unfair it is that she's gone but you got to stay after your MatchBook fiasco."

The pirate ship swings right.

"Don't worry, I'll fill you in," Gigi says. "Mani pedis before brunch Sunday? I looked up Bacchanal, and it's supposed to be brilliant."

"Sure."

I make a few stops before going back to the apartment after work, killing time in case Ben is back, and get a million texts from Aunt Vee.

"Harper, where have you been?" Aunt Vee asks, when I finally walk in with a Barnes & Noble bag in one hand and takeout from Shake Shack in the other. I don't care if it's not allowed in the house; it's definitely a burger and fries kind of night.

"Weird day at work," I say. "So what's this surprise that's so important?"

Aunt Vee is too excited to register that trans fats have breached her foyer. "It's in your room!"

When I open my bedroom door, I see that the "it" is actually a "she."

· 33 ·

AT FIRST I THINK THAT THE COMBINATION OF STRESS
and exhaustion has produced a full-blown hallucination.

"Is this real life?" I ask the mirage.

But as soon as Kristina pops off my bed like a jack-in-the-box,
her extra-long, tan legs allowing her to pounce on me from across
the room in one fell swoop, I'm convinced that she isn't a figment
of my imagination.

"You're back!" she shouts as our bodies collide. The velocity
of our reunion, captured in an all-consuming hug, causes me to
stumble back out the bedroom doorway and into the living room.
The momentum of friendship. "I was so tempted to call and tell
you to get your ass home, but I knew that this would be better. Are
you surprised?"

Kristina's smile takes up half her face, and I return it.

"Considering that you're supposed to be working at Skinny B's
for another two hours, like, three thousand miles away, I'm gonna
go with yes. I'm so happy! How'd you get here?"

"This fabulous invention called a plane," she says. "Or, planes. Since I got the ticket so last minute I had two layovers. Totally worth it, though."

"How last minute?"

Kristina started stalking CheapOair for deals the day I left, but stopped a couple of weeks ago since I "seemed pretty busy." Which is a nice way for her to say that I dropped the friendship ball.

"But after we FaceTimed, I figured you could use the company. So I talked to your parents."

"So you're, like, here to save me?" I ask like it's a joke as I lead her back into my room. I don't want to be the kind of person who needs saving, but having Kristina here makes me feel lighter.

"Duh! And it better happen by Wednesday because that's when the cheapest return ticket was. Wait, why are you eye level right now?"

"Stilettos, dah-ling."

I bend my knee and raise my heel to show off the shoes. Kristina, who is the queen of flip-flops, stares in awe.

"Since when are you wearing heels?"

"You've seen me in wedge sandals."

"Those aren't wedges; they're weapons." She touches the point of a stiletto like it's a needle and asks in disbelief, "Who are you and what have you done with my uncoordinated friend?"

Sometimes I feel like I've turned into someone else, but I don't hypothesize with her about my transformation. Instead I become paralyzed by the sound of dogs barking in the apartment.

"Ohhh yes, bring on the first New York friend!" Kristina rubs her hands together in anticipation. "I'm excited to meet Dog Walker!"

I grab her arm before she has a chance to leave the bedroom. "No," I whisper very loudly.

"What's—"

"*Shh!*"

Kristina plays along and freezes. It's only when we hear the door close and Princess trots into the room, skeptically checking out this new intruder, that she asks me what the hell all that was about.

And so I start to explain.

"Dog Walker *liked* you? How is this the first time I'm hearing that you're in a love triangle? Leave out anything and I'm going after you with that stiletto."

She crosses her arms while I go over every detail, making my debrief anything but brief. Every bit of tension that takes over my body when I explain the Ben situation is released when I talk about Carter. Pretty soon Kristina knows everything from his freshman year Halloween costume to how insanely soft his lips are. And as I get more swoony, any hint of annoyance about being kept out of the loop is wiped completely from Kristina's face.

"I'm really happy for you, Harper. I've never seen you like this before about anybody. I mean, maybe Adam Lockler, but that's different because—"

"This guy knows I exist?"

"You said it, not me."

That doesn't stop me from whacking her with a pillow.

"Don't be a baby; the pillows are made out of goose down," I say as Kristina squeals and tries to duck under the covers.

Not one to be left out, Princess backs up to get a running start so that her stubby legs can catapult her onto the bed. It's the first time I've seen her jump *or* run. Her remaining rolls of fat, which Ben and I have decided should never be walked off because they give her too much adorable character, jiggle as she basks in her own accomplishment. I stop hitting Kristina and scoop the pug up into a hug.

"I want in on this lovefest!" Kristina emerges from under the covers.

Considering how long it took Princess to adjust to living with a roommate, I half expect her to throw a complete, wheezy hissy fit upon realizing that she has to cohabit with a second talkative, Taylor Swift–blasting human. I was expecting the pug to use her roly-poly body as a way to barricade Kristina outside the bedroom door, like she did to me.

But Princess is a changed canine, and soon we are all snuggled up in the bed, binge watching the last season of *Gossip Girl*.

I fall asleep under the glow of Netflix, the laptop still propped up on my stomach.

We wake up early the next morning for a full day of sightseeing and stuffing our faces.

"I'm completely excited to act like a tourist today," I say as I grab a banana from the kitchen. "This is actually the first time I've busted out my sneakers all summer."

"Not for my lack of effort," Aunt Vee pipes in. "Before the end of this summer, I'm taking you to a workout class."

Before we leave the apartment, Aunt Vee slips me an envelope.

"It's from Benjamin," she says. "Maybe it's about the pug prom tonight."

I haven't told Aunt Vee about the Ben fiasco. My face burns just thinking about it.

"Aren't you going to open it?" Kristina asks, when we squeeze in between two manspreaders on the 6 train on our way to the Empire State Building, which Kristina can't believe I haven't been to the top of yet. "Also, what's a pug prom?"

"Later," I say. As much as I want to know what's in there, I don't want to know what's in there. "For now, I just want to focus on me and my bestie's day of fanny-pack and selfie-stick levels of tourist adventure." I fold the letter and put it in my purse, into the zipper pocket I never use so that my hand won't run into it whenever I try to find my wallet. "Tomorrow we're going to brunch with my friends in the Meatpacking District, but today I have you to myself."

Any weirdness between us seems to have evaporated.

"After that brunch, we should check out the High Line," she says, pulling out a dog-eared guidebook from her backpack. "It's right there. It's an abandoned elevated railroad track turned awesome garden."

We push our way out of the subway to our first destination. "Maybe. Let's see what Carter and the rest of them are up to after, though. I can't wait for you to meet him. Oh, and my friend Gigi wants to get mani pedis before."

"Chlorine is brutal on nail polish." Kristina examines her nail beds while we exit through the turnstile and walk up to the street. "But I can just hang while you guys do it. I'm game to meet a cantaloupe."

"A cantaloupe?"

Kristina looks at me in disbelief. "Hello? Cantaloupe. Filler fruit friend?"

Shoot, did I actually forget that? That conversation on the walk home from Bobby McKittrick's party feels like it happened a lifetime ago. I recover quickly.

"Of course!" I say. "It's just, she's actually pretty cool. *Not* mango level, there's only *one* mango"—Kristina grins—"but maybe she's a raspberry or something."

We link arms. Kristina's the perfect tourist buddy except for her ability to power walk forty blocks without getting winded. We do more sightseeing in half a day than I've done in almost two months. And to top it off, I finally get to take my trip to Serendipity for dinner and frozen hot chocolate.

If the Mad Hatter were to switch from tea parties to ice-cream socials, he'd throw them here. Complete with stained-glass chandeliers, dozens of small circular mirrors that pop off the walls, dainty white furniture, and explosions of pink paint, Serendipity has a whimsy that makes me feel like Alice the moment she first beheld Wonderland.

Kristina waits for me to settle into my goblet of icy chocolate and whipped cream before she brings up Ben's letter.

"You can't tell me that you aren't even a little bit curious about what it says."

I swallow so fast, I get brain freeze.

"If you don't, I'll read it for you." Kristina grabs for my bag while I'm distracted by the fact that my brain is exploding. "It's for your own good."

Kristina rips open the envelope and starts to read.

Harper,

We both know who the writer is between the two of us, but I needed to do more than text to let you know what a complete idiot I was. Not for saying I like you, because I do. I'm sorry for making you feel uncomfortable because you don't like me back. I won't bring it up again. But can we go back to being friends?

I really missed you this week. I should have called as soon as those dbags started tweeting about your blog post, but I was nervous to talk to you after Saturday night. I was embarrassed. Another example of how I was an idiot.

Oh, and idiot example #3: Why did I say you shouldn't come to pug prom? Please come. There's something I'd like you to see, and Princess could use the support, too. It took a lot to get her into that dress.

I hope I didn't mess everything up, but I understand if I did.

Your friend either way,

Ben

Kristina reads the end of the letter slowly, her eyes peeking up above the page every few sentences to see my reaction.

"Whoa." I put down my spoon.

"I can't believe he wrote you a letter," she says in genuine awe. "And it was so nice."

"He is nice. He's really nice. I mean, I'm with Carter but . . ."

"Yeah." Kristina carefully folds the paper into the envelope and hands it back across the table. "I think you have to go to pug prom. Apart from the obvious perks of attending the weirdest-sounding event ever, it sounds like he's really sorry and really gets it. And you do want to stay friends, right?"

"Definitely." It's not even a question.

"Although how you could only want to be friends after getting a letter like that—I feel like *I* have butterflies for Dog Walker a little."

Wait, Kristina and Ben.

I won't have to feel bad about hurting Ben anymore if they hit it off instead. As I told him, she's definitely more his type. It will be a win-win-win: Ben gets his post-Delilah, fun rebound; Kristina gets a cute athlete to make out with; and I can stop feeling guilty about both of them. I can't believe I didn't think of this before.

· 34 ·

HOW FANCY CAN A PROM FOR PUGS BE?

Very fancy.

Extremely fancy.

As soon as we breach the balloon archway leading into the ballroom in our sundresses, we're acutely aware of just how underdressed we are. I'm talking ball gowns, corsages, diamond tiaras, and well-tailored suits—on the pugs and their owners. The room might be full of female dogs, but we're clearly the basic bitches of the party.

Walking across the dance floor, under the sparkle of the disco ball, I scan the room nervously, wondering when I'll spot Ben.

Kristina and I pass a tuxedoed man swaying with his little black pug, also in a tuxedo. The man lowers his monocle to ask the person dancing next to them where her dog (wearing a structured dress fit for a queen) got her gigantic, Elizabethan-style, ruffled white collar that sticks out so far, the pug has trouble lifting her head.

"Once I found out that the collar is technically called a 'ruff,'

I had to get it," the woman gushes. "I didn't care if it was five hundred dollars. Do it for the pun, I say."

Kristina squeezes my hand. "Tell me I just imagined that."

I squeeze back. "I should have known there would be a lot of puns at this paw-ty."

"Oh my God, I don't understand how you can still be so terrible at puns."

"Harper, over here!" Aunt Vee is waving to us from across the ballroom. She's standing next to a cluster of pugs lapping up water from a gigantic bowl labeled "punch."

One of the pugs is Princess, a vision in her poofy purple-taffeta dress. And it seems like Atticus has rubbed off on her. Princess is running around the other pugs, making friends and sniffing whatever nonpantalooned butt she can find.

"I can't believe how incredible she looks," I say as I carefully hug Aunt Vee, scratching my bare arms against her dress's sequins. "And so energetic."

"All thanks to Benjamin."

I assume my casual, hand-on-the-waist pose and attempt a casual (or at least not crazy-uncomfortable) voice. "Where is he, by the way?"

"Probably off taking pictures somewhere. Did you know that the pug prom committee hired him to be the photographer? He promised me some glamour shots. . . ."

"You didn't tell me he was a photographer," Kristina says.

"This must be what he wanted to tell me." I look around the room again, this time brimming with excitement rather than nerves. I don't care that things are awkward with us right now. I'm just really happy for him. And maybe a little bit proud. He did it. He actually did it. "Why can't I find him?"

"Maybe try the guy behind the big camera?" Kristina says.

And there he is, not with an iPhone but with a fancy camera I've never seen before. Crouching down to get the perfect angle on a shot of a group of women in chiffon toting their bedazzled pugs around like purses. The pugs' couture aesthetic is only enhanced by the fact that most of their tongues permanently hang outside of their mouths, creating the perfect juxtaposition of goofy and grandiose.

I don't approach until Ben finishes his shot.

"Hey." I tap him on the shoulder as he's examining the pictures on the fancy camera's screen.

"Harper!" Startled, Ben drops the camera, which luckily is secured by a strap around his neck. "You came? I'm so happy you came."

He reaches in for a hug but stops short, jerking back.

"I got your letter. We're good."

"Yeah?" His face relaxes, but not all the way to normal. "I was worried. I didn't want to make you uncomfortable. . . ."

"We're good," I repeat. I try to find the words to ask him how he got the job and tell him that I'm proud of him, but he extends his arm toward Kristina. She's been hanging back talking to a dog—not his owner, the actual dog—to give us space.

"Kristina, right?" Ben says. "The best friend. I hear you're awesome. Nice to meet you."

"Same." Kristina doesn't hesitate in her hugging. It's how she greets everyone, so I don't know why it makes me feel restless. "Sorry I'm so underdressed for your event."

"Don't worry about it. You both look great."

"Nice camera!" I say, unsure of what to say next.

"Thanks. It's new. Thought I should finally put the dog-walking cash toward more than video games," he says, at first to us and then over us. I turn around and see a group of ladies in boas waving Ben to their table. "Um, I have to get back to it. I'll find you. Don't go."

As soon as Ben heads off, Kristina pulls me closer and stares me right in the face. "Are you sure you don't think of this guy as more than a friend?"

"Of course I don't."

"Really? Because he's really cute and I was sensing this, like, weird energy between you."

"Weird energy or awkward energy? I'm one hundred percent not into it."

"It's okay if you are. I've been confused too, you know I have."

"Actually, I was thinking he might be more your type. He's in mega-rebound mode, but it could be a fun way to kill time when I'm at work."

Kristina is studying my face, but my eyes are projecting nothing. This isn't a test. There are no lines to read between.

We spend the night petting pugs and dancing. Aunt Vee spends most of the night flirting with the head of the pug prom committee, trying to secure Princess's vote for prom queen. (Only to be horrified to find out that this year it was a total waste of time because of an unbecoming streak of egalitarianism in the new pug prom committee that eschews titles.) Every so often Ben waves at us in between shots, but he's mostly occupied taking photos of conga lines—which, it turns out, pugs are horrible at.

After Kristina and I belt "I Will Always Love You" along with Whitney Houston for the final song of the dance, Ben reemerges to ask what we have planned for the rest of the weekend.

"Late brunch and maybe some sightseeing," I say. "You?"

"I'm pretty boring. I have to start editing these photos and, I dunno, maybe run the Central Park Loop to get back in shape. Don't wanna die when the lacrosse season starts."

"That's been on my to-do list, too," Kristina says. It is, I've seen the list.

"You should do it. It's really nice and it's only about six miles. Give or take."

"I'm sorry," I chime in. "But did you say *only* six miles?"

"I guess it's actually six point two." Ben's eyes light up and he asks me, "Why, would you be interested? We could go before your brunch!"

The thought of me running any distance, let alone a freaking 10K, by choice is so funny that it's not even funny. Kristina is laughing like Ben just told the most hilarious joke in the world. Which I guess he kind of did.

"Harper has been walking the mile out of protest in PE every year since the fifth grade." Kristina tries to compose herself only to start laughing again. "Remember how mad Coach Kessler used to get that you weren't even trying?"

"It's like he was auditioning to be a coach on *The Biggest Loser!*"
I puff out my chest and lower my voice a few octaves to give my
best middle school gym teacher impression. "C'mon, Anderson.
Every winner was once a beginner. Punch that laziness in the face!"

Kristina grabs my hand. "And then you'd be all like, 'Sorry,
Coach, but isn't physical violence against the student code of
ethics?'"

"So that's a no, then," Ben says, grinning at Kristina.

"That's a hell no." I punch him in the arm, jokingly, like
always. God, this is feeling so much better. "See, I told you we
were incompatible!"

Ben's entire body stiffens. His smile disappears. The dimple is
gone.

Okay, not that much better.

Do I pretend I didn't say it? Do I apologize? DO SOME-
THING.

"You two should do it, though," I say quickly, trying to recover.
I look at Kristina, whose hand is over her mouth. "You didn't want
a mani pedi anyway. You can just meet us for brunch after."

Kristina searches for a response. "I don't think—"

"No need to think." I take both of their hands. "You both like
jogging. You should freaking jog!"

I don't let us leave until they agree.

· 3 5 ·

KRISTINA CHECKS APPROXIMATELY NINETY-SEVEN times to make sure that it's okay to go. "Because I could just check out the Loop tomorrow when you're at work."

"It's *fine*. You need a jog, and I need a manicure." I wave my chipped orange fingernails in front of her face to emphasize my point. "The bouncer won't even let me into brunch if I try to get into Bacchanal with these cuticles."

"Ha. Ha. Such a comedian," she says sarcastically. She pushes my hands away and finishes tying her running shoes.

"You're acting like I'm joking." For all I know, Bacchanal will have a bouncer. The word basically meant "crazy party" in ancient Greece, and I read a *New York* magazine review that says the restaurant lives up to the name. "Get ready to dance on some tables. If you can still stand after your marathon."

"I'm pretty sure I'll survive." Kristina looks down at her wristwatch. "Okay, if you're positive you don't mind, I guess I should head out."

"Go! Just don't be late for Bacchanal. I don't want to keep Carter's group waiting."

Kristina agrees and kisses the top of a slumbering Princess's head good-bye. The pug, who still has residual glitter in her fur from last night, doesn't even stir from her deep, post-party sleep.

I'm picking out my nail polish colors when Gigi pushes through the salon doors.

"I'm late," she announces to me and half a dozen women sitting in a row of massage chairs, their feet submerged in soapy water for their pedicures.

"What do you like better," I ask, holding up an Essie bottle in each hand. "Starter Wife or Where's My Chauffeur? Wow, I didn't realize how horrible those names were until I said them out loud."

"*Definitely* Where's My Chauffeur."

I put the light pink Starter Wife nail polish back down.

"Well?" Gigi says expectantly. "Aren't you going to ask me *why* I'm late?"

"Hot date?"

"Better. McKayla e-mailed me this morning to ask me to write a story."

She hands her manicurist an ivory Chanel nail polish from her purse ("Only amateurs don't bring their own.") and continues. "Jenni Grace went on a Twitter tirade about breaking up with her boyfriend, and McKayla asked *me* to write it up. I think it's because my blog post is doing so well."

"What story?"

"I wrote a blog about purge watching *Gossip Girl*! *And* some other sites aggregated it because they thought it was funny," she says. "This is my first time being on the Leader Board with something that isn't ridiculous. With McKayla asking me to write something this morning, I think I might actually have a chance of getting the magazine spread."

Um, wasn't *I* the one who called it purge watching? I feel a tug in my stomach. I start to turn and say something, but my manicurist slaps at my hand and tells me not to move.

"Well?" Gigi says, examining the cuticle on her right hand. "Isn't that exciting?"

"Yeah, just . . . maybe tell me when you're going to write about one of my ideas next time. Maybe I was going to do a blog about it."

I didn't have plans to write about it before, but now funny lines that I could have written cram into my head. But my annoyance is disrupted by a look of genuine worry on Gigi's face.

"Oh no," she says. "I should have asked if it was okay. I didn't think about it."

Gigi turns away, which in June I would have interpreted as angry but I now register as a sign that she's upset.

"I overreacted," I say. "We're good."

"Yeah?"

"Yeah."

"Good." Gigi pauses and then quickly exclaims, "I'm glad we're friends, Harper."

"Me too."

Not one for a mushy moment, Gigi quickly changes the subject to gossip about Jamie getting fired for the rest of our mani pedi. But we walk out of the nail salon linking arms, careful not to get our heels caught in the Meatpacking District's cobblestone streets on the way to the Bacchanal. There's a big crowd outside the restaurant.

"I hate it when pretty girls make bad fashion choices," Gigi tsks. "A denim skirt and a bright orange backpack? What is this, Bacchanal or homeroom?"

I know that orange backpack. And I have a matching skirt; it's one of my favorites.

"Harper!" Kristina waves from the front of the line.

"You *know* her?" Gigi asks with a frozen smile, eyeing Kristina's flip-flops.

I got so caught up in *Shift* gossip that I must have forgotten to mention Kristina was in town.

"I thought you were *kidding* when you said there would be a bouncer," Kristina says when we walk over. Proudly wearing her Castalia High Varsity Swim tank and a smile, Kristina may still look effortlessly beautiful, but her outfit is definitely more Bobby McKittrick's backyard than Meatpacking District.

Since she always fits in so perfectly at all social functions back home, I didn't think to give her wardrobe tips for the day.

"You must be Gigi," Kristina says, when neither of us takes the lead. "I've heard so much about you."

Gigi puts out her hand when Kristina goes in for a hug. "I don't want to get water on the silk," she says, looking at Kristina's wet hair. "No offense."

"Sorry about that! I had to shower after my run and didn't have time to dry my hair. You know, Harper, even if you just walk it, you should really do the Central Park Loop sometime. It was awesome."

"Shopping is my cardio," Gigi says.

I say the reservation name and we are granted entrance.

"And you weren't kidding about the table dancing, either." Kristina stares at a girl as she spears a waffle on her high heel while jumping up and down over her entrée in beat to the DJ's mix. "I definitely underestimated brunch."

Kristina looks down at her hand. Since she doesn't have a fake ID, the bouncer stamped "MINOR" in big letters across the back of her hand.

"I wasn't going to drink anyway," I say in response to her stamp, right as an explosion of streamers rains down on us from a birthday group who came with their own party poppers. "Isn't New York incredible?"

"Finally," Gigi says exasperatedly when a hostess starts leading us to our seat. She is utterly unfazed by her surroundings and keeps giving me and Kristina weird looks as we slowly take in the extravagance.

"Don't tell your parents, but this is already more fun than my usual pancake-flipping Sundays in your kitchen." Kristina grabs on to my shoulders, re-creating last night's conga line, and we start dancing while we walk to the table, shaking our heads with the beat.

"*Your dripping hair is splashing all over me.* Some of us don't want our outfits sabotaged." Gigi stalks ahead.

"She seems *really* great." I don't have to look behind me to know Kristina is rolling her eyes.

"She grows on you. I promise she's really sweet when you get to know her." I can feel the eyes rolling again but don't look. Instead I'm distracted by the table Gigi's approaching. "There he is! The one giving Gigi a bis-bis?"

"A what?"

"God, he looks good." I speed toward the table. Carter's changed his hair—while it still has the side part, he now has what Brie describes as a "taper and fade," where the hair is longer on top and gets shorter as it goes down, fading into the skin.

I don't know how someone this cool could actually be standing up right now to make room at the table for me. Asking his friends to move down so I can sit next to him, proudly introducing me as "the writer I was telling you about."

He was *telling* people about me? And not just as a girl. As a writer.

"He's a smoker?" Kristina whispers into my ear after taking the other seat next to me, leaving Gigi to sit all the way at the end of the table, her least favorite seat. "Harper, we don't do smokers."

Ever since fifth grade science, when Mr. Whitney displayed a blackened pig lung in the classroom for a week ("This is what tobacco does to your body!"), we swore never to touch a cigarette.

I'm about to protest that he's not until I see a pack of Marlboros tucked into the front pocket of his short-sleeved white shirt. I guess I haven't hung out with Carter long enough to actually know that about him. "Whatever," I say. "I'm sure it's just social smoking. At parties and stuff."

Kristina seems less convinced, but I refuse to take the conversation further. He's in college, in New York. Things are different here.

I am instantly distracted by Carter as he shifts in his seat. I'm acutely aware of our proximity, internally tracking the centimeters and inches between our bodies. Willing our knees to touch, our feet to brush.

I flash back to the last time we were this close to each other. The Hamptons. Carter. Carter's lips on my lips. Carter's teeth on my ear.

Carter is telling everyone about his reporting trip to New Mexico and how he interviewed the reigning meth-smoking champion of America.

"That's a thing?" Kristina asks.

"I had him smoke my Holland Prep diploma on camera, so that I can add that to my story," Carter says confidently, leaning back. "After my exposé on Internet trolls, I think this might be my greatest work."

I shudder. "Don't remind me about trolls. I'm still getting the most horrible messages. And I report them to Twitter but nothing happens. I just want it to stop. McKayla says they aren't serious, but I don't know. . . ."

"Don't be such a little girl about it," Carter says, shoving a mimosa into my hand. I take it. "You can't be a *real* journalist if you care what people think about you. What doesn't kill you makes you stronger."

I want to protest, but I take a sip of the mimosa instead. Then I take another.

"That's what you say to someone who's getting cyberbullied? What doesn't kill you makes you stronger?" Kristina's eyes narrow and then she says to me, "Isn't that a Coach Kessler-ism, Harper? I know how much you love Coach's philosophy."

"Nietzsche's philosophy," Carter says.

"What?"

"A *gym* teacher didn't say that. *Nietzsche* did." He turns to Kristina for the first time since we've been here. I don't like where this conversation is going. I refill my glass.

Kristina gives me a look that I ignore.

"I take it you aren't a writer like this one." Carter rests his hand on my knee.

"She's a swimmer," I say. "She's *really* good. College coaches from Stanford and the Ivies are all over her."

"Don't you wish creatives like *us* had the same admissions opportunities athletes do?" Carter says, launching a tablewide debate about priorities in academic institutions.

"I have a three-point-eight GPA," Kristina says.

"Oh, I'm not talking about *you* specifically," Carter replies. "I'm just talking about the system in general."

Kristina's heard it from me, too. I whined nonstop when D-Bag Dull Man, who I'd say has the intellect of a Pet Rock if I didn't want to be offensive to Pet Rocks, got into Penn, which is on my "super-reach" list.

"You sure about that?" Kristina asks, when the waitress comes to refill my glass.

"Don't be a downer," Gigi says, "just because you can't have mimosas."

"I don't drink champagne anyway," Kristina says. She hasn't

had a sip since she had way too many sips at her dad's wedding. "Besides, I'm not being a downer. She said she wasn't drinking. I'm being her best friend."

"Funny that I haven't heard about you until five minutes ago," Gigi says.

"Tina, it's okay." I fill my glass. This brunch is *not* going as planned. Kristina's usually the most popular person at the party. Any party. Befriending everyone she meets. I want Carter and Gigi to meet *that* girl.

"All right," Carter says. "When we wrap up here, I say we go to Le Bain. My friends have some tables."

"I've been *dying* to go there," I say, confidently putting my hand over Carter's on my thigh.

"What's Le Bain?" Kristina asks me.

"It's at the top of the Standard Hotel and is supposed to have the *best* view of the city. Maybe even better than the Empire State Building. And it's right by the High Line, so we can hit it after." Carter squeezes my leg. "Maybe."

"I like views." Kristina puts her smile back on, *thank God.* "Let's do it."

"Won't it be a problem that *she* doesn't have an ID?" Gigi asks.

"Just remove the 'MINOR' thing and we should be okay," Carter says. "I know people there."

Kristina stands up to go wash the indelible ink off her hands when Gigi shouts, "Stop. You can't tell me *that* won't be a problem."

"What?" I ask.

"No ID is one thing, but improper footwear." Gigi looks at

Kristina's rubber flip-flops and then works her way up to the rest of her outfit. "Make that improper everything-wear, and no way will we get in."

Shit. She's right. How do I fix this?

"If we cab back to my apartment right now, Kristina can change and we can just meet you there."

"I didn't pack heels," Kristina says, brushing back her hair.

"Who doesn't pack heels when they go to Manhattan?" Gigi asks.

"It's fine," I say. "Look at her. She can totally get in with flats. We just have to change outfits and—"

"I'll make things easier for you"—Kristina throws her arms in the air—"I'm out. Just go without me."

"No!"

"Leave her," Gigi shouts after me when I chase after Kristina. I'm slowed down by the dance party in the middle of the restaurant, so by the time I catch up to her, she's already at the front door.

"Kristina!"

"Oh, now you realize I exist." She doesn't stop walking, pushing through the crowd by the hostess and out the door.

"What's your deal?" I squint as my eyes readjust to the light outside. I forgot that it's still daytime. "I'm not used to seeing you like this."

She spins around on her flip-flops. "I'm not used to seeing *you* like this. Downing mimosas like Diet Coke? Kissing the asses of the biggest assholes I've ever met? You think *my* water polo guys are bad? Every time you went gaga over his Nietzsche crap, I had to actively stop myself from throwing up. You're acting like an idiot."

My face starts to flush. And not because I'm embarrassed. I'm mad. I don't say *anything* when Kristina goes through all the jocks in remedial English. And now this objectively gorgeous and smart guy wants me.

"So this is what you're like when *I'm* with the hottest guy at the party?"

"Yeah, right. You think I'm jealous? Have him."

"Like he's yours to give away? Like D-Bag Dull Man? News flash, Kristina, you're not his type. You're not one of his people."

"Are you saying I'm stupid?"

Kristina and I never fight. But now that I've started letting things out, I can't stop. The words keep flowing. I know I'm taking things too far, but I can't stop.

"I'm saying you're pissed that you came here on a humanitarian mission to rescue me, and I didn't need saving. I'm the one who fits here, not you."

"You have truly lost it," she says quietly. "I'm gonna go. Just don't do anything with him you'll regret."

Stop. I should stop now. But I can't. Why is she still pretending she knows what's best for me? I'm not her sidekick anymore.

"That's rich coming from you."

"Harper!"

Suddenly I'm snapped back into reality. What am I doing? "I shouldn't have said that. I'm just really tipsy, and stressed, and new to having a guy actually like me."

"It's fine."

"We can skip Le Bain. We can just go to the High Line like you wanted."

"I said it's fine," Kristina says weakly but resolutely. "I'm feeling kind of tired from the run, so I should go home anyway. I think I should be alone right now."

The brunch hopefuls in front of Bacchanal eagerly part for Kristina to leave so that they can take her place at the front of the line. I forgot that there were so many people here.

With that, she walks away.

· 36 ·

I DON'T KNOW WHAT TO THINK, SO I JUST DON'T.
What did I write in a blog once? Oh yeah, *fake it till you feel it.*

I'm all sunshine and smiles by the time I return to the table. Instead of squeezing back into the booth next to Carter, I sit on his lap. He wraps his arms around my body and it feels good to be in his arms, wanted.

"Did your friend bail?" he asks.

"Looks like it."

"Too bad. We decided to skip Le Bain and hang at my place instead."

Carter's apartment, which allows varsity swimming tanks and flip-flops. I pick up my phone to tell Kristina to come back, that Carter *isn't* a bad guy and changed plans so he could get to know her better. (Okay, so that's probably overinterpreting the situation, but how's she going to know?) But then I stop.

After Kristina's dad left, when Kristina said she needed alone time, she meant it. Sure, she came over and cried the night of. But the next morning she was off and didn't take my calls for three whole days. It was the longest we'd ever gone without talking to each other. Until this summer, that is. I'm not saying our fight is comparable to Kristina's dad cheating on her mom and leaving, but I imagine that if she says she wants some space, she wants it.

We all head to Carter's apartment. He lives in the West Village.

"How long does it take you to get to Columbia from here," Davie, mercifully without the donkey head, asks.

"Who cares," Carter says. "Who wants to live uptown when they can live *here*?"

Here is not what I'd imagine a college guy's apartment would look like. There aren't empty boxes of pizza or an Xbox. The mattress isn't on the floor. But it is exactly what I thought Carter's apartment, probably funded by the Bosh Media conglomerate, would look like. It's decorated with David Lynch movie posters and books. Shelves and shelves of books. While other people are hanging out on the couch—not even a futon!—I'm examining Carter's literary collection.

It's even freaking alphabetized.

"I think I'm in heaven," I say, picking up an old copy of Salinger's *Franny and Zooey*.

Carter leaves the group and stands behind me, arms once again wrapped around me, his chin resting on the top of my head.

"It's a first edition," he says.

"Oh my God." I quickly and very carefully put the book down and turn around. "I don't want to touch that! Have you met me? I'm the clumsiest person alive."

"What are you talking about?" He kisses my cheek and says the next part in a whisper, "You're incredibly smooth, Harper Anderson."

What Harper Anderson is he talking about? I want to correct his egregious misunderstanding but realize that he hasn't seen that side of me. I've never had a meltdown or head-on collision in his presence. So instead I enjoy the tingly aftermath of the kiss.

"That's our cue to go," Gigi says, rounding everyone up from the couches. "Call me later, Harper."

And then there were two.

Then we're alone.

"I've been waiting to do this for weeks," Carter says, and he pushes me up against the bookcase. His lips meet mine in an electric kiss. All-consuming. He holds the back of my head in his hands and I grab his shirt to pull him closer to me, leaning deeper back into the bookcase. I want to make out forever.

And then, bam. My butt knocks into one of the shelves, causing books to topple to the floor.

"The Salinger!" *Franny and Zooey* is now at my feet.

"Leave it." He pulls me in for another kiss.

"See," I say. "I told you I was a klutz. Total disaster."

"I don't do romantic comedies, Harper. Clumsy is not hot. Knocking over the books was a hookup casualty. Much sexier. Awkward doesn't appeal to me."

I like the sound of a hookup casualty, but I also want to clarify that, yes, I am actually uncoordinated as well. Just to make sure Carter knows whom he's actually kissing.

Not just kissing.

I feel Carter start to trace his fingertips up my thigh, teasing the bottom of my skirt. Oh God. This is new territory.

"Let's talk some more first," I say, taking his hand off my skin and dragging him toward the couch.

"Seriously?"

"Yeah, I want to get to know you better." I pat the cushion next to me and he sits down. "So, how was your week?"

"I told you about my week at brunch."

Right. That must have been when I wasn't listening.

"Well, my week was kind of all over the place," I say without prompting. "I checked a lot of stuff off the bucket list. *Phantom.* Empire State Building. Frozen hot chocolate at Serendipity."

"Those tourist traps? What a nightmare. That all sounds terrible. At least you started on a high note with your blog going viral and are ending on a high note with me."

Carter's lips. His tongue. His teeth.

His kiss. It couldn't be more perfect. Until he moves his fingers to my skirt again. I put my hand on his and push it away.

"Come on," he groans. "You don't have to play hard to get anymore. We're finally alone."

"I know," I say, running my fingers through his dark hair but feeling on edge. I don't like feeling on edge. "And I am happy we're finally alone—"

"So don't be a tease!"

What's he talking about?

"I'm not. . . . We're making out!"

"Don't play that game. You made out with me before you knew

my name," he says. "I'll still respect you and whatever. It doesn't have to mean anything."

If we had sex, it wouldn't mean anything?

"But I'd want it to," I say quietly, and look right into his bright green eyes. "Wouldn't you?"

"Aren't you the one who introduced herself to me as the girl who gave no fucks?"

"Yeah, but, that's before I knew you. And now we're dating and—"

"Oh, Jesus." Carter's green eyes narrow and he gets a look on his face like I smell like I haven't showered in a week. *"Dating?"*

"Aren't we? I thought—"

Carter stands up and starts pacing the room.

"This is not what you advertised. You're a cool chick, sure"— *cool chick??*—"but I just want to have fun. And come *on*, after all this chasing, you kind of owe me. Not to mention the fact that I got your blog viral *and*—"

"Because you told *deviant* to aggregate my blog?"

"Nah, Davie was going to do it anyway. I just gave him the picture of us. My tax for being your Make-Out Bandit muse."

"So, why do I owe you?"

"I sent it over to my Internet troll connection so it would get more attention—things aren't really doing well unless there's controversy."

For a second everything stands still.

"You did what?"

"It worked, didn't it? I knew my troll would hate it, and he's not shy about his opinions. I was helping you."

"Helping? People are still being horrible to me whenever I tweet anything. I had to make my Instagram private because angry guys were telling me I'm ugly and should take what I can get every time I posted."

"You're being so melodramatic. If you can't handle this, then I *did* do you a favor. Journalism isn't for the weak. 'To live is to suffer, to survive is to find some meaning in the suffering.'"

"Are you quoting Nietzsche right now? That isn't even relevant!"

"I think I *know* what Nietzsche was talking about. I'm majoring in philosophy."

Carter walks back over to the couch and sinks back into the cushion. He softens his voice.

"I'm probably being harsh. I just want you to have thick skin." He strokes my arm to emphasize his point and puts his mouth to my ear. "Although I also like your skin soft, just like this."

He touches my arm, but what I'm feeling isn't warm tingles. Something is building inside of me. It starts in my stomach and then moves up to my chest, to my shoulders, to my arms, and to my hands, which push Carter away as hard as I can.

Totally taken by surprise, Carter stumbles back and knocks into the table. "What the hell? You really are a spaz."

"And you're insane if you think that after all that, after pressuring me and admitting that you're the reason why my life was hell this whole week, there's even the slightest chance we're going to hook up. I was *so* wrong about you."

"You're going to regret this when you're home alone tomorrow night Instagram stalking me and my hot date hanging out with the most important people in media at my dad's party. . . . I was *going* to introduce you to the dean of the Columbia School of Journalism."

"Of all the things I might regret this summer, not hooking up with you is definitely not going to be one of them."

"As Nietzsche said, 'To regret deeply is to live afresh.'"

"Um, okay, I got an A in AP English Lit. Nietzsche didn't say that, Thoreau did. And as my favorite philosopher Taylor Swift would say, 'We are never, ever, ever getting back together.'"

I slam the door on my way out.

· 37 ·

WHEN I GET BACK TO AUNT VEE'S APARTMENT, Kristina's already in bed.

I change into my pajamas in the dark and quietly crawl under the comforter, careful not to disturb her. But Kristina isn't asleep. Both of us just lie there side by side for a few breaths, unsure of what to say.

"How'd things go with Carter," she asks finally, breaking the awkward silence.

I could pretend it was fine. Prove her wrong. But I don't have the energy.

"You were right," I say. "He's a jerk."

She turns on her side to face me, but I can't make out her features. My eyes haven't adjusted to the dark. "Do you wanna talk about it?"

"Maybe tomorrow." It's still too fresh.

"I'm sorry," she says. "I wish he hadn't been."

"Please. You hated him from the first second you met him."

"No." She pauses. "Well, yeah. But still. I know you really liked him. That sucks."

She pauses and another few seconds pass. Now it's my turn to break the silence. My parents always say you shouldn't go to bed angry.

"After brunch," I start. "The things I said . . ."

"I said things, too. . . ."

Our sentences don't feel like they have beginnings or ends.

"Do you want to talk about it?" I ask.

"Maybe tomorrow."

We're trying to make things better but are so emotionally worn by the day that we don't have the words.

After another pause, another set of sleepy breaths, I say, "Love you."

"Love you, too," Kristina replies. "Night."

Come Monday morning, things might not feel back to normal, but they do feel better.

"I can't believe you know how to do smoky eyes now," Kristina says, watching me put on makeup.

"Brie taught me. She's the Beauty intern; you'd like her!"

Kristina raises an eyebrow.

"No, you actually would this time. Really!"

Before this summer I always assumed sorority girls were really fake, but Brie genuinely *is* that sweet. She really *is* that easily excited about almost everything. And she's better read than just about anyone else at *Shift*, including me.

"You should stop by *Shift* if you have time today," I say. While I'm at work, Kristina has a long list of sightseeing destinations planned. A part of me wants to ask if Ben's going to be joining her for any of her to-do list, but I don't. "The office is awesome. And I *have* to show you the open kitchen. You'll die. There are mountains of pastries that no one eats because they're all afraid of carbs."

"Swimmer. Very pro carbs," she says, still in her pajamas.

"Um, my cardio is typing. Also very pro carbs."

Feeling more confident that we're good now, that yesterday was an anomaly—I mean, every lifelong friendship has to have at least one big fight, right?—I leave for work.

Gigi has a Diet Coke waiting for me on my desk as soon as I get in and demands a debrief of the rest of my night with Carter.

"Ohhh yes." Sunny joins our gossip circle. "Did you guys finally hook up?"

"Kind of?" I pop open the can's tab.

"Did you have *sex*?" Gigi asks, eyes open wide.

I shake my head.

Gigi looks confused. "But why not? I thought you wanted to have sex with him."

"He was . . . I don't know . . . kind of clingy?" I don't want to lie to Gigi, but I also don't want to tell the truth. "You know the type. And all the Nietzsche stuff was getting on my nerves."

"He *did* quote a lot of Nietzsche." Gigi nods.

The day continues as normal. We comb through the Internet

for clicky story ideas to write about and help reporters-in-need with last-minute research projects. Brie and Sunny are huddled together completing the daunting task of making a master list cataloguing every single item of clothing, brand and price included, that appears in the September issue.

"From head to toe, hat to pointy-toed heel," Sunny says. Then she surreptitiously points to the little black dresses that made a field trip to Mode with us. The fully accessorized models might look exquisite in them, but I guarantee we had more fun wearing them.

The issue is complete except for the blank two-page spread that's being held for the intern feature. But that will be filled soon. The internship is over in less than two weeks.

My stomach does somersaults whenever I think about it. What's the word McKayla used again? Shoo-in?

I'm not ready for the summer to end, but I also can't wait to go to school, to walk into the *Castalia Chronicle* room, with my magazine copy in hand. Proving to the world that while people at home just see me as a fact-checker, *Shift* freaking magazine says that I'm the "Teen Journalist to Watch."

Everything is going to change.

Of course, I can't let on to the other interns that it's going to be me. The circulating rumor is that McKayla's going to announce it any day now, so I'll know for sure soon enough.

I want to ask McKayla about it, to make sure that we're still on the same page, but she's in back-to-back meetings "with the dinosaurs upstairs" for the entire day. She didn't even have time to edit my copy of this week's proposed blog.

"What's it going to be about?" Gigi asks. "Ditching the Bosh heir?"

I flash back to last night. How cold Carter was. What an idiot I was. He was interested in someone I was pretending to be. And whose fault was that?

"I don't think I want his Twitter wrath," I say, deflecting. "I wrote about pug proms."

"Huh?" Sunny says.

So then I have to explain about dog dating culture and how it's not a lame topic at all. It's hilarious. The *Shift* Girls are unconvinced, but I know Ben would laugh his butt off. He gets me.

Luckily I don't have to explain my blog choice for long. My work phone rings. Security says Kristina's here, and I have to go downstairs to pick her up.

"I'm sorry, but did you notice the *gigantic waterfall* in the middle of this skyscraper?" Kristina asks, when I meet her downstairs. "It's, like, Yosemite big."

"Did you see the fish?" I point to the pond below.

"Wow."

Kristina isn't wearing a denim skirt and flip-flops today.

"Nice dress," I say.

"Oh, thanks." She smooths the floral-printed wrap dress's hem. "Your aunt lent it to me. I wanted to look the part when I came here. Didn't want to make you look bad in front of your boss."

"That's crazy," I say reflexively. But then I feel a pang of guilt remembering Bacchanal. Shit. "You could never make me look bad. I *never* meant to make you feel that way. Let's go upstairs so I can ply you with free cupcakes."

We take the elevator up to the forty-second floor, and when the doors open I say, mimicking Skirt Suit from day one, "Welcome to *Shift*."

I show her the different signed magazine covers, sneak her past the fashion closet (whispering about our break-in), and take a detour to the open kitchen. When I make it to the main part of the office with the electric-blue desks, I see that McKayla is back from her meetings and is holding court over the interns by the Leader Board, which has both my MatchBook and Gigi's purge-watching stories on display.

"*There* you are, Harper," McKayla says. "Just the intern I wanted to see."

The *Shift* Girls stare, like they were waiting for my return.

OMG, is she going to announce that I have the magazine feature right now, in front of everyone? Am I about to be whisked away to hair and makeup before my coveted photo shoot with a famous fashion photographer?

Not quite.

"As I was saying," McKayla continues to the staff (plus Kristina), "one of the dinosaurs upstairs announced his retirement this morning, so I've spent the day in meetings with Trenton and other Bosh Media executives about the future direction of *Shift*'s magazine and website.

"Aaaaand"—she elongates the word to tease us, happy to have

a captive audience—"I won. We now get to write the provocative material I've wanted to publish on the site since I got here. I used the MatchBook post as an example of the kind of clicks really controversial and bold posts can bring in. So now we're free to write about sexcapades!"

She makes eye contact with me. "Harper, I was just reading your sexcapade post out loud to show everyone what I'm talking about. Forget your pug post. I'm putting this up on Wednesday."

"What sexcapades?" Kristina whispers to me through a smile.

For a second I have no idea what McKayla is talking about either. And then I do.

Shit, shit, shit.

McKayla's talking about the sexcapade blog post I sent in with my application. Or, rather, Kristina's sexcapade that I sent in my application.

The anxious tension starts in my core and then radiates out to the rest of my body. She has to stop talking. This can't be happening.

"McKayla, can I talk to you in your office for a sec?" Maybe I can cut off this conversation before it goes any further. Before she says anything in front of Kristina. I can just make up some other, crazier sexcapades that she can put online instead of this. I just need her to stop—

"I do *not* enjoy being interrupted," McKayla says, putting her hand in the air to shush me. Then, after she fiddles with her iPad for a few seconds, the television screen above her changes from displaying the Leader Board to showing a preview of my to-be-published blog post:

HOW I RUINED MY DAD'S SECOND WEDDING BY . . . GETTING CAUGHT HOOKING UP WITH MY NEW STEPBROTHER AT THE RECEPTION

Clueless is kind of my life.

· 38 ·

THE HEADLINE SMACKS THE SMILE OFF KRISTINA'S face, which contorts into an expression I've never seen before. But it's easy to read: betrayal.

Complete betrayal.

"How could you not tell us about this during the *Clueless* screening in the park?" Brie squeaks. "You hooked up with your *stepbrother*? Gross! No offense."

"Haven't you learned to read past the headline?" Sunny says. "Look at the first paragraph. They didn't grow up with each other like Cher and Josh in the movie. They basically just met." Sunny turns to me with her faint version of a smile. "You just met him. That's way less gross. . . . No offense."

This is not happening.

"I can explain," I whisper to Kristina.

She doesn't look at me. Her eyes are glued to the screen. Her face reddens as she reads through my quippy, snarky, embellished-for-laughs write-up about her actual life.

Her dad's wedding over spring break sophomore year was only the second time, after the cruise I crashed, that she had met her soon-to-be stepfamily. And it was one of a handful of times she had been in the same time zone as her dad since he left her mom. His new wife wasn't one of the women—yes, women, plural—he cheated with. She was his new beginning. New leaf. New family. New life across the country without Kristina in it.

Kristina's soon-to-be stepbrother, Erik, was a year older, really smart, really cute, and just as unhappy about the upcoming nuptials as Kristina. And so, just like they commiserated over strawberry daiquiris on their Faux Family Cruise, they commiserated at the reception over champagne flute after champagne flute. Only this time, instead of some light flirting, things went slightly farther.

After nabbing two extra-large slices of wedding cake—"We'll take these to go," Erik told the caterer with a wink—they traipsed off in search of an ideal hookup destination.

"You ate cake in a bathroom?" Abigail reads in horror. "That's *so* unhygienic. Such a bad idea."

It was a bad idea for a lot of reasons. One of them being that the bridal bathroom at the venue didn't have a working lock. When Erik heard the doorknob turn as he was jokingly shoveling chocolate frosting into a half-undressed Kristina's face, he freaked. His horrible gut reaction to the interruption was to throw the cake in his hands at the intruders.

Also known as the bridal party.

Five bridesmaids barged through the door to accompany his

mom to the bathroom, so that they could lift up her now-cake-splattered, poofier-than-poofy dress while she crouched over the toilet.

"You have bad luck with white clothing," Gigi laughed, reading that bit off the television screen.

"See how Harper makes this a scintillating but still humorous read?" McKayla asks. "The part about the bridesmaids clumsily lifting her 'Stepmonster's' three million layers of tulle, silk, and crinoline so that she could simultaneously pee and yell at them, for the entire reception to hear? Those details are begging to get aggregated all over the Internet!"

It was Kristina's most embarrassing moment. The one dalliance in her otherwise very public love life that she has kept secret, fiercely hidden from everyone in Castalia. No one outside that reception knows the story.

Except me.

And now everyone at *Shift*.

And soon, everyone with access to the Internet.

Everyone will read my humorous retelling of Erik blaming the cake throwing on Kristina. "You don't have to live with them," he said. And while this was true, it was also cementing her future fate. Stepmonster made it very clear that Kristina, a seductress, wouldn't be welcome. And until her dad's recent overtures at resuming a relationship, he seemed to agree with his angry bride.

I turn to Kristina and she backs away. I don't know what to do. There has to be a way to clean up this mess without outing myself to McKayla.

"I'll fix this," I whisper to Kristina. I reach my hands toward her but stop short, as if she were a live grenade and the slightest movement would risk setting her off.

"Now I know how to get you out at Never Have I Ever," Gigi says. "I can't believe you did this."

Kristina answers, no longer whispering, "She didn't!"

"Excuse me," McKayla says, finally noticing that there is another girl in our midst, "but *who* are you?"

"That's Harper's *childhood* friend from San Francisco," Gigi answers, rolling her eyes.

"And we're not from San Francisco," Kristina says, even louder. "God, Harper, did you lie about *everything*?"

Everyone is staring at me.

What do I do?

"What is she talking about, Harper?" Gigi asks, and then stage-whispers to me, loud enough that everyone can still hear, "Is she, like, deranged or something?"

"Should we call for help?" asks Abigail.

Kristina explodes.

"Yeah, I'm the one who needs help. Not the virgin who says she hooked up with the stepbrother she doesn't have! Not the girl who says she's a dating expert when really she couldn't ever get a date if I didn't *beg* a guy to find a friend to double with."

I'm too numb to feel what would otherwise be a sharp jab about D-Bag Dull Man. Kristina's eyes are wide and glassy and kind of wild. She flips her hair and makes a dash for the elevator. I'm stopped before I can follow and try to fix this horrible thing that I've done.

"You aren't going anywhere, Harper." McKayla grabs my arm. "What the hell is going on?"

I close McKayla's office door after I walk inside, but I can see all the *Shift* Girls staring at me through the glass. They're clustered together conspiratorially.

"You'd better start talking." McKayla drums her Picasso nails on her desk. They sound like the drumroll before a public execution.

I don't know what to say, so I go with a tactic I haven't been employing much lately. I go with the truth.

Here goes nothing.

"I never hooked up with my stepbrother. I don't even have a stepbrother, or really any hookup stories to tell, since I've never really hooked up with anyone before. I really wanted an internship at *Shift* this summer, so badly, but I didn't have an interesting 'scintillating personal essay' of my own, so I made one up." She doesn't have to know that it actually happened to Kristina.

"I'm worse than Jamie," I add. "Everything I wrote about myself is a lie."

It feels like a knot I never realized was there has finally been untied.

McKayla's eyes narrow.

"When you say everything was a lie . . ."

"I made things up." I'm unable to stop myself. "Like, I've never had a summer fling in my entire life. Some of the blogs are true, but I'd . . . embellish."

McKayla stops drumming her fingernails.

"Well," she says slowly, "no one has to *know* your posts aren't true, right? Who doesn't embellish a little to get a better story?"

As chief fact-checker for the *Castalia Chronicle*, I know that this is not how journalism is supposed to work.

"Here's what I think," McKayla says. "We post your story anyway. It's going to kill with clicks, I know it will. You told a good story, I don't care how real it was."

Seriously?

"But I don't even have a stepbrother."

"Maybe you changed the identity of your cousin to protect the innocent," McKayla says, searching for any excuse to put up what she thinks is a clicky post. She walks around her desk and crouches so that we're eye level. "Look, Harper, we all lie to get ahead. You can succeed here, you have the voice, and I was going to announce it later today, but you have the magazine feature. Just let this happen."

"You can't." I don't want to feel as tempted as I do.

"Technically, I can. *Shift* has owned the rights to that blog ever since you sent it to us in your application. Read the fine print. I can put it up whenever I want." But McKayla's uncanny ability to sense people's vulnerability is on point. She turns her voice from sharp to soft, puts her hand on mine, pseudokindly, and says, "I'm here for you, Harper. Let me be your mentor. Don't you want that profile in the magazine? Haven't you spent your entire summer—hell, your entire life—working toward being a journalist?"

My resolve starts to waiver as I flash back to my vision of walking down the halls of Castalia High with the *Shift* September issue in my hand, proclaiming to the world that I am the teen journalist to watch.

McKayla continues, "Nietzsche did say that success is a great liar. Don't you want to be successful?"

Those words jerk me back to reality. I try to hold it in, but I just start laughing.

This is not the response McKayla is expecting. She removes her hand from mine and looks at me like I'm about to lose it. Who knows, maybe I am. I've lost so much already.

"Of all the philosophers you could have quoted," I say, "Nietzsche was definitely the wrong choice."

I stand up over McKayla, who's still crouched on the ground, and say, "I don't care if you own the blog, you can't put it up. If you do, I'll tell everyone that I was lying and you knew it. It would be easy to prove—my parents are still very happily married. And ever since the MatchBook blog went viral, people have been watching me. Waiting for me to mess up. Confessing that I'm a fraud would be like giving them an early Christmas present."

McKayla rises abruptly, her eyes as dark as I've ever seen them. Her features look particularly sharp, and somewhat deadly.

"If you do this, it's professional suicide. You're out. And you won't just lose the magazine feature and your internship here. I have connections *everywhere*. So if you ever plan on being a journalist—"

I slap my badge onto her desk and leave before she can say another word. I'm not changing my mind.

"What happened in there?" Brie asks as soon as I leave McKayla's office.

"I was just telling them about how insanely jealous your so-called friend was of you at brunch," Gigi says. "I can't believe she would try to hurt you like that at work, though. What a liar."

I have to pull myself together. I wondered how things could get any worse than when I was in McKayla's office. This is how.

"I'm the one who hurt her," I say, barely able to make eye contact. I might have lost Kristina with all my lies, and now I'm about to lose the *Shift* Girls with the truth. But I just can't keep pretending to be this person I'm turning into, this girl I don't even like.

"I'm the liar," I say. "The only experience I've had before coming here were Dance Floor Make-Outs with guys who wouldn't ever date me. I made everything up. Everything has been a lie."

"What?" Gigi's expression devolves from confusion to anger to hurt. Great. Two friendships ruined in one day. Good job, Harper. "But in the Hamptons, I told you things. And you pretended . . . you let me think—" There's a long, horrible pause. "I trusted you. I don't trust people and I trusted you. I *defended* you."

How could I do that to her? I feel so bad that I want to cry.

"Gigi, I value your friendship," I say. "That's real. And if you'll just let me explain—"

"Don't talk in bad clichés, Harper," Gigi cuts me off mid-sentence. "I don't want to hear it."

Gigi turns away and walks toward the open kitchen. The *Shift*

Girls follow after her, giving me quick, disapproving looks as they go. I silently pack up my workstation and head back home to Aunt Vee's, replaying the nuclear explosion of a morning on a loop in my head, searching for the right words to say to Kristina, if the right words exist.

• 39 •

I STRUGGLE TO FIT THE KEYS INTO AUNT VEE'S front door. Since the elevator wasn't there when I got to the lobby, I ran up the stairs. I'm wheezing by the time I stumble into the entry hall.

"This is a huge mistake; that was never supposed to go online," I say as I trip over . . . Atticus? Pepe and Wagner are eating Princess's food, something that the pug would be territorial about if she weren't snuggling up on the couch next to Kristina.

And Ben.

They're in a familiar pose. Except instead of me crying in Ben's arms, getting mascara all over his Saint Agnes T-shirt, she is.

Kristina's head pops up when I make my grand entrance, and she wipes away her tears almost furtively. She's more comfortable letting Ben see her cry than me.

Her best friend.

Please let me still be her best friend.

"I can't handle this right now," Kristina says, rising abruptly and moving across the carpet to my room in two long steps. She slams the door.

Ben looks at me in total confusion. "Tell me that what she's saying isn't true," he says. "Because you wouldn't just exploit your best friend to, what, go viral?"

"It wasn't like that. I didn't mean to. . . ."

"It doesn't work like that. You either did it or you didn't." Ben raises his voice. He hasn't raised his voice since the first time we met. And he didn't know me then. Now he knows me. All the weird, clumsy, complicated parts of me. And he likes me.

Or at least he did.

I don't know what to say back, so I don't say anything at all.

"I can't believe this." Ben tousles his hair into a mad scientist's poof and looks very sad. "You were right before. We really *are* different."

He knows all the parts of me. And he hates me. It feels like there's a switchblade to my chest.

Kristina clears her throat. She's standing in the doorway. Her face is composed. Stoic. "Thanks, Ben, but you don't need to do this. Would you mind?" She nods toward the front door. "It won't be long."

"Are you sure?" he asks softly. Ben's protection of Kristina feels almost intimate.

How did we get here? And how did we reach a point where she needs to be protected from me?

Ben gathers up all the leashes in his right hand and, before he leaves, crosses the room to Kristina and gives her another hug. He looks back at her with his sweet, concerned eyes as he drags the dogs out the door. Did something actually happen between them? I know I pushed them together, but it feels like that switchblade is turning in my chest, hollowing me out. And not just because my best friend is so mad at me. Justifiably mad.

As soon as the door clicks behind Ben and his canine entourage, I run over to Kristina, arms outstretched. She pushes me away, like I did with Carter last night.

"Please, please, please let me explain."

"Explain how you betrayed me?" She steps back so there's more space between us. "But you managed to write about it so that day seemed quirky, and funny, and like no big deal? Well, it was a big deal! Things were going *slightly* better with my dad—do you even remember that? Now I can barely look him in the face. Stepmonster thinks I ruined her wedding on purpose. I can't face going to Stanford with Erik. He basically told his mom I force-fed him champagne and then jumped him."

"I know it was a big deal. I never meant . . . When I wrote it, I—"

"What's your excuse this time? You wrote it because I said it was cool to *Carpe that Effing Diem*? That doesn't mean it's okay to *carpe* my life." Kristina's face is a thin veil over rage. "This isn't a harmless white lie. This is my screwed-up relationship with my father and his new family. Just because your relationship with your parents is so great doesn't mean we all have that same luxury."

"You have it wrong. I wrote the essay months ago in my application to be an intern. My life is so boring, so I borrowed yours. I know I shouldn't have, but I did. I didn't write this to go online."

Kristina just stares at me. "That makes it even worse! You had months to tell me about this and you didn't. The fact is, you wrote it, and when it goes online, everyone will know it's about me. God knows they won't think *you* had any scandals. Water polo players are one thing. Making out with my *stepbrother*! You heard that girl at your office: *Gross!* And don't even get me started on how you made it so ambiguous that it seemed like we might have had sex, when you *know* we didn't. What, the worst day of my life wasn't dramatic enough for you? My dad's just starting to talk to me again. What will he think if he sees this? What are people going to think?"

"No one's going to think anything because no one else is going to read it," I say. "I made McKayla promise not to run it. Even though it meant giving up that profile I'd been trying to get all summer. She fired me because of it!"

Kristina jerks back when I try to get closer to her. "What, you want me to feel sorry for you? Want me to throw a 'Harper Anderson didn't do the wrong thing' parade? Will that cheer you up? I've been trying to be sympathetic because I get that dating is new for you, and then things were really shitty after all those trolls started tweeting horrible things. But I had a hard summer, too, okay? You didn't just ditch me at Skinny B's, you ditched me as a friend. You walked out on me. And you said that *I* came here as some humanitarian rescue mission for *you*? Maybe I came all the way here because *I* wasn't fine. Maybe I needed *you*. And you wouldn't even take my calls."

The only time Kristina cries is when there's too much chlorine in the water, and even then, it's rare. But I catch her finger quickly swiping away not a tear but a pre-tear that she doesn't allow to come to term.

"I guess *I* was the cantaloupe," she says.

"No," I say. "I love you. I got so overwhelmed—"

"I don't want to hear it. I'm out of here." She picks up her suitcase, which is already packed.

"Where are you going?" I feel like I'm about to throw up. "Please stay. Your flight's on Wednesday."

"I'd rather blow my life savings on a hotel than be here one more minute. Hell, I'd rather go to Connecticut and stay with my *dad*."

"You don't have to do that."

"Stop," Kristina says as she walks to the door. "Oh, and, Harper, of all the things you said—you didn't mean it, you didn't think it would go live, you were busy, you were new to dating—you never once said you were sorry."

●

• 4 0 •

I DON'T KNOW HOW TO MAKE THINGS BETTER.

I go into my bedroom, lock the door (sorry, Princess), curl up under the covers, and close my eyes.

I don't find a compelling reason to move until late that night, when Aunt Vee begins to pound on my locked door.

"Harper?" she screams from the other side. "Are you in there?"

I get out of bed groggily and drag my feet to the other end of the room.

"You look nice," I say as I let her in. For context, I'm wearing ducky-print pajamas and she's in a gold, crushed-silk cocktail dress with long white gloves.

"Thank God you're all right," she says, sinking her butt into the pillow-top mattress of my bed. "I came home as soon as I realized you weren't at the Bosh anniversary party. Weren't you supposed to go with Carter? I got so worried when I saw him with some trollop and you didn't answer my calls."

I was in virtual attendance, though. Under the covers, I was looking at pictures of Carter with a different bookish brunette in glasses on his arm before I decided to unfollow him. I didn't feel upset that I was missing the event, though.

I was right, walking out on him is the thing I regret the *least* this summer. The other stuff, though, I regret a lot.

"I didn't mean to worry you," I tell Aunt Vee. "It's been a horrible day."

"I know I might seem a little . . . out of touch at times," Aunt Vee says, "but do you want to talk about things? Just ask your mother. I gave out some pretty good advice in my day."

"It's okay."

"Tell me. What's the worst that could happen?"

And then I just let it all out. About Gigi and McKayla. About Carter and Ben and Kristina. About the deceptions and lies.

"I think it's too late to be forgiven," I say.

"But you haven't even done anything about it yet," Aunt Vee says.

"Yeah, I did. I stopped McKayla from putting up the post. I lost my *job* over it. If it doesn't make Kristina feel any better to know that I got fired for doing the right thing for her, then I don't know what else I can do."

"Oh, Harper," Aunt Vee says, talking to me like she did our first day together, when I had no idea what a Birkin bag was. "You have so much to learn. You didn't get fired for *her*. You got fired because of *you*. I don't want to sound harsh, but you got your internship on the basis of a lie. That doesn't mean you didn't deserve it or that you didn't do a wonderful job at it, but still. In the real world, that gets you fired."

Oh.

She's right.

"So what are you doing now to show Kristina how sorry you are?" she asks. "What did she say when you apologized?"

I almost can't bear to tell Aunt Vee that I never apologized properly. And when Kristina walked out the door, it was too late.

"I don't think she wants to hear anything from me at this point," I say.

"You don't wait for an invitation to apologize. You just do it. As loudly as possible." Aunt Vee stands up in her dress and walks across the room. Before she leaves, she gives me a final piece of advice: "Forget all the parties and the boys and the drama, Harper. My Studio 54 years were great, but I only have a few failed marriages to show for it. My friends are the ones who have been in my life the whole time."

I spend most of the next day going back and forth on whether or not I should call Kristina. At first I was really worried about where she'd stay. She wouldn't have to go to her dad's place in Connecticut, would she? But I feel a wave of relief when I see Ben post a picture of a perfectly round pancake with a smiling chocolate-chip face.

A Kristina pancake.

"Forget Clinton Street Baking Company. This is the best pancake in town," Ben wrote in the caption.

Of course Ben would invite her to stay with his family. He's such a good guy. So thoughtful and . . . STOP.

Stop, Harper. Stop.

I've missed my chance with Ben. And Ben and Kristina deserve to be happy together. They're the most loyal people I know. Which is why I ignore the gnawing feeling that I get when I think about them together. I have no right to feel that way.

Instead of calling Kristina and interrupting the only good thing that might come from her shitty trip to New York, I put down my phone and open my notebook.

Recently, I've only been writing as a character. I wonder what would happen if, this time, I wrote something as me.

And so I start putting words on the page. Not observations about other people but about myself. I write about this summer and the things I regret. Hurting Kristina. Hurting Ben. Brushing off the only guy I've ever *really* liked, because I was too fixated on the one I thought I should like and too dumb to recognize what was right in front of me.

My sentences keep flowing, page after page, until the sun is setting over Central Park.

I know what I have to do.

· 41 ·

GIGI IS HESITANT WHEN I TEXT HER FIRST THING Wednesday morning to see if she'll meet me at lunch and maybe do me a favor I don't even deserve.

> **Harper:** Please?
>
> **Harper:** PLEASE!!! I miss you.
>
> **Harper:** I'll bring you mac and cheese from Ban Bread.
>
> **Harper:** Please?
>
> **Gigi:** Fine. But only because I've been craving that all week.

I tell Gigi I'm sorry the second she walks out of the Bosh Building to meet me.

"*Shift* Girls don't say sorry, Harper," she says, grudgingly accepting my offering of gluten-free mac and cheese. She walks ahead of me toward the fountain.

"I'm not a *Shift* Girl anymore," I reply, taking a seat on the ledge next to her.

I spend the next thirty minutes apologizing. I don't qualify any of my actions. I don't make excuses. I don't leave out details. There will be no lying through omission today.

"You should have told me in the Hamptons," Gigi says. "Now I feel like a fool."

"I'm the fool. You were the one telling the truth. I was lying because I was a coward and a hypocrite," I continue. "And not just about my nonexistent love life before coming here. I never should have gotten pissed at you for writing about purge watching. Did I ever tell you how good that article was? I didn't, but it was amazing. You deserve to get the magazine feature."

"Maybe," Gigi says, a very slight smile forming at the edges of her mouth. Even though she warned me she was leaving as soon as she finished her mac and cheese, she's still here in spite of her empty bowl. "McKayla says it's really close between me and Abigail right now. I think I need one last clicky story to put me over the edge. Preferably something Internet friendly that I also don't think is idiotic. Artistic, even?"

"Wait! I know exactly what you should write about!" I burrow in my bag to find my phone. Which isn't there. I picture it lying next to Princess's bed, where I used it to take a picture of her lying on her back with her Manolo Bark-nik chew toy hanging out of her mouth this morning. I was going to send it to Ben until I remembered that I couldn't because he hates me.

I make Gigi give me her phone, so I can show her Ben's dog Instagram account.

"Is that dog getting bar mitzvahed?" Gigi asks in disbelief.

"*Bark* mitzvahed! And yes, my friend's an amazing dog photographer. You should do a profile on him and make a slide show of his pictures. Clicky and artistic."

"I'll consider it," Gigi says coyly, but I can see her smiling to herself, already imagining it getting picked up by BuzzSnap.

"Maybe I forgive you." She puts her phone away and takes the key card I asked for out of her romper's pocket. "Here."

"You got Abigail's?"

"I had to," she says. "Abigail is the only one you could pass for with security downstairs. All I had to do was tell her there was an up-for-grabs bag of organic antihistamines in the open kitchen. I grabbed her card off her desk when she went running. Why do you need to get up there, though? McKayla isn't your biggest fan right now."

"I'll tell you if it works."

I use Abigail's ID to trick the security guard into letting me through to the elevators. As planned, Gigi distracts the *Shift* Girls while I sneak into McKayla's empty office.

When McKayla strolls back in from her Wednesday beauty department lunch, I'm sitting on her charcoal couch. Judging from the glare in her eyes, I'm worried she's going to use the eyeliner pencil she's carrying as a weapon.

Her greeting is, "Get out."

"I came here to tell you that I'm sorry."

"You know I hate that word," she seethes. "And I don't care. I know that following directions isn't your strong suit, but get out. It's not that hard."

I ignore the get out part. And the insults. And how terrifying she is when pissed off.

"I know you hate that word," I say. "But sometimes it's necessary. I put you in a horrible position, I jeopardized all the work that you've done to turn this website around, and I want to make things right."

I hand her two printed pages. "I e-mailed this to you as well, but I was worried you'd delete anything from me. I know I'm not the dating blogger anymore, but please at least consider publishing this."

McKayla snatches my mea culpa out of my hands and gives it a quick skim. Probably just to feed her curiosity. "It's *more* than a little too doe-eyed and sincere for my taste."

"Please, McKayla."

"You're not going to *cry*, are you?" McKayla asks. But this time she pushes a box of tissues my way. She sighs. "It galls me to say this, but people have been sending e-mails asking where your new dating blog is since we didn't put one up this morning."

She skims the entire piece. "All right. Some media reporters have been asking questions. Word's out that we dramatically lost two interns in less than a week. This *thing* would clear up any confusion that it was *Shift*'s fault. If I publish it."

"Is that a yes?" I ask hopefully.

"This will never make the Leader Board."

"Thank you!"

"I'm not doing this for you, Harper. I'm doing this for *Shift*. Now get out of my office before I call security."

I'VE BEEN LYING ABOUT WHO I AM

And it's time to say the "S" word.

At *Shift*, we aren't supposed to say "I'm sorry."

It's not the worst rule. Girls often apologize too much.

I'm sorry, I have a question.

I'm sorry, I already have plans.

I'm sorry, you bumped into me—sorry for my own physical presence, sorry simply for being.

It's a bad habit we need to break, being sorry for things that we have no reason to apologize for.

But today I am genuinely and unabashedly sorry. I'm not the girl you think I am, and I am sorry for lying to you all summer.

I got my job at *Shift* by writing a "personal" story about a crazy dating experience that I'd never had. Because, really, I didn't have any dating experience *period*. That's right, a girl who had never been on a real date has served as your dating guru all summer.

I've always been horrible with guys. My instructions on how to dazzle a guy on the street? Those were all hypothetical things that I thought sounded good but had no experience with myself. In fact, when I tried them out, I crashed and burned. But I was too embarrassed to share the truth.

It wasn't all a lie. I did go foraging in Central Park and made out with a stranger in a gallery, but every fact was riddled with fiction and embellishments.

Why did I do it? Maybe because I was sorry for who I actually am.

But, really, where you fall on the dating spectrum doesn't make you any more or less worthy. There's no shame in embracing your truth, and by pretending to be more experienced than I was, I implied that there is.

And when I got caught up in being this desirable "cool girl," that other "cool girls" could look up to and "cool guys" would want to date, I turned boys into my main priority. They became the only thing I cared about. But I was picking the wrong boys and I was ruining the most important relationship I will ever have. With my best friend.

My line about "being a good friend means putting your love life on hold" was good advice, but I wasn't following it. And I hurt people I really care about.

Dates come and go; friends don't. At the end of the day, the jerk you went to homecoming with won't matter. Your friend who kicked him in the balls when he was a jerk to you will. Because she'll be kicking jerks in the balls for you for the rest of your life.

And that's the only relationship advice that I can give.

Carpe your Effing Diem (and no one else's)!
Harper

Editor's Note: The writer is no longer working at *Shift* and her other blog posts are under review. As a publication, we take authenticity very seriously and apologize for this writer's actions.

· 4 2 ·

EVEN THOUGH I MIGHT BE RUINING ANY FUTURE
credibility I could have as a journalist, in eight weeks this is by far
the best advice I have given.

I take my final walk to the *Shift* elevators.

For the first time this whole summer, there are no stops on any
of the forty-two floors on the way down. I wish there were. I want
this to take as long as possible. I'm not ready to leave the sound-
proof elevator. Or the Bosh Building. Or journalism. I'm not ready
to walk into the lobby, into . . . chaos.

Complete and total chaos.

I'm not talking about my own metaphorical struggle; something is happening in the Bosh Media lobby. Someone is getting
patted down by security, there's a lot of splashing in the koi pond,
and the world-famous editor in chief of *Icon* magazine is wearing
only one shoe and screaming, "Someone get that dog away from
my Louboutin!"

I know those dogs. The one with the shoe, the others splashing around the waterfall, and a final pup chasing his tail, spinning himself into oblivion, next to the guy about to get handcuffed.

It's Ben.

"Stop," I yell, running over to the security guard. "Stop, I know him."

"Is this the girl you were talking about?" the annoyed security guard asks Ben.

"Yes, sir."

"So now you'll agree to take your dogs and leave?"

"Yes, sir."

The security guard takes his hand off Ben's back and gives him a stern warning, "Now you know. When I say no dogs allowed, I mean no dogs allowed!"

"What are you doing here?" I ask, picking a surprisingly swimming-proficient Princess out of the koi pond.

"Don't do it!" Ben says. A look of panic is on his face.

"You want me to leave Princess in the water?"

"Haven't you been getting our texts?"

"Our?"

"Me and Kristina's?"

"Oh. No. I forgot my phone today. I was kind of preoccupied."

"Whatever, that doesn't matter." Ben grabs me by the arm and says, "I'm here to tell you, don't hand in that story! Kristina texted me that I had to stop you from coming clean. She wanted to run down here herself, but she's on a plane right now. Am I too late?"

"What are you *talking* about?"

"Look," he says. "You made a mistake. A huge one. But Kristina accepts your apology! She doesn't want you to ruin your whole career before it ever gets started."

Gigi and McKayla weren't the only ones on the receiving end of my truth overdose. After spending hours writing in my notebook last night, coming to terms with everything I had done wrong, I realized that Kristina was the most important person to see the blog post—whether or not it got published.

I e-mailed it to her this morning with an overdue apology and the promise that I would never take her friendship for granted again. If she would consider still being friends with me.

Ben takes a crumpled piece of notebook paper out of his gym shorts pocket.

"I wrote it down so I got it right." He reads his scrawl. "Kristina wanted me to tell you, and I quote, 'to stop smoking Bobby McKittrick's bad pot. We never stopped being friends, we just had a really bad fight. But we'll work it out. Don't wreck your career to fix it. It's already been fixed.'"

I hug Princess a little tighter. My best friend doesn't hate me.

Ben takes a step closer to me before the security guard grabs him by the back of his T-shirt. "How many times do I have to tell you to take the damn dogs outside?"

"Right. Sorry," Ben says.

I walk with him to the front of the lobby and watch the dogs squeeze into a revolving door.

"You should have seen them in the cab," he says.

"You took a cab?"

"I was in the park when Kristina started calling from the air-port. I had to stop you. Did I stop you?"

"No."

Ben looks like someone punched him in the gut. He sinks onto the ledge of the fountain with a look of utter defeat.

"It's a good thing!" I sit down next to him. "I want people to read it. My other blog posts have been funny, but this one feels honest. It feels like me."

"Yeah?"

"Yeah. Sorry you wasted the cab fare."

"It's not a waste," he says. "I had to see you anyway."

There's that dimple. I didn't realize I'd missed it so much.

"Why are you looking at me like that?" I ask.

"I have to show you something, but I'm afraid you're going to kill me when I do."

He smooths the paper where he wrote Kristina's message against the leg of his cargo shorts. It's riddled with bite marks. He hands it to me. The other side is filled with familiar handwriting. My handwriting.

"How did my notebook get ripped up?" My heart stops beating when I see what's actually written on the page. "Wait, you didn't *read* this, did you?"

"It was an accident! Atticus got to it when I was picking up Princess. I tried to put the pages back together again, but when I saw my name . . ."

No.

No, no, no.

"So I took it with me on the walk," he says. "Maybe I read it. I couldn't help it. I had to talk to you, but then Kristina called and—"

I left my cell phone behind and my notebook out. Brilliant. "No. You should ignore every word of this! You and Kristina are great together. You have so much in common. You and Kristina—"

"Are friends," he says with great finality. "We've only been *friends*. She knew I was crazy about someone else. She said it was obvious. I didn't believe her when she said you felt the same way . . . until I read this."

Ben takes his big hand and brushes a wisp of my hair behind my ear. He leans in slowly enough for me to stop him, but I don't. I lean in too, until our lips are touching. His lips are softer than I thought they'd be. And also more intense. Carter's kisses felt dangerous. Ben's feel like home.

There are no tourists. There are no selfie sticks. It's me and Ben and this amazing endless kiss.

Until Princess takes a running leap into my lap.

But Ben isn't looking at Princess. He's looking at me. In a way I've never been looked at before.

I have to catch my breath. "So, you and Kristina didn't . . . ?"

"No."

"And you're sure, after everything, you don't hate . . . ?"

"No."

"How did she know I liked you?" I didn't put that in my mea culpa e-mail to her. I didn't want her to feel guilty if she and Ben had hooked up.

"I asked her the same thing. She just said a best friend always knows."

I smile.

"So what happens now?" I ask. "I leave in a week. And I don't know how to do . . . any of this."

Ben grins so big that another dimple emerges. One that I never knew existed. "We'll just have to figure it out as we go."

Carpe that Effing Diem.

· Epilogue ·

WE DID CARPE THAT EFFING DIEM. AND THE DIEM
after that, and the diem after that. I helped walk a lot of dogs and
played a lot of Frisbee with boys. Ben came to Shakespeare in the
Park with me and actually liked it. Until it was time to go back to
Castalia, with a Saint Agnes Lacrosse T-shirt packed snugly in my
bag next to a lot of Aunt Vee's hand-me-downs, and face reality.

The glossy pages of *Shift*'s September issue are spread across my
polka-dot bedspread.

"She might be terrifying, but she sure does look beautiful,"
Kristina says.

After my departure, Gigi was awarded the title of "Teen
Journalist to Watch" and the promise of an internship for next
summer. We FaceTime every few days when it's early in California and dinnertime in Geneva.

"I can't believe you're seriously going to wear that to school,"
she says. "It's a denim skirt!"

"I am. And I'm going to look damn good in it too."

She sighs.

"Just don't wear it when you pick that dog-walking boy up from the airport," she says, rolling her eyes. "I'm telling you this as a friend."

It's only been a week, but I missed Ben so much.

I'm swaying with him at Bobby McKittrick's "Sayonara Summer" party the Saturday night before the start of senior year—surrounded by couples whose Dance Floor Make-Outs are so intense, so ravenous, I'm kind of worried someone's going to drop down dead due to suffocation—when I get what might be the most unexpected e-mail of my life.

"Oh my God, Ben. You won't believe it," I shout over the loud music blasting in the middle of Bobby's yard. "Kristina, get over here!"

FROM: McKaylaRae@Shift.com
TO: HarpAnd32@gmail.com
SUBJECT: The "S" Word

It turns out that I miscalculated the impact of that godawful doe-eyed blog post of yours. I underestimated how much sentimental sap resonates with our readership. The clickability was outrageous, and Trenton Bosh wants you back as our dating blogger next summer. I think it's a mistake, but I can let him find that out for himself. One misstep and you're gone.

All the best,

M

"Um, what was that?" Kristina asks after we finish reading.

"I think that was the least enthusiastic job offer ever," I reply.

"I think that's us in New York next summer," Ben says, squeezing my hand.

"There's just one teeny, tiny, infinitesimal problem," I say. "Do you think they'll let me be a relationship blogger instead?"

Acknowledgments

There are so many people who helped make this book possible. To those who gave me their emotional support, their business savvy, and their permission to incorporate pieces of their lives into my fiction (Princess was based on a real pug!), thank you, thank you, THANK YOU.

A gigantic thanks to my agent/therapist Dan Mandel at Greenburger Associates and the team at Simon Pulse: Mara Anastas (I'm forever grateful that you saw something in those bachelor blogs and Tinder testimonials at *TIME*), my incredible editor Alyson Heller, Jodie Hockensmith, Lucille Rettino, Tara Grieco, Mary Marotta, Katherine Devendorf, and Karina Granda. My thanks also goes to Sara Sargent (the wonderful editor who acquired this book), Jason Richman at UTA (Gaieties forever), Lucy Truman (I hope the book lived up to your dazzling cover art), and everyone at JKS Communications.

Thank you to my early readers that I am lucky enough to call my friends: Emma Gray, I love you and want to be a feminist superhero like you one day; Samantha Grossman, your pug GIFs kept me going; Kate Hutchison, metaphor master and creator of the cantaloupe; Abby Rogers, for telling me "and this is where I start to hate her"; Dana Sherne, I can't imagine what life would be like if we hadn't drawn the lowest housing numbers sophomore year and become roommates; Brittany Wallace, for your positivity and for bringing Princess into my life; and Rebecca Yale, you were there from beginning to end, for my smiles (posing as you took my author photo) and tears (as you cleared your schedule to expertly plot this book out in Post-its on my living room floor.) And of course, thank you, Maurice Goldstein, for more than can fit on a page.

Although *Shift* and the ridiculous people who work there are 100 percent fictional, I want to thank all of my editors and colleagues who have been instrumental in my growth as a writer and reporter. I'd also like to thank teen whisperer Taylor Trudon, Megan Reid and Zander Bauman (for enduring my many publishing questions), Dasha Jensen and Kyle Torrence (for enduring my late-night, dramatic readings), Allie Miller (always a hilarious brainstorm partner), Megan Delis (Carpe Fucking Diem), and Kimberly Rosenblum (my pre-K friend-maker). Thanks, Amy Lombard, whose photography inspired many of the canine formal events depicted in the book, and Jo Murphy, whose art inspired "The Ladies Who Give No Fucks." Thank you, Paragraph, for providing such an incredible writing space, and the NY Writers Coalition teens, whose incredible writing inspires me to let go and put pen to paper.

While I'm fairly certain I wouldn't have been able to write this book without Oreos, an IV-drip of Diet Coke, and Taylor Swift's *1989* album playing on loop for months on end, I'm absolutely positive I couldn't have done it without my friends' (those listed and the many more who are not) and family's love and support. A big thank you to the Stamplers & co., particularly Grandma M, Jay, Grandma L, Michael (you are so talented), and my parents. Mom, it is such a gift to come from such a talented and insightful writer and person. Dad, thank you for always being there, advising and encouraging me. Thank you both for always listening, no matter how late at night, no matter how irrational my fears. Thank you for always telling me that I could. I am so unbelievably lucky to be your daughter.